TRUTH

WOLVES OF WALKER COUNTY

KIKI BURRELLI

CONNECT WITH KIKI

Join my newsletter!
And stay up to date on my newest titles, giveaways and news!
Want a free—full length— wolf shifter Mpreg novel? Join my newsletter when you get Finding Finn!

———

Join the Pack! Awooooo!
Come hang out with your pack mates!
Visit Kiki's Den and join the pack! Enjoy exclusive access to behind the scenes excerpts, cover reveals and surprise giveaways!

EXPERIENCE THE WOLVES OF WORLD

Wolves of Walker County (Wolf Shifter Mpreg)

Truth

Hope

Faith

Love

Wolves of Royal Paynes (Wolf Shifter Mpreg)

Hero

Ruler

Lovers

Outlaw

1

BRANSON

"Have you gotten your invitation?" Aver asked. A low but steady beep told me he was on site, hopefully pouring the concrete to reinforce the posts for the Lanser's dock.

"Invitation? Oh, that's right. The winter solstice." The last time I'd seen Aver had been this morning when he'd left for the day. I should've gone with him, but the paperwork was already piled high. The Lanser's was a big job, and they'd opened the doors to us booking up for the rest of the season. Aver hadn't been back to check the mail.

"Don't play dumb with me, Branson. You know what invitation, just like you know why you've been running us both ragged with endless consultations these past weeks."

"We're running a construction company. I thought that was what we did."

Aver made a sound that was half growl, half snort. "You should've seen it. Hand delivered. Gold foiled edges. The paper was heavier than a rock. Good stock."

I could only imagine the hours Aver's mother would've

spent on choosing the card stock. She probably had her spies reporting back to make sure she was the Walker family with the thickest paper.

I scanned the untidy stacks of paper on my desk in the office Aver and I shared in the house we lived in with our two other cousins. Carbon copies of pastel pink, blue, and green fluttered each time a breeze blew from the cracked window. "Maybe mine was lost in the mail."

"You wish. Your mom makes mine look tame. If I know Delia Walker, she's enlisted an entire parade to bring it to your door. Oh yeah, unrelated, I'll be late tonight."

An alert popped up on my computer screen telling me the perimeter sensor alarm had been activated. I groaned.

"Uh oh, is that Mommy Dearest now? Was I right? Is it a parade? Or just a full marching band?"

I yanked open the curtain to the driveway that wound down from the main road. I couldn't see anyone coming. "I don't know. Maybe it was just a raccoon. I'll check it out later. I've got three proposals to finalize as well as updating those numbers for the Forstein addition. Maybe, if you see them, you can try and explain why the granite specially shipped in from Italy would be more than the original locally sourced stone we'd quoted them."

Between the two of us, Aver had a better way with words. His father had groomed him from a child in public speaking, in hopes that it would help him assume leadership of the wolf pack. Now, Aver lived off pack land and co-owned Walker Construction. How the mighty had fallen— according to Aver's father. "If I see them. But I doubt I will. I'll be at the club—"

"Say no more. I don't want to be roped into whatever scheme this is, and I will take no part in you playing this part."

"Things aren't that easy, Branson," Aver replied tiredly.

"It's as easy as 'Mom, Dad, I'm gay, stop setting me up with female shifters you think will lure me back to the pack.' It's what I said."

A knock at the door made me frown. I hadn't heard any of the other sensors. The perimeter alarm had gone off, but not the porch or the door. I pulled up the front door camera but didn't see anything. I'd told Aver that camera was angled too high.

"Awesome, now I get nagged at from both sides. Would you like to also criticize my other choices in life? How many beers I have at the end of the day? The many ways in which I am disappointing my family by living outside of the pack?"

I grinned, but I didn't feel any happiness from Aver's annoyance, just grim acceptance. Which I imagined he felt as well. Sometimes, it was easier to give a mouse a cookie. At least then it got them to stop asking for the whole bakery —for a while. "I'm sorry, you're right. Agreeing to a date now will get them off your backs, but not for long with the Winter Solstice Celebration approaching. Have you spoken to Nana? I have a voicemail I haven't checked from her waiting at the end of my to-do list." At this rate, I wouldn't be getting to the end of my list likely until Aver had returned from his ill-fated date.

"I have a voicemail too. I'm afraid to check it. I never know with that one. Either she wants us to come over so she can stuff us with pies and tell us we are smart and brave like when we were kids, or she needs to warn us of the latest apocalypse the stars have brought to her attention. It's a gamble I just won't take today. She probably called Wyatt too. Let him handle it."

Another knock sounded. I frowned. "Hold on, there's someone here. That sounds good, about Wyatt. If he is going to claim to be Nana's favorite, he can fend off her endless prophecies." I exited the office, not bothering to close the double doors and walked down the hallway to the front door. "I've been telling you, we need to lower the front door cameras..." I saw the vague outline of a small body through the frosted glass oval insert in the center of the door. So there had been someone there.

The figure was alone, not in a band or parade, so that knocked Aver's suggestions out of the running. I opened the door, my eyebrows lifting as my mouth dropped open.

"What is it?" Aver's voice spoke from far away. Except he was where he'd been the whole time while I'd found myself in a load of shit.

"Who sent you?" I barked, and the young man on my porch flinched.

He was short and slim with silky brown hair and blue eyes. He wore hardly anything, despite the frost on the ground that still hadn't melted from the night before.

"Do I need to come home? What is going on, Branson? Dammit! This camera is too high, I can't see anything!"

"Maybe you should. See if Dave can handle the site for the rest of the day." I slipped the phone in my pocket despite the fact that Aver was still speaking.

The young man on my porch had begun to shiver. My treatment of him could have started the trembling, or the fact that he was dressed like a virgin fit for sacrifice to an angry god. He'd recently bathed, adorning himself with so much cologne I should've smelled him long before the perimeter alarm had gone off. His shirt was white and so thin I could see through it. I imagined that was the intent. But, I couldn't ask him in or even offer him something to warm him up, not if he was sent from my mother.

And he was definitely a shifter.

"P-please, Alpha Walker—"

"Don't call me that," I snarled with more menace than this poor boy deserved. I sucked in a calming breath, shoving my fingers through my hair. "Who sent you? My mother, right?"

"Elder Delia said I wasn't to return if you weren't with me." He clasped his hands in front of his body, lowering his head so deep his chin rested against his chest.

I wished I could believe him, ask him in, give him a blanket, and then send him on his way, but Delia Walker had been trying to bring me back to the Walker family since the four of us—Aver, myself, Wyatt, and his twin brother Nash—left together at eighteen.

An act I'd followed by coming out.

Now, Aver got set up on blind dates, while I got barely legal, or possibly not at all legal, meat offerings.

My lips twisted into a scowl of disgust. I was sure the young man was very nice, and maybe, with a few years and pounds on him, he'd make some man very happy. Right now, he reminded me too much of my nephew, and when I thought of the types of things Delia, my mother, would've suggested to this kid to help him persuade me to return with him, I wanted to throw up. "What's your name?"

It was odd that I hadn't known him by scent, but maybe the cologne was blocking anything familiar about him. He was probably sixteen or seventeen now... Since it had been over ten years since myself and my cousins had left, I should have had at least an inkling of recognition.

"Paul, Al—sir."

"Paul?" I didn't remember anyone by that name from the pack families.

"Paul Tyson, sir, I wasn't born in this region. My family comes from the south."

I frowned. "Oregon?"

Paul shook his head. He wore a light coverage of makeup, and as he turned his head, dark blue splotches shadowed underneath. "Texas. I hate it there, and I'm not going back. You can turn me away, but I ain't... I'm not going back." He tugged at his shirt, covering more of his midriff and telling me he wasn't any more pleased to be in that outfit as I was to have him there.

It would have ended my problem, but I couldn't block out those bruises. "Now hold on. Don't go running. I will not be going back with you, but I can't order you into the cold. Hold on." I lifted a finger to tell him to wait while I dug in my pocket for my phone.

He jerked back, toward the door.

"No, just wait—"

"Sir, I don't mean to disrespect you, but I told you I won't go back, and I won't. I thought I'd find safety here, but if that's not the case..." His attention swung up to something behind me. His jaw slackened.

"Fucking fuck, Aver, he's alive. I'm looking at him right now," Wyatt griped into the phone as he moseyed down the stairs. Aver's call had clearly woken him at the early morning hour of eleven forty-five. He wore only holey jeans, and his shaggy hair flopped long enough to cover his eyes. "And what's this?" Wyatt crooned, coming to a stop at the bottom step. "He's got a friend." Wyatt winked.

I rolled my eyes. Wyatt would flirt with a rock. But Paul had stopped trying to run out the door.

"Wyatt, this is Paul Tyson. I was wondering if you would wait with him while I make a call?" I stepped to the corner, never leaving the two.

Paul's gaze flitted toward me. "Who are you calling?" His tone was unmistakable. He didn't trust me.

That wouldn't change by me lying now. "The police. I know that might not be what you want, but I know the cops around here. They can help you. They won't make you go home."

"I know the sheriff," Wyatt said, but out of his mouth, the words were husky. "He's an alright guy. Can't quite keep up spotting me at the gym, but he tries."

I waited for Paul to start laughing, but the kid was lapping out of Wyatt's hand. "I'm eighteen, though..." Paul said instead in a half-hearted attempt.

Wyatt's gaze flicked to mine long enough for him to turn back to Paul and say, "Still, it's better to go by the book with these things."

I would've mentioned Wyatt had no idea what *these things* were. He was just good at dropping into a situation and assimilating to what was needed. He would've been much angrier had he known that Delia Walker had sent this kid to seduce me. As if I'd find my omega in a shifter who was still a child. She'd crossed the line this time, though. Maybe Wyatt didn't know enough to be angry, but I was livid.

"Sheriff Maslow." Jake answered on the second ring.

"Hey, Sheriff, this is Branson Walker. I may have a kid in trouble here."

"Kid? How young we talking? Are you at home? What's a runaway doing way out there?"

It wasn't like we were in the middle of the woods, but we were a few minutes out of town by car where the Lynx River emptied into Walker Bay. If Paul had come from pack lands, he'd likely run from the other side of the bay to here, but I wasn't going to tell the sheriff that. "Not sure. He doesn't seem like a bad kid, though..." I looked briefly over at the two of them. Wyatt had Paul's full attention talking about some superhero movie that had just released. "He might have been abused?" If my mother had knowingly sent an underaged male to seduce me, I wouldn't protect her. Pack pride be dammed.

"I'll be right there. This is good timing. Well—you know what I mean. That fancy hire from Seattle came in this week. He's been on my ass talking about updating our procedure and policy. I tried to tell him we don't have enough of those kinds of trouble in Walker County to have all that rigmarole." He stopped speaking suddenly and cleared his throat, making me wonder who had walked in on him. When he spoke again, his tone rang with polite authority. "Thank you for calling. We'll come up now. Keep him there, keep him calm."

I hung up, wondering how I was supposed to keep a skittish shifter kid from running, but Wyatt had that under control. His habit for flirting was an advantage at the bar he owned and operated, and, I guessed, it was an advantage when trying to keep impressionable youths from fleeing. I lingered around the border of the room, still keeping an eye, without interrupting. And yes, I got a vindictive amount of pleasure seeing Delia's trap circle down the drain.

If this was the type of shifter she thought would lure me back into her clutches, then she didn't really know me at all.

Suddenly, my driveway was a parking lot. First, Aver in the white work truck with Walker Construction written in blue blocky letters on the side. Behind him was a firetruck, lights spinning but thankfully not the siren, and then Sheriff Maslow in his cruiser.

"Holy shit!" Paul exclaimed when he caught sight of them all.

"It's okay. Only one of them is here to talk to you," I said. "The rest are just nosy." I'd recommended Aver come back to the house, but that was before I realized Wyatt had been asleep upstairs. He didn't always sleep at home, choosing to crash at his bar sometimes instead. And I hadn't meant for Aver to blab to our cousin Nash. He was Wyatt's twin brother and a fireman, as well as the fourth of the Walker cousins to live in this house. And apparently, the town could spare a fire truck. "Stay here," I ordered, mostly to Wyatt.

Aver was already crunching over the gravel. "What's going on?"

At the same time, Nash hopped out of the firetruck and strode over.

"Listen, both of you. Delia sent me... a *gift*," I said with a snarl so they would understand. "He's shifter—"

"If he's shifter, why is the sheriff here?" Nash asked, hackles raised as his dark eyes flit back to where the sheriff was just now getting out of his car.

"Because he's got bruises, and I'm pretty sure Delia sent him for a specific purpose. If he's underaged, I don't care if she's my mother—I'll report her." I'd have reported her even if Paul was of age, but at that point, Paul was responsible for his own decisions in the eyes of human law, and shifter law was just about useless at a time like this. "He might have come from somewhere worse. He said he traveled here to try to join the packs and make a new life, I don't know. But I won't feel comfortable until we check it out."

The sheriff walked too closely for us to continue talking. A second man approached in step beside him. He stuck out immediately in an outfit that was probably called business casual where he came from, but on this side of the bay, he might as well have been in a tuxedo. His light blue button-up and gray wool blazer fit over a broad chest. The creases in his black slacks looked like they'd come straight off the ironing board. With an outfit like that, I expected some shiny loafers or equally impractical leather dress shoes, but I grinned at the tri-colored canvas sneakers.

"Branson." The sheriff offered his hand. I shook it, and then he turned to his partner. "This is our new representative from the Washington State Social Services, Riley Monroe."

I stuck my hand out, but the other man just nodded stiffly in my direction. He had a narrow face and sharp cheeks. His dark brown hair stuck out in a style I could only describe as artfully messy. Already, he had a dusting of facial hair shadowing his chin and jaw. There were faint dark circles beneath his deep blue eyes. A late night? Or early morning?

I pulled my hand away before the moment could get any more awkward. There were any number of reasons why he wouldn't want to shake my hand. It couldn't have been something I'd said—I hadn't spoken to the man yet. But, as the moment stretched on, I needed to say something quick. "Welcome to Walkerton."

The sheriff cleared his throat. "Mr. Monroe, this is Branson Walker."

"I was wondering when I would meet a Walker. Your name is everywhere in this area. I was sure the family wasn't far behind," Riley Monroe said. His tone was pleasant enough, but with an edge I was used to by now.

"Walker is just my last name. I'm afraid you'll have to go to the other side of the bay to meet the impressive Walkers of the family." My great-great-great-great grandfather had helped develop the island. We were one of many coastal islands located between the north-easternmost tip of Washington State and San Juan Island. Accessible from the mainland only by ferry, we lived a sheltered, quiet existence.

Most of the time.

But my ancestors hadn't been all that creative when it came to naming things. We lived in Walker County, the city was named Walkerton, and I looked out onto Walker Bay every morning.

Riley's gaze drifted to the house behind me. "I don't know, this is pretty impressive."

Pride filled me. The four of us had made this home with our own two hands. It had acted as our first symbol of independence from the packs. I rarely had a chance to show it off and had thought that the more than ten years—closer to fifteen—living in it with three other bachelors might've soiled the original feeling, but, there it was again.

I heard the door opening behind me and Riley's expression transformed. When he looked at me again, there was none of the polite friendly demeanor from before. Only judgment. His dark blue eyes narrowed, his gaze searching me with a new purpose. "Is that the child in question?" he asked, his voice all steel.

"I'm not a child!" Paul shouted back, despite the fact that Riley had spoken too quietly for Paul to have reasonably heard. He was either emotional or not used to ignoring his senses around humans.

Riley's eyebrows rose. "Nothing wrong with his hearing." He stepped by me without a glance in my direction. In fact, I got the distinct impression he hadn't looked at me on purpose.

I had no reason to care about what this stranger thought of me. I knew how bad this looked; it was one of the reasons I'd called the police so quickly. I could've sent Paul away with some money and a ticket to the wolf packs in the next territory over. But if he'd been stopped, it would've been harder to explain my involvement at that point.

"Hello, my name is Riley Monroe. I work with Washington State Social Services." Again, Riley skipped shaking hands. Was it a city guy thing? Cold and flu season? He pulled a small, leather-bound notepad out of his pocket and began writing as he asked Paul questions.

The only thing I knew for sure was that I was too busy to be hanging around, especially if my presence was no longer required. And yet, when I turned to make my excuses to the sheriff, what I said was, "Would you like to come inside? It might be easier for the interrogations to happen in the dining room."

I very nearly clocked myself in the face, I reminded myself so much of my mother. She was vindictive and manipulative, but she would never say a mean word—to your face. Every guest was offered food and beverages, never mind if Delia Walker didn't know how to turn tap water into tea.

Riley approached, having left Paul at the front porch. "I'm going to need a list of everyone who lives in this household. As well as the number to a Mrs..." He checked his notepad. "Delia Walker. Any reason why Paul might've gone to her home? Is she known for housing runaway youths?"

I snorted. Delia Walker was known for being one of three elder households, garden parties and always getting her way. But I was sure she would've loved being associated with something so altruistic. "Delia Walker is my mother. She lives on the other side of the bay with all the other fancy Walkers." There were four official Walker households: my grandfather, my mother, Aver's parents, and Nash and Wyatt's parents. But once we started splitting the names off, it became impossible to explain without a graph and a bottle of booze.

Riley's eyes narrowed on me again. I wished I could go back to the moment before he'd seen Paul. At least then Riley hadn't looked at me like scum. "Do you know why your mother would've sent Paul here? He's dressed extremely provocatively but claims he got the clothing from your mother."

"I can't begin to pretend I understand my mother. We aren't close, not since I moved from home."

"Hm."

I didn't trust that single noise any more than I trusted the situation at hand. Until now, I'd been pretty polite, but I wouldn't have this stranger thinking something about me that was wholly untrue. "Do I need to remind you that I called the cops here, Mr. Monroe? From my side, I found a young man, clearly down on his luck. And I called the police first. I'm not asking for any sort of reward, but I'll ask you to stop concocting whatever scheme you've decided is at work here. I want Paul safe. That is all."

Riley's eyebrows rose again, only this time, they didn't settle into suspicion. "Forgive me. I'm new and still getting the hang of things. This is unusual, but for what it is worth, Paul has not claimed to have done anything he didn't want to do. I'll need to run his identification through our systems. If he's eighteen as he claims, that changes my next steps significantly."

He was clearly attractive with a level head. That didn't entirely explain my sudden interest in the man, but I wondered if maybe it had been too long since I'd traveled out of Walker County and mingled with fresh meat. I frowned at the term. I was so out of the game, I'd practically assumed Riley's orientation. He could like women... stranger things had happened.

Riley must've assumed the expression was meant for him. "I'm only doing my job, Mr. Walker. Caring for the welfare of those unable to care for themselves."

I smiled, trying to infuse as much warmth into the expression as I could. We'd gotten off on the wrong foot. I could understand why, but I was still eager to get back on the right foot. "I understand." I pulled out my card. "When you get some answers, please let me know."

Riley took the card gingerly, carefully grasping the very corner between his thumb and pointer finger. "Walker Construction," he murmured with a small smile. His finger traced over the embossed lettering on the card, and I bit my cheek, suddenly wishing his finger would trail over me instead. "I guess it's good to be proud of your name."

Alarms rang in my head as Riley's smile turned sad. I only had about a thousand questions all piled on top of each other. But the longer I stood there, the more I noticed the sheriff standing there with Paul. They were ready to leave.

"Don't be a stranger," I called out as the three of them turned back to the cruiser.

Nash walked up behind me. "Don't be a stranger," he mimicked in a high-pitched tone. I couldn't exactly elbow him with Riley looking. I was still trying to get the man to not think the worst of me.

"Shouldn't you be doing something?" I snapped instead.

Nash's smile never wavered. It hardly ever did. He was the spitting image of Wyatt, except his black hair was close-cut in a military style. "I know what you want to be doing," he teased before shutting the door and ensuring the final word.

Wyatt and Aver waited at the porch. They'd have their

own annoying taunts locked and loaded. I sighed, looking back down the driveway. This wasn't the morning I'd planned for, but it was likely the morning I deserved. I could only hope that everything with Paul checked out. And I would secretly hope that Riley was the one to call me when it did.

2

RILEY

"Thanks, Hal. And you're sure there isn't anything else on his record? A runaway report? Was he ever picked up for solicitation?" I hated that in my line of work, I was required to ask the tough questions. But if I didn't ask them, who would?

"Nothing here," Hal my colleague from Seattle, said. He was the only one from my old life who knew where I'd gone. "You got an easy first case. Everyone seems to be who they said they were." He paused, but the silence felt heavy, like he had more to say. "Doing okay out there?"

The first day had been the worst, going from the bustle of Seattle to the absolute quiet of Walkerton. And then the fear that I hadn't gone far enough crept in. Hal didn't know a lot about why I'd accepted the hurried transfer or the reason for the conditions I'd required. "It's been an adjustment," I said with an airy laugh.

"Don't act like it's all roses, Riley. You left here like the devil himself was chasing after you."

Being threatened by the man I'd thought would protect me would do that. I'd saw my life flash before my eyes and decided that I didn't want it to end there. Blaine's face would not be the last one I saw. "It's not all bad," I told him. There was no reason he needed to worry. "I've already got a place. It's small but has everything I need. And it's so beautiful here. Lots of room to explore. I might even get a dog." Having one in the city hadn't been possible.

Hal sighed heavily. "If you say so. Don't hesitate to call. Even outside of working hours."

"Hal." I drew his name out, making one syllable into two. I'd asked him several times not to worry. Being connected to me wouldn't do him any favors when the wrong people came asking.

"Okay, okay, I'll stop nagging. I pulled the previous caseload from the guy you replaced. You should at least have plenty of time to get settled in. Perfect some of those projects you always have."

Hal—a married black man in his early sixties—and I had bonded over our love of DIY. At first, the hobby had been necessary. I'd been alone, trying to afford to live in an expensive city. I'd barely had enough money for rent, much less furniture. But anything could be turned into furniture if you had glue, paint, fabric, and a staple gun. Now, we both had a habit of starting projects before the previous ones were finished. He liked to joke that we were kindred spirits who enjoyed doing everything the hard way. Looking at my current situation, I couldn't say he was wrong. "That will be perfect. I've got a new space to furnish."

I thanked Hal again, ensuring I would call the next week before hanging up and turning back to my computer, which was more of a paperweight at this point. When I'd asked the sheriff about an internet connection, he'd replied with *it comes and goes*. He hadn't been joking. I could check my email, but anything more than that, and the connection dropped so many times along the way that the entire thing just became a lesson in frustration with no payoff. I'd finally given up on trying to get any information on Paul's case and had called Hal to check the databases in the city. Of course, even a highspeed fiber optic connection was slower than how I could have gotten the honest answers, but I was done doing that. I'd said that before, time and again, but this time, I meant it. No shortcuts. I'd take the long way and live.

These extra steps were still better than winding up dead in a ditch, which was what would have happened had I stayed in Seattle. I'd been lucky to get this quiet transfer. And I was my own boss here. Sort of. I was the only social worker in the county, which would have been daunting if it weren't for the fact that I'd been told this position was mostly symbolic anyway. Walker County, while secluded and accessible only by a series of ferries from mainland Washington, was large. Though the county was sparsely populated, it was too large not to have any one from social services on hand. I wouldn't be extremely busy, but at least I wouldn't burn out.

Though you might burn up.

Unbidden, Branson Walker's face formed in my mind. He was the epitome of tall, dark, and handsome, but with a trimmed beard and warm hazel eyes that had effortlessly thawed my icy shell. They certainly made men tougher out here on the islands. But unprofessional didn't begin to explain the attraction. When he'd held out his hand, I'd wanted to touch it, if only to find out if his hands would feel soft against my skin or if he had calluses that would scrape.

I gulped and readjusted in my squeaky office chair. It made no sense to run away and then immediately get involved with one of the town's most famous citizens. I wasn't even sure if the guy was gay. Besides, the idea in Walkerton was to fly under the radar. Only a few people knew of my transfer; only Hal knew *where* I'd been transferred. He was also the only one who knew I'd changed my last name in the process. People would still be searching for me, if they hadn't already started, but out here, I was counting on seeing them coming long before they got close. Which I couldn't do if I was making moony eyes at the first hot—*extremely gorgeous*—man I met.

I dialed the sheriff to get my mind off Branson Walker and because it was my job to inform him what I'd learned. The phone rang three times.

"Is that you calling?" Sheriff Maslow called from his cubicle down the hall.

I hung up with a low growl. "Yes, that's me." He could probably tell by which button had been flashing on his phone. I wasn't used to such a small, mixed office or working with people who seemed to make a sport out of clinging to their ways.

"We're real informal around here," the sheriff said, filling my doorway in the next moment.

"I just wanted to tell you I heard back about Paul. His story checks out. He is eighteen. He has no runaway or missing person reports on him and no rap sheet that I can find."

The sheriff adjusted his belt. "Good to hear. Though I figured that was the case. Those Walker boys are a good sort."

I'd been in social services long enough to know it didn't matter how people seemed. Actions spoke louder. But in this case, I was inclined to believe the sheriff. *Because you have a stupid, high school crush?* I was thankful for the desk; it hid most of my fidgeting.

"Did you let Branson know? I think he was eager to hear."

That didn't sound like a good idea. "If you have better rapport with him, you can make the call."

The sheriff snickered. "Nah, you go ahead. Seemed you two hit it off."

Had he not seen the part where I'd assumed Branson was some unfortunately attractive pedophile? That he was even nice to me after that was more than I could have hoped for. Suspecting the worst was part of my job, and I hadn't been about to stop just because the man looked like he'd walked out of every lost-in-the-woods fantasy I'd ever concocted. Though I wondered if this wasn't the sheriff's way of implying they were gay friendly. I'd never look down my nose on acceptance, especially in a more rural area. "I can make the call." I patted my pockets for the business card. "Sheriff Maslow..."

"You know you can call me Jake," the sheriff said.

"Yes, sorry, Jake. What is up with the Walkers? I mean, the ones on the other side of bay too." I recalled the way Branson had described them. "The fancy ones."

The sheriff gave me a knowing look, though I wasn't sure all of what he thought he knew. "They're a curious bunch. I'm surprised it's taken you this long to ask. The easiest explanation is that they are old money. They were here before the ferry routes. They made this town and still own a lot of it. But, for all that money, they stay on their side of the bay."

"You don't get many calls over there?"

The sheriff shook his head. "Never. Rich and private. All that land is privately owned and not just by the Walkers. A few other families have made the other side their home too. They must work together or help each other out because not a one of them travels across the river for work. Only the four Walker cousins and Nana Walker live on this side of the bay. For the most part, we don't bother the other side, save for the spare noise complaint."

I opened the internet browser on my computer and clicked to a search engine, but a few seconds later, there was still just a spinning loading icon. I cursed under my breath. Guess I wouldn't be digging up any dirt on my own. "Noise complaint?"

"Yeah, they own show dogs or something. Sometimes, they get to howling, and it's like the whole island is surrounded. Been a while, though. I think they got this litter trained right."

Wealthy recluses who lived on a commune and raised show dogs...

Sure, that makes complete *sense.*

"Sorry, just one more thing. I can't seem to find that card Mr. Walker gave me."

Sheriff Maslow ducked his head, peering at me from under furrowed eyebrows. "The card there in your hand?"

I had to look to see. I'd been holding the card the whole time, though I couldn't be sure when that had started. If the sheriff had suspected I was gay and earlier had been his attempt at inclusivity, he likely knew without a doubt now that I'd been attracted. And if he didn't, he would just think I was brainless. "Right. Here in my hand. Good eye. I'll just...make the call then."

I set the card down and picked up the receiver, only to set it back down quickly. "Is anyone going to lunch?"

The sheriff looked over my head at the clock hanging on the wall. "It's four PM."

"So it is." And I'd already had lunch earlier while trying

to access the national runaway database on my phone. It had not been optimized for mobile.

"He's a good guy. He won't bite your head off," the sheriff said, stepping inside my small office. His cheeks burned a little pinker than they'd been while he'd been lingering in the doorway. "And I happen to know that he is a gay man, if that is anything that would interest you."

I sat with my spine straight, which only made my tailbone press uncomfortably into the lumpy cushion. "I'm not sure why you think..."

The sheriff's entire face blazed red, and he lifted his hands out in front of him while taking rapid steps backward. "It's none of my business. But, you could do worse. And around here, I don't know that you could do better."

Great, it wasn't so much that he wanted to show how accepting they were, but that I was likely the only other gay man he thought he knew, which meant I had to be attracted to the other gay man he knew.

The fact that I was just annoyed me further.

Once the sheriff left, I had no reason not to make the call. It was Friday; I could find something to do for one more hour and then call on Monday. Unless there was a special case, I worked regular office hours. I was still getting used to my small apartment in the center of downtown Walkerton. I could relax, unpack, *spend every one of my forty-eight hours rehearsing this call...*

Before I could come up with another reason to talk myself out of it, I dialed. My throat constricted, and I clenched the plastic receiver, debating hanging up. But it had rung, and there wasn't a phone in the world, except the one I was on, that didn't have caller ID.

"Branson Walker speaking."

I leaned over my desk as if I was trying to jump into the phone—or maybe away. "Hi, this is, Mr. Riley. Uh, no, Monroe. This is..." I took a deep breath. This shouldn't have been the difficult part. "This is Riley Monroe from Social Services."

Branson chuckled. "Mr. Monroe, you work fast."

"I like to get right to business." My eyes rolled so hard, I feared they'd be stuck that way. *I like to get right to business?* There'd been no better way to phrase that? I knew there was; I just couldn't do anything about it now. "I got in contact with my superiors in Seattle. Paul is eighteen, and right now, there isn't any evidence that anyone is looking for him."

"That still doesn't explain how he got all the way here from Texas," Branson said, surprising me. Most people in his situation would've wiped their hands of it. Actually, most people would've sent Paul away.

Nothing that I'd learned had explained why Delia Walker had gussied up a young man before sending him to her son's house. "I don't have an answer to that. If he isn't underage or being abused, my hands are pretty much tied." I'd offer him help now that he was here. Affordable housing, food, and classes, if he needed them, but I couldn't make Paul do anything.

"Tell you what," Branson replied smoothly. "Why don't we talk more about it over dinner tonight?"

I couldn't tell if he meant on a *date* date, or if he was being literal, and he wanted to talk about the case. "I'm not legally able to share information with you past what you've supplied us." I licked my lips, glad that I had the phone between us and Branson couldn't see that my mouth had gone so dry, I'd had to force the words out.

"Okay, then just dinner. We don't have to talk at all.

We'll just sit there silently and then eat." He laughed, and my ears soaked the noise in, like water to a sponge.

I'd planned to say no, politely yet firmly, but when my lips parted with a rejection, I heard myself say, "Sure," instead. By the time I'd hung up, Branson had told me when and where, and I was left to sit there in silence and blink, wondering where the heck I'd gone wrong.

———

THE WHEN WAS THAT NIGHT. The *where* ended up being a quaint but charming restaurant that offered wide views of the river. Branson had offered to pick me up, but considering he was the one driving into town from just outside of it, I thought that was a bit silly. The restaurant, the White Otter, was within walking distance of my apartment.

I showed up ten minutes early, fully expecting to wait in the lobby, but found Branson already there, chatting with the hostess. When he saw me, he smiled and excused himself. The hostess, a woman in her late twenties, eyed me curiously as Branson approached.

"Prompt. I had a hunch," Branson said, offering his hand.

Normally, it didn't take people more than twice to stop doing that with me. I didn't love rejecting the gesture but had learned long ago it was better to reject it than face the consequences. Instead, I clapped him on the shoulder, but he thought I'd been going in for a hug instead. Fully clothed, his skin never brushed mine—at least, I didn't think it did. His scent enveloped me during the awkward embrace, fresh and woodsy. When he stepped back, his hazel eyes several shades warmer, I knew we hadn't touched because he gestured to the side for me to follow him.

That's one catastrophe avoided. I only had to endure countless more before the night was up.

In Seattle, where I hardly ran into the same people day after day, it had been easier not to touch without drawing attention to myself. But here in Walkerton, it was going to be an issue. I'd have to start wearing gloves like I'd done when I was younger. That was clear to me now. And maybe, when I was going to be around the Walkers, a full body suit.

Branson brought us to a table right next to the wide windows. It was too dark to see much out the window, but the moonlight glinted off the river beautifully. "It sure is pretty here," I said, catching Branson's pleased smile.

"I'm enjoying the view," Branson said, but he wasn't looking out the window.

I blushed, and, as always, the flush didn't stop at my cheeks. It traveled down my neck and arms, evident in the large red splotches against my skin. I cleared my throat. Coming here had been a poor choice, but it wasn't too late to set the record straight. "Mr. Walker—"

"Please, call me Branson."

"Branson... I'm new here in Walkerton, and though I've only been here a few days..."

"Hey there, I'm Alexis, and I'll be your waitress today," Alexis chirped, setting two menus down on the table as well as two ice waters with lemon. "Our special today is a black-ened sockeye salmon with zesty lemon pepper pilaf. For dessert we have a marionberry shortbread, and for drinks, our bartender has featured the lemon-ginger Grey Goose martini. He calls it the Sour Goosetini."

Branson handed the menus back. "That all sounds amazing. What do you think?"

I normally hated when other men tried to order for me.

There was simply too much implied in the gesture, but the way Branson took charge, but then checked to make sure, had me nodding. "That sounds great."

"I hope you don't mind," Branson said after Alexis left. "That all just sounded too good to pass up."

I reached for my glass and enjoyed the ice-cold water against my throat. Being around Branson brought my body temperature up by several degrees. I'd be lucky to make it out before my pits started sweating. I'd known he was handsome. Now, I could add effortlessly confident to that list. He owned a business, and he didn't look like he spent his weeknights chugging beers on the couch. Did he have some horrible gambling addiction? A weird fetish? I imagined in an area this secluded, he would be a catch, snapped up along with the rest of those cousins he lived with.

Though I'd been busy interviewing Paul, I would have been blind to miss that they'd all been ridiculously good-looking. Like, too much for any one person to claim.

"You haven't spoken for thirty seconds," Branson said with a smile.

"I'm trying to figure out what's wrong with you," I blurted. Normally, other people were blurting personal things out around me. It wasn't fun the other way around.

Branson laughed, and I enjoyed the way the humor colored his skin and made his hazel eyes sparkle. "Plenty, I assure you. You were saying something before Alexis stopped by."

I was? Oh yes, I was letting him know that, while I appreciated the invitation, nothing could come of this date. I didn't want to say that, but I needed to. Then I could put this crush behind me and concentrate on doing my job as quietly as possible. But, as I opened my mouth to put a stop to the warm fuzzy feelings building in my stomach, I spotted Alexis coming from the other side of the dining area. I smiled, which prompted Branson to turn to see what I was looking at. "We're on the same schedule," I said when Alexis set down our drinks. Branson chuckled, but the waitress just looked pleasantly confused.

"I'll be back with your bread," she said.

"I got a warning this time," I murmured under my breath, surprised when Branson chuckled. Everyone better hearing out here where the noises were drowned out by the constant thrum of the city.

I sipped the martini. It was sweet, sour, and spicy all at once. Shadowing it all was the unmistakable burn of alcohol. I didn't drink a lot—it wasn't safe for a person like me—and a single sip was all it took for my head to feel light. "Better take it easy on that," I commented, nodding to the drink.

"Don't worry, I'll keep an eye on you," Branson said, managing to not sound creepy, but genuine.

I frowned and blocked my mouth with another quick sip. I was too trusting—laughable, considering my past. There was something warm about Branson, a certain quality I couldn't put my finger on. Well, I could put my finger on him and then learn a whole lot, but that would be opening the same can of worms that was trying to kill me now.

Alexis returned soon after with the bread. I dove for a slice, snagging the closest piece from the basket before she'd walked away from the table. I'd lunged too quickly, though, and the side of my hand brushed her thumb as she set down the butter I hadn't noticed on her tray.

"I think you're both hot, and when I go into the kitchen, I imagine you together," Alexis said suddenly. Her lips parted in shock, along with her eyes, and for a second she just stood there, gaping at the two of us.

I pulled my hand back, folding it into my lap while looking down at the tablecloth.

"I'm so sorry. I don't know why... I... just said that."

"It's fine," I said quickly, trying to put her out of her misery. "I mean it," I smiled, aware of Branson's curious gaze. "I mean, look at the guy," I said with a brisk wave in Branson's direction.

The waitress let out a frustrated puff of air that lifted her bangs from her forehead. "I am really sorry. That just... well, let me get you a free appetizer. How do mozzarella sticks sound? They are a specialty."

She left before either of us could decline.

"Huh," Branson said when Alexis was out of earshot. "That was strange. I've never heard her say something like that before. Maybe she's been taste testing too many of those sour geese."

"Sour Goosetinis. You should try yours." I demonstrated by taking another sip. My toes curled, though not all because of the booze.

"I'm a little afraid now that I see their power." Branson smiled. His right arm rested on the table. He'd rolled the sleeves of his form-fitting black sweater up to his elbows. "So, what brought you all the way out to Walker County?"

This was an answer I had rehearsed. "I wanted to get out of the city for a bit. Seattle is nice. There is a lot going on and just about anything you could ask for in terms of food and entertainment, but—" *Too many people want me dead.* "...it was time for a change," I finished with a shrug.

"A long-term change?"

I smirked and leaned back in my chair. "It's a little early to be talking long-term, don't you think?"

"I believe in being prepared. I've got to know if our next date should be something that extols the virtues of Walker County, or if you are sold."

I appreciated the honesty more than he knew. People weren't ever so forthcoming—without help. "Our next date?" Despite his honesty, I couldn't let that slide.

Branson leaned forward. "I mean, this one is going so well, people are writing fanfic about us."

I was still laughing when Alexis came back with the appetizer. She set it down quickly, mumbling something about giving us some time before she brought out our entree. I felt bad, but I couldn't offer any explanations. Getting so close had been a mistake, one that had already been smoothed over and that I wouldn't make again.

By the time our entree plates were cleared and dessert arrived, I was on my second Sour Goosetini. Branson was still on his first. He'd kept up an easy conversation, asking me all the normal questions that I'd already prepared for. When the bill came, he grabbed it before I could reach for my wallet. He insisted on paying for the cheese sticks, despite Alexis telling him he didn't need to, that she was really sorry, and she still wasn't sure why she'd said what she said.

I'd kept my head turned away, worried that either pity or guilt would shine on my face. I didn't understand my ability. I'd never met anyone else who could do anything remotely similar. My ability had only ever brought me trouble. People didn't spill their deepest secrets for a reason. I'd heard countless things I wished I hadn't, and even more that I'd thought I'd wanted to hear, only to regret it after the fact. And things always got worse the moment anyone else found out what I could do. This last emergency move was proof of that.

We lingered outside the restaurant. I'd shoved my hands into my pockets, and they'd have to stay there. The food and conversation had been better than I'd had in a while. The drinks only heightened all those happy feelings. I wasn't out of control or anything like that, but I was enjoying myself. I'd gone almost all week without looking over my shoulder, and Branson was easier to get along with than I'd imagined.

"I don't want to say good night," he said, stepping in front of me on the path from the restaurant to the sidewalk. He was taller than me, and my gaze rested naturally at his chest level. "You don't have to work tomorrow, do you? My cousin owns a bar near here. They have other drinks too."

I wanted to say yes, but I was beginning to sense a pattern and worried that if I didn't put my foot down soon, I never would.

But even while I knew and acknowledged that, I wanted to say yes. So I resorted to drastic measures. I stuck my hand out.

Branson eyed it as if already aware of the trap that it was. "A goodbye handshake?"

"Maybe it's a hello one instead."

He grabbed my hand. His was warm and larger than mine. We'd pumped once when he said, "I hope tonight ends with a kiss." Branson immediately dropped my hand and stumbled back.

There wasn't normally a physical sensation associated with my touch, but Branson acted like I'd shocked him. Was he insanely good at putting two and two together?

"I don't know why I said that," he said, sounding exactly like Alexis. His lips turned up in a broad smile. "Since it's out there, what do you think?"

It was my turn to be dumbfounded. I was often surprised by what people said, but not usually in a good way. I couldn't even be unhappy that my plan had failed, or, if it hadn't failed, backfired. I was in Walkerton under duress, technically hiding for my life. But that had still been the most effortless date I'd ever been on. Listening to my impulse, I grabbed his hand again. I didn't have a lot of control of my ability, but normally after the first touch, it simmered to a more manageable level where people weren't randomly blurting out their most shameful secrets. Branson accepted my hand with a wince, making me wonder what he was expecting to happen. I tugged him closer and kissed his cheek. "I think you should show me your cousin's bar."

3

BRANSON

Riley sat on a tall stool at the other side of the circular table. We'd both ordered waters from Wyatt, earning me an eye roll—Riley still got a winning smile.

"The four of you live together? For how long?" Riley asked.

The music at the Greasy Stump wasn't so loud that I couldn't hear him, but I watched his lips move anyway. Watching him talk was hypnotic. Almost as good as listening to him speak. I couldn't pinpoint the exact thing that drew me to him; *every part* of him appealed to me. I sat a little taller, casting my gaze to those sitting around us in the busy bar. A few looked like they were on dates, but most had rolled in after the end of the workday.

Wyatt's bar was the type of place that had something for everyone. But the only thing I was interested in sat across from me.

"We grew up together, actually. Our houses were next door," I said, leaving out the parts where the four of us had to sneak out to see each other. It was all well and fine when we'd been little children, but the older we'd gotten, the more our parents had tried to keep us apart. Of course, the reasons for that had become clear on our eighteenth birthday. "We moved to this side of the bay when we turned eighteen."

"We?" Riley asked, toying with his straw. "You were born close together?"

"The same day," I said, knowing that would only bring on a round of new questions. I didn't want to talk about me, though. I wanted to talk about Riley. Maybe then I would figure out why I felt so drawn to him beyond his obvious physical characteristics.

Do you need a second reason? Normally, I didn't.

When the four of us had broken free of the packs, we'd gone hog wild. We'd been four eighteen-year-old alphas finally free of the stringent rules and regulations that had governed our lives. What was an hours-long ferry ride when there was the chance of getting laid with no strings attached on the other side? Back then, nothing about sex had been complicated. But these days, I spent more time behind a desk or on a job site than sitting across from an attractive man.

I was out, which was more than I could say for Aver, but while I had the freedom to live how I wanted no matter who was watching, lately, I hadn't had the time.

"That must be nice," Riley said. "It's like a built-in support system." He grabbed his glass and avoided my gaze.

"That's kind, though I wouldn't let any of them hear you. They'll feel important for weeks."

Riley laughed, and I was doubly glad since it wiped the frown away. Maybe he didn't have a family. By the way he talked about support systems, that was my hunch. "And that would be bad? If they felt important?"

"It would be terrible. Wyatt's already too self-important

for his own good." My gaze drifted to my cousin, who was currently pouring shots for a group of girls who couldn't be much older than twenty-one. He winked as he passed the shots over, making the girl in front visibly swoon.

Riley followed my gaze and snorted. "I see what you mean."

I cleared my throat and scooted my chair over, partially blocking Riley's view of the bar. It was childish, and I wasn't used to having such a jealous streak, but I felt possessive of Riley's gaze. He looked away from my cousin easily, smiling when our gazes collided again.

"I'm having a great time. I don't remember the last time I've had so much fun, actually," Riley said.

I slid my hand forward on the table, meaning to grab his, but he'd let his fall beneath the table. He'd been strange about touching, all the way until the end of dinner. What had changed then, and how did I get back to that moment? Was I so out of practice that I didn't know how to seal the deal?

Except sealing the deal wasn't at all what I wanted to do. I wasn't in a rush to have sex with Riley—okay, I wasn't in a rush to *only* have sex. While spoken a little premature, I'd been honest when I said I hoped the night ended with a kiss. But I wanted to skip all of this "getting to know you" stuff, the banal small talk and meaningless banter. I wanted to get to the heart of him, but I couldn't expect something like that right away. I'd done nothing to deserve more of Riley. I wanted desperately to change that.

I stretched my leg out under the table, meeting his foot. Riley gasped quietly when our legs collided, and I couldn't tell if he was skittish or extremely responsive. I left it there, my foot just barely touching his. I felt young again, stretching through my limits slowly so as not to scare him off.

It hadn't been too difficult to hide my shifter nature from romantic partners. But there was a fair amount of being careful and mindful. Perhaps that was why I recognized the same actions in Riley. Even when he seemed relaxed, he had an awareness about him that never completely faded. "I want to kiss you again," I said, deciding that, when I was able, honesty was the best policy.

Riley jolted, jerking his hands and feet closer to him. "Sorry."

I frowned. "Sorry... you don't want to kiss me?"

His face blazed red. *This was going well. Had I misread the situation?* No, he'd just said how much fun he was having. "I do," he whispered. "I want to kiss you. I just...I wasn't sure if you meant to say that."

I'd had less to drink than he had, but what other reason did he have to wonder if I was letting things slip that I didn't mean to?

Things had seemed that way with Alexis. My cousins and I were regular customers of The White Otter. She'd never said anything remotely risqué before. Maybe it all had more to do with Riley's presence? He had an honest face. Perhaps he made people want to tell the truth?

I'd have to be careful, but I wasn't about to back off. Especially not after he'd just admitted to feeling the same way. I scooted my chair over, around the table, sitting next to him. He was nestled against the wall while I sat partially in the walkway, but it was worth it to be close enough for our knees to bump. I grabbed his hand, and he hissed, his eyes flying to my lips. Letting him see my smile, I tugged him closer.

I didn't worry that I was moving too quickly. This felt right. Riley felt right.

His lips were soft and yielded to my mouth, but the rest of him was as stiff as the tabletop in front of us. He didn't push away, but he didn't hold me closer either. As I worried again that I'd read him wrong, a peace that I could not claim ever having felt before settled inside me. I knew, without a doubt, that I was doing the exact thing I was meant to be doing. Kissing Riley.

I deepened the kiss, sliding a possessive hand up to cup his nape. He moaned softly, but it was all I needed. My tongue brushed his lower lip, and he shivered. I wished I could have felt him tremble in my arms, if only so I could hug him tightly and let him know that whatever this was he felt crackling like static electricity between us, I felt it too. "Come home with me," I murmured. I hadn't thought the request over; I'd spoken it the moment the words had formed. But I didn't regret it. Even if his answer was no, I couldn't regret it.

"Okay," Riley whispered.

I caught hold of his trembling bottom lip between my teeth, making Riley gasp again, softly. "Wait here. I'll just go settle up."

I got to my feet, but Riley kept hold of my sleeve, tugging me back shyly. "We ordered water."

My lips stretched into a smile. "That's right." I couldn't blame booze for my goofy grin. I hooked my right arm over Riley's shoulders, and he settled into the crook of my body as I grabbed our waters by their rims with my other hand. Dropping them on the end of the bar, I gave Wyatt a small goodbye wave, and he gave me a ridiculous double thumbs-up.

I pulled Riley out quickly so he couldn't see. Wyatt couldn't understand what was going on or what I thought I felt. To him, this was a normal date that was going very well.

To me, it felt like a beginning. And I couldn't wait to get started.

4

RILEY

How COULD I be so sure and yet so uncertain? I wished I could touch myself and force the honest answer from my lips. Sitting in the passenger seat of Branson's truck only made me want to touch myself more, but in a way that might have caused Branson to crash us into the ditch.

He wanted me—I had no questions on that. He was upfront and open, two qualities that I appreciated. And he was hot. Insanely-talking-down-my-dick-all-night hot. His every gesture and motion was intentional. His confidence was infectious, making me feel like a better version of myself just from being around him.

And when we touched, he didn't say things that made me want to die on the inside. The opposite.

At the same time, I'd been down this road before. I'd fallen deep for a man so skilled at making me feel like I was the one in the wrong, even when I had the truth right in front of me. It had taken me an embarrassing amount of time to realize that, and by the time I had, I'd been forced to run. I didn't know if I could trust my emotions anymore.

Not even when Branson turned down the lit driveway that led to his beautiful home.

I'd been too busy earlier worrying for the client to truly appreciate the architecture. The lights were on inside, giving the front-facing windows a warm glow as Branson parked at the end of the driveway. At the most basic level of description, it was a rustic log cabin, but I hesitated to call the sprawling home in front of me a cabin. It was large and impressive while also matching its surroundings perfectly. There wasn't a neatly trimmed lawn that lined the walkway to the front porch, but rather, the outside had been left to look as if the house had grown out of the landscape, complete and ready to be lived in. Both charming and extraordinary.

It was a testament to the home that I noticed and appreciated it long before I spotted the wide expanse of the bay behind it.

Branson cut the engine, and the dome light illuminated, shoving all thoughts of the view to the background. Was I really going to go home with a man I'd met that day? A man who I likely shouldn't have been getting involved with anyway? He played a role in my case, my first case since coming to Walkerton. He'd been cooperative, and while I still didn't have a clue as to why his mother would've done all that he said she did, I didn't think Branson was responsible for anything.

"You're as stiff as a board."

I angled toward Branson as he did the same. He'd been honest with me, so I could be honest with him. "I'm freaking out."

"Do you want me to take you back?" he asked, though there wasn't any annoyance or anger in the question. I truly felt like if I'd said yes, he would've dropped me off at my apartment without a sour word. And maybe that's what I should've done.

But it wasn't what I wanted to do. And why did I have to hide in the shadows? Because I'd trusted the wrong man? There was no comparison between Branson Walker and any other man I'd ever dated. I'd known him a day and was already sure of that. "No, I don't want to go back."

"Take a walk with me?" Branson asked.

It was dark out. I could see what I had of the land thanks to the clear sky and full moon. "Isn't the forest dangerous at night?"

Branson grinned. "I'll protect you." Any other man might have sounded cocky saying such a thing, but from Branson's mouth, it just sounded like fact.

I pressed the button on my buckle, and Branson did the same. I got the idea he'd been waiting on me to make a choice before unbuckling himself. I got out and shut the door, turning to find Branson close by. He gestured wide with his arm toward a cement walkway, and I headed down it, smiling.

"We have to thank our Nana Walker for the land. She owned it when my cousins and I left home."

"She gave it to you?" I asked. The route around the house turned into a cobbled path.

"She tried to. We paid her every penny of the land's worth. Though she refuses to spend it. Stubborn woman."

My toe caught the edge of one of the stones, and I lurched forward, sure that I would fall. Branson caught me before I could, setting me right. His hand trailed down the length of my arm to my hand as I regained my balance. When I was ready to continue, I gave a little nod, but Branson never let go of my hand.

His palm was heavy but warm, and I was in no hurry to drop it. "Your grandmother sounds like a nice woman." Was that envy in my tone?

"She's our great-grandmother, and she is. Though, now that we're talkin' 'bout her, I'm feeling a little guilty."

"Uh-oh..."

"No, it's nothing all that bad. She called me today, and I didn't call her back. She is a fierce, wonderful woman, but she has a tendency to catastrophize or speak in riddles. She's big into fortunes, not a fan of explaining her cryptic messages." Branson rolled his eyes, but, coming from him, even that was attractive. "I'll call her in the morning. She'd threaten to skin my hide if she knew I was taking up valuable date time talking about her."

I smiled, even though I had no idea what that would be like. A doting grandmother? A family that worried? Those were foreign concepts. Hal was the closest thing I had to a relative, and we'd only met outside of work once. "I don't know my grandmother." My lips formed the words before I thought to stop them. What sort of date banter was this? I cringed, peeking up at Branson when he didn't respond right away.

But there was only compassion. Compassion and something else that had me swallowing hard.

"I'm sorry," I said, tugging at the hand he held. He had to be done with the romance part now, right? Hadn't I killed it?

But he tightened his fingers, reminding me of just how much stronger he was. "For what? I like knowing about you. I only have a trillion questions I want to ask but am holding back so you don't think I'm nosy."

His words could've been spurred by our holding hands, but I didn't think so. For the first time in my life, I'd met a man who spouted honesty all on his own. "There isn't a lot to know, I'm afraid. I was a child when my parents died. I don't have many memories of them. They were close with our neighbors who had a child around my age. I'm not sure if they had a pact or what, but when my parents died, they took guardianship of me."

"And you got to live with your friend," Branson added, trying to spin a happy end on my sad tale.

"For a bit," I conceded. "But when we were eight, he got sick and passed. It was horrible, and after, his parents... I don't know. I think they resented me." Why was I telling Branson all of this? It was the truth, but that was just the problem. My childhood had been bittersweet. I'd had all the basics—food, shelter, clothing, an education—but none of the warmth. Back then, my ability was sporadic, but as I grew, it became more powerful. For the last few months before I left for college, my guardians wouldn't even be in the same room as me. "Sorry, this isn't date talk."

Branson pulled us to a stop and turned me around toward the water. I'd been so wrapped up in spilling all my dirty secrets that I noticed the view for the first time. My breath caught in my throat, and for a moment, I could just stand there.

We were behind the house, at the edge of their yard. Ahead of us, the grass sloped gently downward where it eventually became sand. The water of Walker Bay lapped gently at the shore, while the moon shone so brightly the light reflected off the ripples. "It's beautiful," I whispered, shivering against a cold wind.

Branson moved, occupying the space behind me. He let go of my hands and wrapped his arms around me, clasping them together at my front. I settled my hands over his, leeching off his warmth but also enjoying the feeling of simply being held. Branson had no way of knowing, but the constant touching would help. The only control I'd ever managed to find over my ability was continued proximity. The longer someone was around me, physically touching me, the less my ability affected them. "Is that better?" he asked as my breathing turned shallow.

Could he hear my heart beating? It pounded against my ribs, though not from fear. Tendrils of excitement wound around me like vines, urging me closer to the man behind me. He'd meant to warm me up; I had to remind myself that was why he'd touched me in the first place. I wasn't cold anymore.

I burned for him.

"Yes, thank you," I whispered because he'd asked me a question, and it was polite to answer. My tongue felt thick. In fact, everything on my body felt weighted with desire. "You're so lucky to have this. The house, the view. In Seattle, you'd have to be a millionaire, and even then, you'd have to choose one."

Branson made a rumbling noise, like a groan but softer, higher pitched. Whatever the sound was, I knew, without a doubt, that it was one of contentment. *But how?*

"We are lucky for this land. We cleared this section and used the lumber to build the house."

Holy crap, now that *was* impressive. I spun around, excited at this new information. "You built it? By yourself?"

Branson was already smiling, but it stretched a little wider at my questions. "I can't claim to have done it alone, no. Me and my cousins, though, we built it from the ground up. We had experts come in to check the plumbing and electrical. I like to do things on my own, but I don't mind stepping aside when a job requires more experience than motivation. The house used to be the image on my business cards. The very first project for Walker Construction."

A take-charge guy who knew when to hand over the reins... that wasn't something you saw every day. "Sorry, I must sound like a kid who wants to be a construction worker when they grow up. I like to build things, mostly stuff around the house."

Branson's eyebrows flared. He'd kept his arms around me, and his clasped hands rested at the small of my back. "Oh really? You're a carpenter too?"

I'd been so distracted at the thought of Branson creating the beautiful home behind us that I hadn't noticed the way he pressed against me. When he'd been behind me, I could distract myself with the moon or the water. Now, Branson was everywhere. His warmth and strength made my stomach clench, sparking a need that blossomed even lower than that.

"No, not a carpenter," I said, nervously licking my lips. Great, now he thought I was comparing my milk crate nightstand with his beautiful house. "I like to dabble. Mostly, I repurpose other people's trash into something usable. I guess I've always liked the idea of taking something that was thrown out and giving it new life." A bubble of emotion welled up in my throat. My emotions were all over the place. I couldn't keep up.

"That means you're creative. You can look at something and see what it could be."

He'd taken what I said and put the nicest possible spin on it. But I still couldn't look at his face.

He sighed, the noise sounding resigned yet uneasy. "What you must think of me. After the way we were introduced, and now, I can't keep my hands off you." As he spoke, his arms tightened around me.

I had a million reasons to tell him to stop, that it would be better if we slowed things down. But his face was so close. His breath tickled my cheek. He seduced me without effort. His presence made my knees weak. "I don't want you to." Even if things never progressed past this night, if this was as much of him as I got, I still wanted to experience the warmth and safety of his arms. I hadn't felt truly safe in an embrace for so long.

"I keep telling myself to slow down..." Branson murmured, his lips lowering closer. "...that I'll just scare you away."

Maybe I should've been scared, but fear wasn't what made my pants tight. Fear wasn't rushing up my spine. I angled my face up, as open an invitation as I could manage.

It was an invitation he accepted. His lips were soft, but unyielding, gentle, but persistent. He held me tight, and for good reason. My legs buckled, and I would've fallen otherwise. I opened my mouth to him, and he deepened the kiss, teasing my tongue with his. I sighed, sinking harder against him. Something deep in me, my soul—or essence—called to him, like recognizing like. Though, maybe it wasn't that we were the same, but that we matched.

Perfectly.

My arms wound around his neck, tracing lazy circles along his nape. He made a deep, rumbling noise, unlike the one he'd made earlier. This one sounded distinctly like a growl. The noise shot right to the core of me, sending blood rushing to my throbbing cock.

Branson unclasped his hands and cupped my bottom, letting me get used to the feeling before he gently kneaded the soft, rounded flesh. I had him so close, so very nearly where I wanted him, and yet each caress teased me higher. My hips moved of their own accord, thrusting softly. No matter the direction—forward, against his body, or backward, into his hands—I found pleasure.

In the distance, a wolf howled, the sound long and lonely. I pulled free with a gasp. "Did you hear that?" It was a stupid question. Of course he had. It had sounded so close. I peered in the direction that I'd thought the sound had come from. Somewhere to the right and just behind us. On the other side of the river...

Branson led me up the path, continuing straight toward the house instead of going back around. "Let's get inside," he said, his carefree tone at odds with his stiff body language.

"Do you have wolves up here?"

Branson opened the back door, one of two elegant glass double doors that opened into the kitchen. The lights turned on the moment I stepped inside. The kitchen was bright, airy, and most surprisingly—considering four bachelors lived there—clean. The exposed beams of the vaulted ceiling matched the natural grain of the cupboards and counters. The floor was hardwood as well, but a darker shade that glistened while also looking like it would be soft to the touch.

When I made my projects, I had paint and ingenuity to cover my mistakes, but *this* was pure craftsmanship. Unable to stop myself, I strode deeper into the kitchen, brushing my fingers along the grain of the countertop. He'd kept the natural characteristics of the wood intact. There had been no attempts to make the wood look like something else or to hide that it had once been a tree. I could imagine it, tall and proud, and though it no longer stood, it didn't feel like the trees had been destroyed, but made into something new. Something that would be appreciated and respected for generations to come. "You are amazing at what you do," I said.

When I lifted my gaze to him, Branson wasn't looking at his handiwork, but at me. "I like watching you admire it," he said sheepishly.

He'd stepped close again, and all thoughts of the cabinetry or woodwork fell from my mind. I turned to face him as he settled his palms against the counter on either side of me. I watched his mouth, the supple curve of the bottom lip, the small space where his mouth was parted. He canted his head, covering my mouth in a kiss that stole my breath away. I didn't care, I'd die gasping if that meant Branson's were the last lips I tasted. He kissed like it was his last act on earth. Desperation mixed with desire.

I felt like I'd been tossed into a stormy ocean, Branson's arms were my lifeboat, and all I had to do was hang on while we floated into ecstasy.

I broke the kiss with a ragged gasp. "Where is your bedroom?"

Branson lunged for me, as if the moments that we hadn't been kissing had been too many. He walked back, keeping our faces together as he navigated his home without looking. We stumbled together down the hallway, banging against the walls on either side like a pinball. When he kicked open his bedroom door, jackpot bells rang in my ears. I didn't second guess if this was the right move; I was too eager to see if Branson was as good commanding the rest of me as he was my lips.

He closed the door, blanketing us in darkness. I gripped the hem of his shirt, tugging it over his head. The collar snagged on his chin, and although I couldn't see him clearly, I felt his exposed muscle. My hands smoothed over every rigid curve of his chest. The collar lifted inches higher, and my eyes adjusted to the dim light, letting me see just Branson's smile. I paused, a wicked idea coming to me. Stepping back, I dropped to my knees and pulled his pants down.

"Riley?" Branson murmured. He'd kept the shirt the way I left it and reached blindly out in front of him.

Half of me expected him to rip the shirt off his head and reestablish his control. Clearly, he was a take charge kind of guy, but, when his fingers found my head nestled between his legs, he only carded his fingers through my hair.

He stood before me, blindfolded by his shirt, wearing only his briefs. His pants pooled at his ankles, and even in this half-undressed state, he commanded respect. He was rigid and hard *everywhere*, an apex predator if there ever was one. I hooked my index finger under the waistband of his underwear, and Branson made that rumbling sound.

I'd planned on going slowly, using my tongue first to grow accustomed to his length. The moment it was before me, jutting out at an upward angle—thick, long, and veiny, with a bulbous head—I couldn't help myself. I opened my mouth, filling it with him. I relaxed my throat, allowing Branson to slip down and earning me a sharp hiss and a curse. I paused there, swallowing around his hardness, massaging him with my throat muscles. I needed to move though, not only so I could breathe but because I wanted to keep exploring. I wanted to know every part of this glorious man.

I bobbed my head, flattening my tongue along the underside of his length as I memorized every inch of his hardness. My thoughts drifted away along with my worries. I had no worries, not now.

Branson's hand cupped my cheek, neither stopping nor guiding me, but just touching me as I serviced him. I peeked up at his uncovered face peering down at me.

"I don't mind letting you have your way with my body, but I will watch those gorgeous lips on my cock," he murmured. I spotted the shirt crumpled on the ground behind him.

Knowing he was watching only urged my desire higher. Power filled me, not because I was the strongest or fastest, but because I was bringing this man pleasure. *Me.* It was my lips that forced a groan through his lips. My tongue that had his hand flexing along my jaw. I lost myself, my mind reduced to only a few phrases that urged me to take more of him, suck him deeper. My eyes watered. Branson tenderly wiped the tears from my cheeks as his hips thrust with a lazy, steady rhythm.

He tapped my cheek, and my eyelids fluttered up, opening wide to look into his face without stopping. "I'm going to come," he said, caressing my face as he spoke.

I understood he was giving me the option, but he was crazy if he thought I didn't want a taste of him. Everything about this man told me he was dominant, masculine to the extreme, and I appreciated that. He didn't hide who he was, not like me. I tried to tell him with my eyes that I wanted his essence. I wanted it dripping off my tongue, sliding down my throat. I wanted him to claim my mouth with his dick as thoroughly as he had with his lips.

He got the message, and I felt the mood change. The playful, exploratory feel from moments before was gone. Branson took charge.

He guided my mouth, controlling the depth and speed. His growls grew louder, more frequent until the first jet of cum splashed against my tongue, and Branson roared as he filled my mouth. I swallowed as quickly as I could but hadn't been ready for there to be so much. It leaked from the corners, gliding down my chin in a carnal display.

I expected the mood to mellow after his orgasm. Most men would be done—if not for the night, then at least a few hours. But when I looked back up at Branson, his eyes held pure desire. His lips twisted, uttering a single command that made my dick twitch. "Get on the bed."

5

BRANSON

I DIDN'T WAIT for Riley to obey. I reached down, lifting him gently under his armpits to his feet and then off his feet to the bed. I set him down on the mattress. He was still fully clothed, a fact I remedied quickly. In seconds, he lay naked beneath me. Though I wanted inside of him more than I wanted anything else, I had to appreciate so much of his flesh on display. He had a naturally tan complexion and curves that I couldn't wait to get lost in. He wasn't overly muscled or too thin. He was soft, particularly along his hips and stomach, and my inability to not constantly be touching him increased tenfold.

I'd sensed Riley was different from the very beginning, and now, I was even more certain. I couldn't pinpoint the exact thing, only that my reactions to him were stronger, *purer* than they'd ever been. I wanted him—on his knees, in my bed, in my arms, I didn't care—as long as he was near enough for me to protect, care for, and love.

I lowered my face to his mouth, kissing along the edge of his lips, down his chin and to his neck. He held on to my arms. Every so often, his nails dug into my skin, letting me know I'd discovered a sweet spot. I memorized them. Before I was done, I wanted to know every spot on his body that made him feel good. Dimly, I remembered this was our first date, that maybe, things were moving more quickly than they should. Riley had seemed more than eager on his knees, and that zeal was still clear in the way he looked up at me, but there were things about me that he didn't know.

That I could turn into a wolf, for one. Being a shifter didn't grant me any magical powers—other than the obvious. If I thought he was in any danger from what I was, I'd put a stop to the whole thing, or, at the least, give him the information he needed to make an informed decision. But, at this point, knowing what I was would only place him in danger.

I pushed those thoughts from my mind. Being a shifter had controlled most of my life. It would not influence this moment. I licked down the middle of his chest to his stomach, stopping at his belly button. Riley giggled and wiggled. I tightened my grip on his hips, continuing my inspection of his body. My throat vibrated, a noise I couldn't remember making before. It was like a purring chuff, though I figured it was because I was so very happy with Riley naked beneath me.

I slid to the side of him, rolling him over so that he faced the other direction. I hated not seeing his eyes but loved the way my cock slipped between his cheeks. "I want to touch you all over," I murmured into his ear, biting his earlobe.

Riley's back bowed as he thrust his ass back as well as turning his face around, offering his lips to me. "Don't stop. Never stop. I've never... you make me feel like I'm floating." The apples of his cheeks tinged with a light blush, and I kissed those too before licking back down his neck, massaging his back. I snagged the lube from my nightstand and coated my fingers.

Riley hissed at the first brush of my fingers over his puckered hole. "You're so tight and hot. I can't wait to feel you tighten around me." The rest of Riley had been perfect; I wasn't sure why I'd be surprised he was perfect in this way as well. His body drew my fingers in, as eager for the intrusion as I was.

"Oh God, that's too good. It feels too good." He arched his back, throwing his head back as he bared his neck to me.

I latched on, sucking the sensitive flesh into my mouth as I delved between his cheeks. I was in no hurry, and the longer I took here, the easier it would be for Riley to accept my size. I scissored my fingers, earning another gasp. Sweat accumulated on our bodies, and I licked his shoulder, enjoying this new taste of him—salty but with a sweetness that came from him. Only him.

I switched hands, probing Riley's backside with my right so I could reach around him with my left and grasp his erection. Immediately, he humped into my hands, coming so quickly I couldn't help my low chuckle.

"Oh no, I'm sorry!" he gasped as he filled my hand.

"Sorry for what? That was just the first." I recalled the box of condoms in the bathroom and cursed softly. "Hold on, I need to get protection."

I rolled away, but before I could move very far, Riley snagged my arm. "You don't need to," he said shyly. "If you don't want to. It's been... a while for me. And I've been tested. I have my results online if you—"

I couldn't believe my ears. He was going to let me inside of him without a barrier? With nothing separating our bodies?

"I mean, that is... if you are..." He looked away with a

timidity that had no place between us, not when we'd been so open. I'd fallen hard and fast for this man.

"I'm clean," I told him. "Not only has it been more than a year, but I was recently tested." I had my own test in a drawer in the office. With as secretive as Aver needed to be, I made him get tested regularly, testing myself each time as well.

He didn't say anything, but he didn't have to. It was as if the air changed between us, growing thicker and sticky, drawing us nearer. My fingers were still coated with lube and his cum. I fisted my length at the base, swiping my cock with the slick mixture. Riley reached back for the rounded globe of his cheek and pulled, opening himself to me.

My heart pounded. This beautiful creature wanted me, was asking me to bring him pleasure. I would not disappoint or deny him. I flexed my hips, lining our bodies up as I probed him. His body was relaxed—my fingers and his orgasm had ensured as much—and I slipped inside of him with little resistance. He accepted me beautifully, inch by inch, until I nestled against his backside, the two of us spooned together, connected. He was everything I wanted, and way more than I deserved.

He bowed his back, drawing me deeper. "I feel you everywhere," he gasped.

I moved my hips slowly, but with deliberate, deep strokes inside him. Each forward drive allowed me to touch more, to claim more of him. In the pack, there were laws about claiming and naming an omega. They governed who could claim what and under what circumstances, who could be an omega. I'd always ignored it, uninterested in the concept of binding someone to me. But I could see the appeal now. I wanted Riley like this forever.

He shuddered as I probed him. His gasping moans grew

sharper, and I caressed his dick, rewarded with a burst of precum and a keening wail. "I can't... I have to come!" He cried out, his muscles contracting tight a moment before he screamed with pleasure.

I couldn't help myself. The stiffness of his body, his racking cries, the warmth of his release on my hand—I followed him into the abyss. My orgasm exploded through me. I licked his neck, not wanting to hurt his ears with the roar I barely held back. I nibbled his soft flesh instead, drawing it inside my mouth to lick and suck.

But, as my orgasm subsided, I felt the same stirring again. My cock was as hard as it had been before.

"Again?" Riley gasped, craning his neck around to look at me.

I felt the residual pleasure from the orgasm; it only added to the building anticipation. I'd never had trouble in the stamina department, but this was unusual even for me. Further proof that Riley was perfection on two legs. "Again," I growled, continuing my forward thrusts.

His body was covered in sweat, allowing my palm to glide over him to his chest where I gathered a nipple between my fingers and squeezed. Riley yelped, the sound transforming into a moan when I squeezed again, alternating between sides. "This is insane."

I captured his face, keeping it in place as I covered his mouth with a kiss. "This is what you do to me."

He slipped his tongue in my mouth, twining it around mine. His body wasn't his anymore, not in this bed. It was mine to pleasure, just as my body was his. I snaked my hand around his throat, holding him gently but firmly against his throat as my other hand gripped his hip. This wasn't sex. It couldn't even be lovemaking. It was a surrender.

Riley came several more times, I'd lost count of his and

my orgasms. Each time I filled him, my dick remained as hard as ever. The urge to pound into him only increased. I lost track of time. Nothing else mattered, not as much as what was right in front of me. I didn't care—I was doing the exact thing I wanted to do and never wanted to stop.

As the sweat cooled, so did my thrusts. I kissed his shoulder while dancing my fingers up his ribs. He was squishy there too. I loved every soft, welcoming part of him. I didn't know what had brought him to Walker County, but I was glad for it. Riley's breath grew soft and deep. I'd worn him out, literally.

I stayed inside him, content to snuggle, but unwilling to separate. Already, I thought about tomorrow, the next day, and the day after. How did I keep Riley exactly where he was? Did he even want to be there? My instincts told me yes, but so much could happen. For now, I would have to be satisfied holding him, knowing he was safe in my arms.

———

The moment my eyes opened again, I was aware of only one thing. Riley wasn't beside me.

I launched out of bed, scanning the room and confirming Riley was not where I'd left him. We'd had sex for hours. I'd come so many times, I wouldn't be surprised if my dick started shooting out dust. But now, he was gone.

He just isn't in your room. Calm down.

I ignored my own recommendation. I tried to remember where he'd lost his clothes. They weren't in this room either. Who was home right now? I wouldn't be so worried if Aver was up, but Wyatt didn't know when to shut his mouth, and I didn't even want to get started thinking about Nash.

I pulled on my jeans, not bothering to button them

before yanking my bedroom door open. I could still smell Riley's presence in my room. The scent was stronger when I opened the door. Exhaling, I relaxed a fraction, until I smelled someone else.

Riley wasn't alone.

And somehow, he was with someone worse than Wyatt and his loose lips, way worse than Nash and his insufferable arrogance.

I sprinted down the hallway, as the voices in the foyer grew louder.

"I was unaware he had company," my mother said stiffly.

I rounded the corner as Riley was trying to step around Delia Walker, but my mother pretended not to notice as she remained firmly in the middle of the doorway. Her pale eyes narrowed on Riley, who was obviously wearing clothes that had been thrown off in passion and had spent several hours crumpled on the floor.

"I, um, I met Branson yesterday. I'm the new social worker for the county," Riley said, clearly uncomfortable. He'd clamped his hands together in front of his body as he strained away from my mother, doing everything in his power not to bump into her. I strode forward to rescue him.

"And you were making house calls?" my mother sneered. Her dark hair was pulled back in a perfect low bun. Not a strand out of place. Her outfit looked expensive, not that I'd know a brand name from another. But with Delia Walker, it was a given.

"No," Riley replied before I could speak. He'd transformed from the man the night before, limp from having his every sexual desire satiated. His spine was stiff and straight, his chin raised. "I was called down here first to investigate a young man that I was told you sent here."

Delia straightened, clearly affronted, but if Riley

thought his words would make her step back, he would be disappointed. "I'm sure I don't know what you mean."

"I'm sure you don't," Riley muttered. He hadn't noticed me; neither of them had. But I'd been so blown away by Riley's gumption, I'd been paralyzed. He moved to step around her again. This time, Delia couldn't mask her refusal to step out of his way. I wasn't sure what this game was that she played. Delia had disdain for anything that she thought responsible for *tearing me from the pack*—her words. But this seemed heightened as well. She didn't normally resort to getting physical.

She thrust her hand out, snagging Riley's in a handshake he'd clearly been trying to avoid. Before Delia could pump their hands once, she said, "It was me. I sent the pup to my son to seduce him and bring him home." Delia gasped loudly, like she was wrenching back whatever other dark secret waiting to pour from her lips. Her eyes were wide now with shock and horror. She'd ripped her hand free as she stumbled from Riley to the porch, where she finally spotted me at the hallway.

"You've brought evil into this home!" she shrieked.

Riley was as white as a ghost. I toed out from the spot I'd been lurking and hooked my arm around Riley's back. "Evil *was* in this home, but you've just stepped out..."

Delia made the same noise I imagined a fish would make when it's ripped from the river and left to flop on a deck. She clutched a handkerchief and brought it up in front of her face. "My own son..." she muttered. "Can I assume you won't be attending the Winter Solstice Celebration?"

I nodded and tightened my grip. "You can assume."

Delia frowned, giving a believable performance of a person experiencing sadness. I waited for that guilt that had kept me under Delia's thumb for years to rise up. All I felt was Riley's warmth and softness under my palm. His spine was still stiff, but some of the color had returned to his cheeks.

When it was clear Delia was on her own and would remain that way, she turned with a huff back to the shiny black town car parked in the driveway. Her driver, Linus, sat in the front seat until he spotted her coming and jumped out to open her door.

We were silent as she got in, and the car drove down the driveway.

I dropped my arm, turning cautiously to Riley. We'd been united in front of my mother, but Riley had been sneaking out. My mother didn't stop by often, preferring to get others to relay her manipulations. She'd probably been pulled from her mansion when Paul had returned empty-handed—he'd mentioned he would go back, after I told him Delia didn't actually have the authority to keep him out of pack lands. Only the pack leader could make those decision, and that title had reverted back to my grandfather after my father, the last pack leader, had died.

And Alpha Walker didn't give two shits about Paul, Delia, or their schemes. He'd been ready to give up the leader position when my father had assumed the role. There'd been a Walker alpha leading the packs from the beginning. But, with my grandfather only growing older, and my cousins and I no longer interested, that was going to have to change.

Which was probably why my mother's antics had only grown more desperate.

"You didn't tie your shoes," I said, wondering where I'd gone wrong. I woke that morning ready for the next round. We had the weekend, and I'd planned on spending every one of those hours getting to know Riley. But he'd been trying to leave—without saying goodbye.

"Thanks," Riley mumbled, blushing as he dropped to tie his loose laces. "I'm sorry. She was there when I opened the door. Scared the crap out of me."

"Don't worry about her. She would've made a scene no matter who answered the door. I am sorry you had to be subjected to that." My fingers itched to reach out and touch him. His hair had flung forward, tickling the corner of his eye. I wanted so badly to brush that hair back, cup his face, and kiss him as openly as we'd kissed the night before.

"She's...something. It is very good Paul is a legal adult, for her sake." Riley's face hardened. "I don't care who a person is or how much clout they have in a community."

I loved his devotion as much as I loved how he'd stood up to my mother. But I couldn't express either of those thoughts because Riley had been *running away*. That fact kept repeating in my mind, yanking me through a range of emotions so anger turned into concern. The longer I remained silent, the thicker the tension between us grew.

Riley still stood just inside the house, right next to the door that was still open to the chilly winter morning. Aver would complain we were letting the heat out. Hell, I would make the same complaint, but I didn't dare move. Riley was giving off the vibes of a trapped animal, and even though I'd caught him trying to turn our night into a one-night stand, the way he acted now was like I'd caught him stealing my finest silver. "I was going to make some coffee," I said, gesturing toward the kitchen. "Unless you're in a hurry?"

Okay, so that was a little snarky, but it hurt. While I'd been rapidly falling in love, he'd been planning his escape.

"I was going to call." Riley kept his face down.

I ignored that voice that told me to back off and moved

closer. It was the reasonable side of me that said if this man was trying to leave, he must not have been the man for me, and yet, telling that voice to shut up was the easiest choice I could make. Maybe I was headed for heartache, but at least I'd rush toward it, instead of drawing the process out.

I stopped just in front of him, hooking my finger under his chin to lift his gaze. His dark eyes were full of uncertainty. "I can call you a cab or drop you off in town myself. Or, you can come tell me what you were going to say when you called over coffee."

6

RILEY

ONLY I COULD RUIN a perfect night as spectacularly as I had.

I sat across from Branson. He'd busied himself for a bit preparing our coffees, but now, I had a steaming mug of black coffee in front of me, and Branson was loading his own cup with cream and sugar.

"I know," Branson said after catching me looking. "Do I want some coffee with my cream? That's what you were thinking, right?"

When he'd first come down, finding me in an impromptu standoff with his mother, he'd worn only his pants. He'd found a t-shirt since then. He'd wiped most of the sleep from his eyes, but his hair had clearly been tousled. No wonder. I'd spent the night running my hands through it, tugging on the strands when it had all gotten to be too much.

Branson had started as a man straight from my fantasies, and he'd yet to do anything to disprove that illusion. The opposite, actually. He was perfect in every sense of the word. Perfect body, perfect job, kind, friendly, amazing in bed. Why couldn't I be normal? At the very least, why couldn't I have skin that didn't make people spout their deepest secrets?

He had to know by now, and if he didn't, that scene with his mother had clued him in. Most people didn't get right away that I had an ability. Instead, they found themselves shying from me without knowing exactly why. It was their sixth sense, their instinct, the thing that told them to take the left route instead of the right or to smile at one person but avoid another.

I was a thing best left avoided.

"I wasn't trying to hurt your feelings," I murmured, pouring a drop of cream into my cup. The earthy, nutty scent called to me despite the discomfort of the situation.

Branson set down his mug. "You didn't think I'd mind falling asleep inside you but waking up alone?"

My cheeks burned, and I looked around us. I knew he had roommates. They were his relations, but still.

"No one else is here right now," Branson said. He cocked his head to the side and was silent for a second. "Scratch that. Nash is here, but he's snoring."

I couldn't hear it, but I figured Branson was much more accustomed to picking out that specific sound.

"I'm not trying to embarrass you, Riley. I just want the truth. I had a great night last night. I thought you did too."

Lordy, last night had been... I'd get hard if I thought about everything we'd done, the number of times Branson had released inside me. I should've known right then that something was different. I'd always been so careful. Even with Blaine, he wore a condom every time, or he kept it in his pants. But sharing that first with Branson had felt as natural as breathing. "I did," I said, biting on my lip immediately after. "It was... amazing. You were..."

When our gazes met again, Branson was smiling. "I'm not gonna lie, that's good to hear. But why were you runnin' then, babe? It isn't like I wouldn't see you again."

Another reason why I should've exercised more caution.

"I know. I should've..." I couldn't say the words that would say last night was a mistake. I didn't regret a single moment. It was only after, waking up and remembering all the sweet nothings Branson had whispered the night before. I'd been running from the regret I'd been sure *he* would feel. He didn't seem at all regretful, though. Upset, maybe. Did the man have no instincts? "There's more to me than you see. I have... secrets." I couldn't expect him not to have questions after saying something so vague, but I felt stuck. I'd never had a good experience telling someone about my ability. A few people, like Blaine, had figured it out or had figured out enough. And that had ended tragically. The other times, the end had just been abrupt.

How could I blame them, though? Who wanted to be around someone who made it impossible to keep a secret? I couldn't control what people said. It seemed to be just what was swirling at the top of their mind, what they most wished to keep to themselves, that they spoke out loud. The waitress had likely been thinking her lustful thoughts the moment before our skin touched. The same thing with Branson when he admitted to wanting a kiss. With Branson's mom, I'd guess she'd been feeling guilty, and that had been what was at the forefront of her mind. I didn't see suspicion in Branson's stare, though. I saw understanding.

"We all have secrets," he replied.

Ugh, no. How did I explain I didn't mean secrets like emotional baggage? Not like *I peed the bed until I was thir-*

teen secrets. Still, that sounded better than *Even though I am a man who can make you tell the truth by touching you, I was fooled by my last boyfriend, cheated on more times than taxes, and then tricked into becoming an accomplice in murder. Oh, and now he wants me dead too. Because I have a big fat mouth.*

For some reason, I didn't want to share all of that.

But I was being stupid. I didn't have to tell Branson the complete truth. Wasn't it enough that I'd tried? I couldn't be blamed if he'd assumed the wrong thing.

If he weren't so very perfect, this wouldn't be an issue. I'd say *thank you, I had a lovely night* and *goodbye*. But I didn't want to say goodbye. Sneaking from his room had been hard enough. Now, he was awake, right in front of me.

With coffee.

I brought my mug to my lips, pausing from the drama unfolding to appreciate the nutty, oaky, lifegiving flavor.

Branson smirked.

"What?"

He slid his hand closer on the table like he was going to grab my hand but stopped with our fingers inches apart. "The look on your face. I should've led with coffee. Woken up early and had it ready before your eyes opened."

My expression matched his. "There isn't a lot I won't do for coffee."

"I'll remember that," Branson murmured. I was aware of just how close our hands were, and Branson was too. His eyes kept lowering, a wistful look filling them. "I'm sorry," he said quietly. "You're sitting right there, right across from me. And it still doesn't feel close enough. This can't be attractive. I'm not all that hip with the dating scene, but I know intense clinginess is never a good look."

After being pushed away for so long, he had no idea

how good that sounded. But my skin was dangerous. By some miracle, he hadn't noticed that, and I'd been so smitten, I'd gone along for the ride. His gut would kick in at some point, and when it did, I didn't want to be around to get hurt.

I put my coffee down. "I think you're a great guy. A really great guy—"

"Hold on, now. This sounds like—"

I had to say it, before I couldn't. What was the point of waiting for him to hurt me? We'd only spent a night together so far. His feelings might be hurt, but with as gorgeous as he was, someone was probably already waiting, eager to tend to his emotional boo-boos. "But I think I'll take that taxi after all."

He pulled his hand back, and I immediately felt the loss of his warmth. His expression was shuttered. "I'll go call them now. Finish your coffee. You were enjoying it so much." He got up, leaving me alone with my coffee and my sadness.

It's for the best. I'd known from the beginning that this was where we would have to end. This was why I'd been so hesitant. But how could I know every other part but this moment, and the unfortunate run-in with his mother, would be so amazing?

Branson was gone for several minutes. When he returned, he was dressed in worn blue jeans and a red-and-black flannel shirt. "They're on their way," he said. "I could probably make you something to eat, if you don't mind taking it to go." He opened the fridge and grabbed several items. A carton of eggs, milk, and a container of orange juice.

My throat tightened with emotion. This wasn't what normally happened at all. "No, I'll be fine."

Branson just nodded as he got started cracking eggs into a bowl. "Suit yourself," he said, not unkindly. He wasn't being mean at all. His attitude had cooled, but I'd just rejected him. What did I expect? He busied himself for several silent minutes.

I hated that this was how our perfect night would end, with awkward silence. "I really had a great time. If things were different..."

Branson set the whisk down, his chin jerking up along with his face. "If what was different?" he asked with narrowed hazel eyes.

Squirming, I wished I'd kept my mouth shut. "Just things. I accepted the transfer to Walker County as a chance to start new. A lot has changed for me in the move." *My name, for one.* "And I don't think it's the best time to..." I trailed off, the words escaping me. What could I say? It wasn't the best time for him to blow my mind sexually? To show me more orgasms than I'd been aware I was capable of experiencing? "It's just not the best time."

He stared at me for a long time. Then his face jerked up over my shoulder like someone had called his name from the front door. "Your taxi is here."

I frowned. "How do you know?"

A honk sounded from outside, and Branson made that growling sound. Though this time there was no warmth in the rumble, only annoyance. "I didn't tell him to honk." He kept grumbling as he led me to the door.

A yellow cab waited in his driveway. I couldn't see the driver but read the words Walkerton Transportation Service on the side of the car in peeling black decal letters. I didn't imagine there was a huge need for a cab service in this area. Likely just a few people with free time and cars.

"Thanks," I said, giving him a little wave. That didn't

feel nearly appropriate after the time we'd had, but I couldn't exactly pull him into a kiss. "It would have been a long walk."

"I never would've let you," he replied quickly.

"Let me?" I shot back. Of all the overbearing... I took a deep breath. This was for the best, my leaving. I took the first step toward the door when Branson blocked my way.

"A hug is probably out of the question, but at least let me shake your hand. I can't imagine what makes this the wrong time for us—I'll still respect your decision—but there's no need for you to run out of here like we fought. If you ever change your mind, I'm here." He offered a smile that looked friendly on the surface, but I was in possession of the knowledge of what Branson looked like when he smiled for real, in ecstasy, in anticipation, in desire...

I eyed his hand as the taxi driver revved his engine, prompting another wave of rumbling growls from Branson. Man, that was a sexy sound. Animalistic, but comforting. Still, I needed to make a choice. It wasn't often that I was afraid of what people might say under my influence. Generally, I was just afraid *for* them.

This was for the best even if I despised using my curse. Let Branson blurt out one last thing he hadn't meant to, and then he'd see how lucky he was to be free of me. I met his gaze, trying to let him know that I was sorry already. Our hands touched. He held mine tightly. He pumped once, twice.

His eyes widened a moment before his mouth opened. "I can turn into a wolf. So can my cousins. We're alphas and live together because our families tried to get us to fight to the death more than ten years ago."

If he hadn't still been holding onto my hand, I would've

fallen back. As it was, he tightened his grip, stopping my momentum a moment before he reached around, holding me at the small of my back. Our lips a hair's breadth away from each other. My mouth felt dry, my brain buzzing. But when my lips parted, all I could say was, "What?"

7

BRANSON

I ACTED ON INSTINCT, tugging Riley closer. Something had happened when we'd touched. I wasn't sure how I hadn't sensed it before. Perhaps I'd been too wrapped up in my initial attraction, the way I'd felt inexplicably drawn to him. I still felt that draw, but that time, there was something else as well. A numbing calmness, followed by the urge to say the one thing I wished I could tell him.

None of the feelings had come from me, and as a shifter I was pretty in tune with my inner power. I felt my beast lurking at all times. It wasn't like I had a tiny wolf in me, scratching and pacing to be free, but more like a second consciousness, a primal one that urged me to live just as I wanted at all times. Only, as an alpha, my voice was louder and more insistent. That beast also told me there was some-thing different about Riley, more than what I'd initially thought.

I shut the door, commanding him to stay as I trekked out to the cab and gave him a fifty for his troubles. He rumbled away, and I took the moment to regain my composure. Riley had been trying to tell me he had a secret all morning. I just hadn't listened.

I would now.

When I went back inside. Riley was huddled beside the coat rack like he was trying to hide. "Are you afraid?" I asked because I needed to get that clear first. I couldn't handle Riley's fear. He should never have needed to be scared. He didn't answer and kept his face turned away. Not seeing his face was maddening. "Despite what I just told you, you aren't in danger from me."

"You can turn into a wolf," Riley said, blinking several times. It looked almost like his brain malfunctioning as it tried to process what I'd said.

There was no point denying it now. "I can. Though you aren't supposed to know that."

"Wh-what are you going to do to me?" His gaze twitched to the door, to the taxi that was likely down the road by now.

"Whoa, whoa, what's with all the tension?" Nash came down the stairs in jogging pants and his long-sleeve workout shirt. He stopped a few feet away, his stance casual, but I sensed his suspicion.

"Nothing," I spat. I didn't need everyone knowing I'd spilled my secret. There were rules about humans knowing about shifters. It wasn't like there was a shifter police force, and I knew Nash would keep my secret if I asked. But, this close to pack lands, they were bound to find out sooner or later. And then protecting Riley would be much more difficult

Nash didn't respond to me; his eyes were on Riley. As a fireman, he had a hero complex that his arrogance only heightened. He'd never leave a person in trouble, but he should know that Riley wasn't in danger around me. "Are you okay, Mr. Monroe?"

Instead of getting angry at Nash for stepping in, I tried to look at the situation from his point of view. It had looked like I was cornering Riley. *Probably because you were cornering Riley.* I was giving off harsher vibes than I'd intended. I exhaled slowly, letting my shoulders drop and my hands relax from the fists they'd been tightened into.

"I'm okay," Riley replied. "Thank you. I'm afraid you know my name, but I don't know yours." He didn't stick out his hand to shake, and now I knew why.

"Nash Walker," he replied with a toothy grin. "Welcome to Walker County. Despite the impression my cousin is giving you right now, we aren't all wild animals."

Riley made a choking sound that turned into a series of coughs. My uncertainty couldn't stop my grin, but I hid it quickly behind my hand. Meanwhile, Nash had no idea of the significance of what he'd said and stared at us both now like we'd recently fallen on our heads.

"Nice to meet you, Mr. Walker," Riley said.

"Call me Nash." My cousin oozed forward, and I couldn't help my instincts to move between them. He was my cousin, and I loved him. Our love for each other was why we were all here, learning to live outside of a pack. But Nash was shameless when it came to his sexual love life.

Riley was claimed. He just didn't know it yet.

Nash backed up, finally sensing he'd walked into a situation that he didn't understand completely. "I better get going. Those miles aren't going to run themselves." He winked at Riley before heading out the door.

Riley watched him leave, but his face wasn't one of admiration. "He's pretty full of himself, isn't he?"

My mouth broke into a smile. "You have no idea. When he and his brother get together, hide your sons."

"All three of you are gay?" Riley asked.

I shook my head slowly. I hated lying, but Aver's secret was not mine to share, despite how cavalier I was with it when Aver and I were alone. "The three of us are."

"And you can all turn into wolves?"

I grimaced. "You can't tell anyone that you know." I lifted my hands to reach for him but let them fall between our bodies. "There are rules. If the pack knew you knew—"

"The pack?" Riley gasped. His head swiveled away, toward the kitchen. But I realized he wasn't looking at the kitchen: he was looking at the backyard, the mouth of the bay, and the land that lay on the other side. "The show dogs, the wolves... you can all..." He stumbled back, stopping only when he hit the wall. "I thought it was strange your mom said *pup*."

"Just as I thought it was strange she said anything at all," I said, bringing attention to the other secret lingering between us. I didn't have to give Riley more context; he understood what I'd referred to. "Is it your skin? Or just your presence?" I was pretty sure it was the skin.

He looked at the floor. "My skin, specifically my hands. Well, strongest in my hands."

"Are you shifter?" I'd heard whispers of shifters with extra abilities. Nothing like magic, but heightened senses. I'd never met one. I would've thought they were made up if it weren't for Nana's insistence that they were real. But the spectrum of things Nana believed was wide and unreliable. She'd told us so many insane stories as kids, and that hadn't changed when we'd left the pack.

"No. I didn't... I had no idea other people could do... extra stuff too." He lifted his face, but suspicion made his mouth tight. "I haven't met anyone who could lie when I touch them. Some have... well, they've learned to think of *other* truths, blocking their minds, but..." He wrapped his arms tightly around his middle.

"So other people know about you?" This wasn't the first time he'd reminded me of a caged animal. Not all the time, but occasionally, he acted like someone living on the run.

"Not many. It isn't something I like to... well, who wants to be around someone like me?"

The wistful edge to his words gave me an idea. "Is that why you were leaving this morning?"

Riley sucked in his bottom lip, biting and rolling it between his teeth. He nodded. "I figured you'd put two and two together, and even if you didn't get it right, you'd realize there was something off about me and that it was easier just not being around me." He sucked in a loud gulp of air. "Or you would figure out a way to use my curse, which is just as bad. I won't use it for—"

I'd held back as long as I could but hearing the reason why Riley had been running—and knowing it had nothing to do with me or how he felt about me—was like being given an early Christmas gift. I wrapped my fingers around his nape, pulling him flush with my body, silencing him with my lips. I wanted to hear what he'd been saying—I wanted to hear everything Riley wanted to say. I needed to kiss him immediately, before something else tried to crop up between us.

I was surer now that there was something else between us. Two mystically inclined people couldn't just happen to bump into each other, and then bump inside of each other. I thrust my tongue into his mouth, swiping along the ridge of his teeth before toying with his own tongue. Riley relaxed into me, and I took more of him, sliding my leg between his.

Once I started, it was nearly impossible to stop. I wanted him naked, now, begging for me.

"Wait, wait, wait." Riley turned his face to the side, ripping his mouth free. "If we keep on with that, I don't see us getting much talking done."

Talking? Who wanted to talk? He was a human truth serum, and I turned into a wolf, no big deal. I was ready to be over it and move on to the parts where we got naked. I nibbled at his neck, as a compromise. "What else did you want to talk about?"

Riley squeaked. His mouth gaped. "Well, what are we going to do about... what we know?"

I shrugged. "How does it change this? Us?"

"You'd still want an us? Even though you can never lie to me?" His face hardened. "I won't be used."

"There's only one way I'm concerned with using you." I buried my face behind his ear and inhaled.

"But what about the pack rules?"

I barely heard his question over the roar of my libido. I swayed back on my heels. The pack. That's right. There'd been a time when I'd been afraid of them as well—mostly of what they'd been capable of—but that was enough to not let me continue to take the moment lightly, despite how much I wished I could be doing other things with Riley. "No one can know that you know, but I don't see why anyone would expect you to. You're not on my mother's list of favorite people, but she'll be too afraid of a scandal that would come when the rest of the pack found out what she pulled with Paul. The elder houses have an image to uphold."

"It sounds like a complicated and very in-group dynamic." Riley rested his palm on my chest. "What would happen if they found out that I knew?"

I led us away from the door, back to the kitchen.

"They'd hold a council. Your case would be argued, and the leader would decide if you're a danger or not."

Riley accepted the seat he'd been in. I dumped the cup waiting at his chair and poured a fresh one. "Who is your leader?" he asked, tracking my movement through the kitchen.

"My grandfather. He's the Alpha, with a capital A, not like the lowercase alpha that my cousins and I all are. Alpha Walker isn't so bad on his own. He's a grouch and traditional to a fault, but he resents his position. He's done leading the packs."

"Why doesn't he quit?"

"A Walker has led the packs since they first settled there. Walkers built this island. He won't step down until there is an alpha Walker to step up."

The next question was obvious, but Riley didn't ask it. He glided his index finger around the rim of his mug. It had to be hot, but he did it once, then again. "Does what you are... your being a shifter, does it change anything about you? Will it change anything about me?" He gulped, his lower lip trembling.

"Nothing." My reply was instant. My words sure. "I just turn into a wolf sometimes, that's all."

He snorted, grinning. "That's all?"

"And all you do is make people tell the truth."

His smile turned pensive. "That's all."

I might as well continue my honesty streak. Riley wouldn't give me a choice anyway. I rolled that over in my head. I could never hide from Riley, could never keep anything from him, not even for his own good. That option had been taken by what he called his curse. And I found I didn't care one bit. "The way I feel for you, from first sight, to right now, it feels different. New."

That wasn't just my dick talking either. The draw I felt to Riley was stronger than anything I'd experienced. I'd have been afraid of it if I wasn't so busy enjoying every moment.

Riley licked his lips. I wished he'd let me do that. "Me too," he whispered. "Do you think it has something to do with what we are? That we're both different?"

That was as good a guess as any.

Riley brought his mug up and looked at me over the rim. "So now what?"

I felt like a racehorse at the starting line, pawing at the ground as I waited for the pistol's crack. "Now we finish our coffees and head back upstairs."

His fingers tightened on the handle, and the gaze that met me over the rim of his mug was as heated as the steam drifting between us. "Just like that?" he whispered. I couldn't see his lips move, but I felt the tremulous hope. He couldn't believe I'd still want him after what I knew, but I felt the same about him. I'd never told a human. I'd always assumed the truth would be too strange, but it wasn't for Riley.

"The only thing keeping me from sweeping you off this stool is that I think you might fight me to keep the coffee, and Nana gave us that mug—I'd hate for something to happen to it."

I winked, and Riley lifted the mug, hiding his eyes now too. Only the tips of his red cheeks were visible.

As much as I despised ruining such a cute image, I was so hard, I'd probably find an imprint of the zipper along my shaft. I gently lowered his arm and leaned in. "What do you say?" I murmured.

Riley stretched forward, and his lips grazed over mine.

He pulled back suddenly, clapping a hand over his mouth. "My breath is probably nasty."

Cocking my head to the side, I scratched my eyebrow. "Is that your clever way of saying I should go brush my teeth first?"

His eyes widened. "No! I just mean I should brush my teeth, oh my God, and shower. I need both of those things before we..." He wiggled his finger in the air between us.

"Dance the cha-cha?" I guessed.

"Ha, ha." Riley rolled his eyes.

I liked it a little too much. "I still don't hear a problem. We'll start in the shower. I'll give you a toothbrush."

"No. I want my own."

I leaned back. Was I coming on too strong? The answer to that was definitely yes. But was I coming on stronger than Riley wanted? That was the only question I cared to have answered. "Okay, I'll call the cab back and instruct him to return in two hours. That will give you time to freshen up." I hated the idea as I spoke it, but I needed to give Riley his space when he wanted it, or I'd scare him away.

He batted his eyelashes. Why did he have to look extra adorable when I was trying to do the right thing? "Could you... would you have time to take me?" he asked.

My lips stretched upward in a wide smile. "Of course."

―――――

RILEY'S APARTMENT was right in town. He'd be able to walk to work and just about anywhere else worth going to in Walkerton from this location.

He made me wait in the hallway as he rushed in his apartment ahead of me. When he opened the door again, he stepped aside, gesturing for me to come in. "Nice place," I said, looking up at the high ceilings and then down to the wood flooring. There was thick, gray carpet in the living room area that continued down the hallway to the single bedroom. "Excellent craftsmanship."

Riley frowned. "Thanks?" His eyebrows lifted a second later in shock. "Did you—I mean, your company...?"

"These apartments were our first big commercial job. During construction, there wasn't a person in Walkerton that wanted work who didn't have it. It was a shame to see the job end, but the building has held up."

"You built my apartment. That's..."

"Strange?" I offered.

"Pretty cool," Riley replied. He must have changed while he'd made me wait in the hall. He wore khakis and a soft sweater with a holiday print knitted in a pattern. He looked ready for a cozy night by a fire, cocoa, moaning carols as I thrust into him—

I cast around, looking for something to distract me. He had a small end table on the other side of his couch, and at first look, I hadn't seen that it was made out of wooden crates, stacked and nailed together. "This is interesting. Is it one of yours?"

Riley looked over. "That?" he scoffed. "*Interesting* is a word for it. Yes, I made it. I made most of the furniture in here actually. Except the couch."

My initial description didn't really do the piece justice. Somehow, he'd transformed the crates into a functional, attractive end table that was one of a kind. "This is gorgeous."

He shrugged and looked away, clearly made uncomfortable by my praise. But why should he be? He had obvious skills.

Now that I knew more about the furniture, I examined

every item. The coffee table was especially impressive. The top was a mosaic, bits of broken ceramic all placed together to form a full moon glinting off a watery horizon. It was peaceful and serene and completely made by Riley's hand. "You're an artist."

Riley had been coming down the hallway, a pack over his shoulder. Good. He planned on staying. "I'm a dabbler," Riley replied. "With Seattle's prices, I had to get good or have a rickety coffee table."

I shook my head. "Maybe it started that way, but you've got talent. I could use your eye for detail and design."

Riley's dark eyes twinkled. "Are you offering me a job?"

"No." I turned to face him. "Because then I couldn't do this." I'd waited just about as long as I could before kissing him again. I tasted his minty toothpaste, though I wouldn't have minded a morning-coffee breath kiss either. He lifted his face, offering me easier access. I immediately took advantage, deepening the kiss as I molded my palms to his hip, sliding lower to cup his ass. This wasn't second-date behavior. Technically, we were still on our first date. But we'd blown past what was expected or proper during dates. From the first moment to now, I hadn't ever wanted to date Riley. I wanted much more than that.

I stepped back, and Riley's eyes were still closed. He leaned forward, as if trying to keep the kiss going, but landed on my chest with a soft, "Oof."

"Do you have everything you need?" I asked. I wanted to add, *for the weekend*, because I wanted Riley for as long as I could have him.

"Depends on what you have planned," Riley said. "I'd be pretty unprepared for any black-tie events."

I reached for his pack and hooked it over my shoulder

before reaching for his hand. "I don't have anything planned that will require you to wear more clothes."

He squeezed my hand like he still hadn't noticed how easily he'd let me hold it in the first place. I'd noticed. I couldn't wait to see more of the true Riley that would come out when he felt more comfortable around me, but I wouldn't postpone our plans any longer. "Let's get home."

————

I PARKED IN OUR DRIVEWAY, still empty. I wasn't sure where everyone was. I knew they weren't staying away for my benefit. Riley fit perfectly under my arm as we walked to the front door. He fit everywhere. His body had been made for me, and I was going to spend the next several hours proving that exact thing—

"You're home!" Aver's overly friendly voice spoke first, while Wyatt grabbed my collar and pulled me the rest of the way in. Riley, connected by our hands, had no choice but to come with. When we were clear of the door, Nash shut and locked it.

"Really?" I said, lifting a single eyebrow his direction.

He shrugged as if he had no idea. "I saw you had company, saw you were hitting it off, and figured you would be delighted if we all gathered to meet him." In the living room, they'd pushed the coffee table aside and replaced it with a card table.

I had no doubt this cockblock was revenge for some time I'd done the same to him. We loved each other, but sometimes I had to remind myself of that more than others. "Where'd you all come from?" I grunted, pulling Riley close. Who knew how he was taking this embarrassing scene?

"I was on my way home already when Nash called,"

Aver said. His hair was wet, likely from a recent shower, and he had bags forming under his eyes. I knew he'd had his date, a female from the pack no doubt. I believed Aver could handle himself, but I also knew how much those blind dates his parents kept sending him on took out of him. We all pretended to be something we weren't but Aver had to do that twice.

"I'm not due back at the bar until this evening," Wyatt said. "We were just about to get started."

They led us into the living room, where they had cards and snacks set out on the table. So it was a three-way cockblock.

"You don't have to play, of course. But we'll be down here, playing, listening..." Nash let his meaning linger.

Those dicks. The table was already set for five players. "Were you expecting company?" I asked, arching my eyebrow.

"Nope, just you," Nash replied cheerfully. Shamelessly. He'd known my date with Riley was something special; my actions toward him were so unlike how I normally was. And he'd come in right after I'd blabbed our secret. He'd likely heard enough to be concerned.

And this was his answer.

"You can sit here, Riley," Aver said, indicating a chair between him and Wyatt.

"He'll sit by me." I sat down next to an empty chair, probably taking Nash's seat in the process.

"Is it all right if we call you Riley?" Aver asked, ignoring me. "Using surnames would get confusing pretty quick. Mr. Walker, Mr. Walker, Mr. Walker." He pointed at each of us.

Riley chuckled. "First names are fine."

"He probably still calls Branson Mr. Walker," Wyatt

mumbled jokingly. After leaving the pack, I'd found it most difficult to transition from titles and positions to just names.

Riley wisely ignored him. "What's the game?"

"Just a little Texas Hold'em. Do you know how to play?" Aver asked.

Riley reached for the deck in the middle and parted the cards in two. He shuffled them together with a perfect arch. "Not at all, will you teach me?" He batted his eyelashes. I didn't trust that for a second.

Neither did the guys. "Whoa, watch out." Wyatt plopped down on Riley's other side. He pulled his stacks of chips toward him, cupping his arms around them like a hoarding dragon.

Nash returned with a coffee pot, pouring everyone a fresh cup before donning the dealer's visor and sitting down. "All right, chips start at one, then, five, ten, twenty and fifty, in that order."

"Is this for actual money?" Riley whispered, his eyes tilted with worry.

"Something better than money," Aver replied. "Chores."

"How does that work?" Riley handed the deck to Nash.

We'd skipped over the introductions, and I wasn't going to slow things down. Riley seemed to know who was who, and they all knew him, thanks to Nash. This wasn't at all what I'd planned on the two of us doing the moment we got back, but Riley was smiling, and I wouldn't do anything to put a stop to that.

I set his pack down, a motion Riley noticed. He winked. "Are you okay with this?" he asked quietly.

"Of course he is," Wyatt replied.

I reached over the table and snagged a pretzel out of the pile in front of Wyatt. "He was asking me."

"It must be hard to keep private conversations private in this home," Riley mused, lifting the cards Nash had dealt.

"Ante starts at one," Nash told us. To Riley he asked, "Why do you say that?"

Riley slid his ante into the pot, watching Nash's hands as he dealt the center cards. "Since you all have the hearing of wolves."

I hadn't told him that, but he'd already proven he knew how to put two and two together. I'd wondered how much the rest of them knew, how much Nash had heard or told them.

Aver didn't say anything. He just reached for his wallet and pulled out a twenty, placing it in Wyatt's outstretched palm.

"He said there was no way you would blab our ancient secret to a hot piece of ass, no offense," Wyatt added for Riley's benefit, though he was grinning from ear to ear.

"That's okay. I was basically giving the twenty he already lost back. He said you wouldn't be dumb enough to bring Riley back here to continue your sexcation."

Riley had just taken a sip of his coffee and was now coughing it back up. "Sexcation?"

"Sex vacation?" Aver handed him a napkin that Riley accepted.

"I'd hardly call it that," Riley said. He met my gaze, that same twinkle still in his eyes. I wanted nothing more than for this circus to end so I would have Riley to myself, but clearly, he got something out of being around these guys. "More like a sex-long-weekend."

So he had planned on staying for the weekend. Knowing I had more time with him, at least one more night —two if I was lucky—let me relax enough to lift my cards. Ace and eight. Crap. "Thanks to all of you for really trying to show me in a good light to my new friend," I said, knowing they wouldn't feel guilty in the slightest. We'd always been more like brothers. Loyal to the end, but with a lot of teasing along the way. And I had considered staying at Riley's, but I knew where everything was here. I was doubting that choice now.

"Eh, stop trying to distract us from the fact that you were dealt a crap hand," Nash said, calling for bets. "The chips are more of a point counter," he explained to Riley. "Play them like you would if they were worth money. The first to go out—lose all their chips—has to clean the bathrooms for a week. Next takes out the garbage. Second place gets to buy the beer for the week, and the winner, me, gets to bask in their victory." There were plenty of grumbled curses from Aver and Wyatt at that; I didn't need to add mine. Meanwhile, Riley listened attentively. "If a hand goes heads-up, meaning it is down to two people, you can start betting more chores. Ask me how many times I've had to clean the gutters around here."

"How many?" Riley responded dutifully.

"Zero," Nash replied proudly. "Seriously, if there is something on your to-do list that you aren't looking forward to, remember that when a hand is down to two."

The game got going after that, and my earlier suspicion proved true. Riley played skillfully, and he had the advantage of none of us knowing his tells. The rest of us had been playing for so long, I didn't need to look at the cards, just their faces. Riley quickly raked in his chips, nearly taking Wyatt from the game during an intense stand-off that had ended with Wyatt having to promise to tune Riley's bicycle. "It's been on my list for months," he said as he revealed his pocket rockets over Wyatt's pair of kings.

The guys didn't try to show off too much, especially once Riley had shown his skill.

"Brought a card shark to our pond," Wyatt mumbled, clacking his small stack of chips together.

It was Riley's turn to deal. He accepted the cards, declining the visor. "I played a little in college. Sort of like how you all do it, but for food instead of chores. We all lived like slobs anyway."

I would've liked to have seen a younger Riley. He wasn't old now, but I'd always been fond of those college sweaters. He'd look great in one, with nothing else. Something slid up my calf. I looked to Riley, who winked. He'd toed his shoes off under the table and rested them against my leg. Even a touch as mostly innocent as that had me tensing. I wanted to flip the table over, order the others away—into the woods, the river, I didn't care—and bend Riley over the couch.

"So you're an old pro," Aver said. I barely heard him through the thrum in my mind that urged me to take what was mine. This feeling was getting out of control. A card had stubbornly stuck to the table, and Aver pried it loose, handing it to Riley. Their hands touched for only a moment. "I hated every moment of my date last night and stood under a scalding shower for hours after in the gym."

No one said anything. Riley ripped his hand back, his eyes opened wide and pleading to me. I hooked my arm over his shoulders, drawing him nearer on instinct. The others weren't sure what to do. Nash and Wyatt's mouths hung open, and they looked from Aver to Riley, tucked under my arm. Aver's face was redder than I'd ever seen.

"I'm sorry," Riley muttered. He pushed back from the table, sliding out from under my arm. "I'm so sorry." He searched the floor, likely looking for his bag. I had it on the other side of me. "I'm so sorry." Riley kept apologizing.

Aver's shocked look had faded, replaced by suspicion, directed at me. "I didn't mean to say that," he said, likely for Wyatt and Nash's benefit. "I handed Riley the card, and then it was like I couldn't stop the verbal diarrhea."

Riley grimaced. "It was me. I thought maybe you all knew that too." Riley spoke quietly. He'd stopped trying to get up from the table, but sat a foot away from it, his hands folded in his lap. "I figured... I guess not. I'm sorry. I'll go."

Tearing my gaze from Riley was difficult. I met my cousins' stares individually. The mirth of a few moments ago was gone, and I was met with three concerned, wary gazes. They had questions. Understandable. Too bad I didn't have any answers. "It's something he's lived with, like us."

"I can't do that," Nash said.

"I meant it's just an extra ability. Like how we have extra abilities. Only being able to hear a conversation from the other side of the room is much more invasive. If it makes you feel strange, just don't touch him." I took the cards from Riley's spot and began shuffling them. "In fact, that's a general rule. No one touch Riley. Except me." I smiled to Riley, earning a weak smile in return.

Wyatt cleared his throat. "Are you trying to tell me that when Riley touches someone, they start telling their own secrets?"

I looked to Riley first. He'd scooted back to the table, and I took that as permission to hold him under my arm again. He nodded, giving me permission to speak for him. "Basically."

"Do you rent him out?" Wyatt asked with a laugh.

Riley stiffened. "I won't be used." He clenched his hands, his knuckles white from the pressure.

The humor in Wyatt's face evaporated. "I'm sorry. That was rude. You aren't a party trick."

"That's right. He's not." I kissed Riley's temple, and he sighed gratefully.

"But you have to touch him for it to happen?" Aver asked. He stared at his stacks, choosing to rearrange them rather than look up at the four of us.

"Yes," Riley answered. "And I am sorry. That wasn't information I was meant to hear, and I'll do my best to forget it."

"I've already struck it from my memory," Nash said, raising his fingers in a Boy Scout's promise.

"Struck what?" Wyatt added.

Aver exhaled heavily. "Thanks," he whispered.

I dealt, and the table threw in their antes. Wyatt was down to chips enough for a hand, maybe two if he played conservatively—which he never did.

"Okay, so I know it isn't a party trick, but I'm so curious," Wyatt said before I could flip the first flop card. "Will you touch me?"

I growled low as Riley gaped at Wyatt.

"Wyatt," I grumbled.

"Hold on, hold on. This isn't weird. Believe me, you've staked your claim. You couldn't do a better job than if you lifted your leg and peed on the poor guy. He's yours. But I like new experiences. This is a new experience."

Riley's mouth closed and then opened again. "You *want* your deepest darkest secrets ripped from you?"

Wyatt touched the side of his head to his shoulder in a shrug. "Why not? These jerks are nosy. There isn't anything they don't know or won't know about me."

Riley just shook his head. He'd called this ability of his a curse. Wyatt wanting it must've seemed so odd to him. But,

I understood Wyatt's curiosity. Perhaps a different group of guys might've been more weirded out, but growing up the way we had, there wasn't a lot that could phase us. Riley lifted his hand tentatively to the center of the table.

"It probably won't even work." Wyatt brought his hand up, their fingers hovered near each other.

"You asked for it," Riley said before bridging the gap and grabbing Wyatt's fingers.

"I've always wanted to wear a bra so I could feel how good it would be to take it off," he blurted. Nash burst out laughing. But Riley hadn't let go. "I sleep with my closet door closed because even though I know there is nothing in there, how can I be sure?" Wyatt ripped his hand free with a ragged gasp. "Whoa." He rubbed his hand, blinking in amazement. "Nash, you try."

"No, thank you," Nash said, not unkindly. He looked down at his coffee. "Am I the only one who thinks it's late enough for beer?"

"I agree," Riley said quickly. He still stared at Wyatt like he wasn't sure if he was crazy.

None of us were.

Nash hopped up, and Wyatt went with him to help. It wasn't like Nash couldn't handle carrying five beers. Technically, Wyatt was the youngest of us, born minutes after his brother. They'd grown up close. What our families had tried to make us do had hurt them especially hard. My mom had only asked eighteen-year-old me to kill my cousins— Wyatt and Nash had been instructed by their parents to murder their own brother. Only one Walker alpha was meant to survive. Instead, we all had. And then we'd left.

"You okay?" I asked Aver in a low voice.

He scratched the back of his head as he nodded. "Yeah. It's stupid anyway, right?" he asked, a hard edge to his voice.

In any other instance, I might've pushed him, agreed that, yes, it was stupid for him to live like he was. But he'd yet to give up complete hope. Sure, he joked around about our families like the rest of us, but he'd been happy living on the pack's land. He missed that life. He'd been devastated when they'd asked what they had, and from then on, he'd claimed they would never accept him. He agreed to the dates because at least then his mother would talk to him. It made me furious to think about, but at the end of the day, he was a grown man, an alpha. His problems were his to deal with and mine to support him through. "It isn't stupid. I don't think you should put yourself through them, but I understand."

Riley looked between us, probably feeling as awkward as hell. I pushed my leg against his under the table, and his shoulders relaxed.

"Thanks. This is helping. You guys are a good distraction. At least someone had a good date."

Technically, this was still our first date. We were going on almost twenty-four hours.

The guys returned, passing beers and the rest of the bag of pretzels. It didn't take Wyatt long to claim bathroom duty for the rest of the week. Aver followed after, earning a week of trash. I went out third, and the showdown between Nash and Riley was long. They were equally matched in skill, so it came down to luck. And in the end, Riley was just that much luckier.

"Because you had me at your side," I joked as Riley gathered the chips. They were stacked in piles in front of him. He looked like a cute banker, and I was willing to do anything for a loan.

"It's a nice day," Nash said. "How about some touch football?"

I groaned.

"Got to get ready for work," Wyatt said. "Thanks for duping me, all of you." He left, jokingly whining as he did about being raked over the coals.

"I've got some things to do in the shop," Aver said.

When Nash looked hopefully at Riley and me, I tugged Riley from the table. "We're on a date," I said. "And it's time for me to make my moves in the hot tub," I said more quietly.

"You've got moves?" Wyatt called from the other room.

Riley laughed, allowing me to pull him out of the living room, through the kitchen, and to the back doors. We hadn't explored the other side of the house the night before. If we had, he would've seen the hot tub on the side porch with an expansive view of the bay. I hadn't intended on going out there, but it was just about the only place near the house with enough walls between it and everyone else that we could have some privacy.

"Hot tub? I didn't bring a suit," Riley said.

"That's okay," I replied cheerfully.

"You've got an extra suit?" he asked.

"Nope."

8

RILEY

"You LIED." I tugged at the waist of the swim trunks Branson had loaned me. He'd waited outside the kitchen bathroom for me to change, and now his eyes raked up my body. I covered my chest, feeling silly but also on display. Maybe if I had a tighter body, but it wasn't like I had the cash laying around for a gym membership, and most days I was lucky if I ate food that didn't come from a takeout carton.

I wouldn't mind as much if I hadn't been standing in front of perfection in the male form. Branson's body was chiseled, his six-pack as pronounced as his wide pecs. And he expected me to stand there with my General Tso's pooch? No thank you.

Branson continued his visual exploration of my body. Moving from the kitchen counter to where I stood, his thick thigh muscles rippling with each lithe, purposeful step. He tugged my arms down to my sides, where he rubbed from my shoulders and then back down. "You don't ever need to hide yourself from me," he murmured.

I pushed him back with my shoulder, I wasn't uncomfortable with his touch or closeness, but he didn't need to ply me with kind words. I was already here on the world's longest date.

Branson frowned. "What are you thinking right now?"

"I'm wondering how long the record is for the longest date," I replied automatically.

His chuckle was low and slid over my senses like melted butter. "Tired of this one? Or looking to set a record?"

I lifted my face to look into his but concentrated on his nose instead. It wasn't completely straight. There was a slight bend at the very end, making me wonder if he'd been a fighter in his early years. "Neither. It's just... I'm already here. I'm having fun. You don't have to keep... trying."

Branson grabbed my hand so that we stood face to face, our hands palm to palm between us, fingers interlaced. "I'm touching you, so you know this is true. You don't ever need to hide yourself from me. I love every inch of your body." He dipped his head down. All I saw was his dark hair lowering to my stomach before his lips brushed over my right love handle.

I was frozen by his gesture. My mind clouded, and I saw us, but it wasn't us as we were right now. In my mind, Branson was ducked over in front of me the same way, but something had happened to me. In the image, my stomach was round, like I'd started hitting the beers too heavy after work. I gasped and jerked my head back, bumping it softly against the wall.

What had that been?

Whatever it was, the picture was gone from my head, having taken the same rapid path out as it had in. But what had it meant? I'd never gotten visions before, I wasn't psychic. I shook my head, deciding to ignore the disturbing picture and concentrate on the man with me now.

He'd migrated across my stomach—blessedly somewhat flat but still soft—to my other side, where he kissed up my ribs.

I giggled and reached for his shoulders. "Is there a real hot tub, or was this a trick to get me in my—your—under-wear?" He'd told me the pair I wore were actual swim trunks, but they'd been meant for a body Branson-sized. The legs were baggy over my own thighs, and I'd had to pull the drawstring as tightly as it would go.

"Good idea, but yes, there is a hot tub. It's also located in such a way that we can't be heard." Branson stepped back and grabbed my hand. "So feel free to be as loud as you like."

My face burned, both at his implication and remembering that everything we'd just said could have been overheard. I needed to find out the limits of their abilities if I was going to be hanging around here.

That thought brought me nearly to a halt. *Would* I be hanging around here? This was turning into the opposite of the plans I had for my time in Walker County, but why couldn't I do both? Hide from Blaine, try to do some good, *and* let Branson sex my brains out? The whole "turning into a wolf" thing was a little strange. I still needed him to show me that—*was it a rude thing to ask?*

I figured I wouldn't truly believe something like that until I'd seen it. But he'd been under my truth influence when he'd confessed. No one could lie in that circumstance. They could only tell other truths while keeping the one they really didn't want me knowing out of their mind.

At least, that's what Blaine had done.

Branson took us around to the side of the house. His hand remained in mine, a warm, insistent tugboat leading me to an oasis. With as much beautiful craftsmanship as I'd seen, I had no reason being shocked at the gorgeous brickwork surrounding the hot tub or the ivy-covered driftwood lattice that offered protection on three sides. Just the front view had been left unobstructed.

While Branson busied himself with the hot tub cover and getting the dials set how he wanted, I turned around. I couldn't get enough of this view. It was heaven before my eyes. Then I remembered who lived on the other side, where Branson and his cousins had come from, and I frowned. Why live with the memory of your worst day in front of you?

Like before, Branson slipped in behind me, his arms wrapping around my middle as he rested his chin on my shoulder. "Dare I ask what you're thinking again?" he murmured.

I shook my head. I'd done plenty of mood killing things since this date started, but bringing up what was on my mind would be the king daddy of them all. I reached up to cup his head, turning my face up to his. "I'm still waiting for this hot tub you promised. I've got a crick right..." I stuck my ass out, nestling it in the warmth of his crotch. "...here."

"Well, let me help work that out for you." Branson slid his hands down, cupping before he pinched my ass. I jumped forward, and he continued pinching, alternating cheeks and hardness as he used my ass cheeks like a rudder and guided me to the tub. He picked me up bridal style and stepped in first.

The warm air wafted from the bubbling surface to kiss the bottom of my feet. He'd mentioned something earlier about needing to turn the tub from maintenance mode to get the water up to the right temperature. When it was, it would feel glorious.

I looked up at the warmth in his hazel gaze. A warmth that was replaced by something much more mischievous as he looked from me, cradled comfortably in his arms, to the water. "What?" I asked.

Branson looked away, mumbling something I couldn't decipher.

I reached down to where he held me, grabbing his hand.

"I'm going to drop you," Branson said.

I shrieked, laughing as I struggled.

"That's cheating!" Branson said, carrying me to the center of the circular tub.

"Don't you dare!" I screamed back, unable to stop laughing. I wheezed, choking on my mirth. I knew the moment before his arms disappeared out from under me, but like an unlucky man in a carnival dunk tank, I could do nothing about my imminent plunge.

My butt hit the water first. Branson followed me down, catching my weight before I hit the bottom with too much force. The water wasn't quite hot yet, but it was warm, like a huge bath. I bobbed to the surface, wiping my hair back so it wouldn't clump in my face. "I take my screaming back. This feels amazing." I did a backstroke. There was only room for me to do one before I bumped against the side. The outer rim of the tub was lined with a ledge like a bench, and I sat down, settling my feet over a jet to the right while snow glinted off only the highest trees in the distance. "Oh yes, this is nice."

"I agree," Branson said, but he wasn't moving around or enjoying the weightlessness. He stared only at me.

I stretched long, kicking my legs lazily to bring me by his side. He lifted his arm in a silent invitation, one I accepted. His warm, muscular arm settled over my shoulders, and I leaned my head against his chest. "This is the craziest date I've been on."

Branson squeezed my shoulders. "Definitely my longest. But I don't want it to end."

It would. If not because he finally grew tired of me, but because Sunday would end at some point, and I was due back to work Monday. Branson was no slacker either. I'd peeked into what looked like a home office this morning when I'd been trying to sneak out. If the messiness of his desk was any indication, Branson would be busy for the foreseeable future.

Why was I so morose imagining a single moment without him?

He kept talking about how fast he'd fallen, but I felt like a new man after meeting him. My old worries just didn't seem to matter. Even my curse felt like something I could manage a little more easily. I needed to remember this dissonance later when I was back at my apartment, wondering why he wasn't calling.

But Branson's hand dropped to my upper thigh, and I forgot what I was trying to remember. His shorts swam on me out of the water. In the water, the leg portions floated up to my waistband, covering nearly nothing. "This is where we should've come the first moment. But I wouldn't miss watching you wipe the floor with my cousins for anything."

"I might've hidden something," I said, biting my tongue as Branson's hand inched toward my inner thigh. He dragged his fingertips along my skin, drawing something that I couldn't decipher. I was too busy trying to forget how close his hand was to my dick. I was hard, no surprise there. Combine that with my oversized trunks, and I was mostly indecent—a fact Branson didn't mind at all.

"What did you hide?" His words dipped persuasively as his pinky grazed the underside of my balls, sending pleasure zinging through me.

"I've played a little more poker than I let on."

Branson tilted his head back and laughed. "Oh really?"

"I've always played. From high school to now. There are some bars around my area in Seattle with five-dollar games that last several hours. I guess I've always liked activities that were non-contact. Nash is actually really good. I was surprised he came so close."

Branson sighed and leaned back, looking exactly like a man who was completely content with where he was and who he was with. "Again, we don't need to tell him anything that would make him more confident of himself."

These four liked to tease, but there was real affection under their jabs. I imagined the four of them more than ten years younger: first, called upon to do something heinous, losing all faith in the ones they loved; then breaking out into an unknown world together. They had the type of bonds that took years, blood, sweat, and tears to form. And for all intents and purposes, they seemed to treat Branson as a patriarch of sorts. If not that, then an unspoken leader. "You don't really mean that," I said.

"No, I don't. I'm glad overconfidence is his problem now. We were all pretty messed up after... everything."

I snuggled in, still on fire from his touch, but I didn't think that was a feeling that would go away anytime soon. "Do you want to talk about it? About before? I am a trained listener."

Branson replied by lifting me from the bench and setting me down so I faced him while straddling his lap. I lost the view, but gained a virile man between my legs. "I do want to talk about it with you," he murmured, cupping my face before resting his forehead against mine. "I want to tell you everything. But we'll have time for that. If I have my way, we'll have lots of time."

I worried what I had to say next would burst this bubble of bliss we'd slipped into, but if it was important enough to lodge into my brain at a time like this when my body wanted less talking and more rubbing, it needed to be asked. "Will we? I don't know the rules here, Branson. We sort of jumped in blindly. If people were reading the story of our lives, they would've rolled their eyes long ago. Not because you can turn into a wolf or because my touch compels people to tell the truth, but because I've fallen so hard and fast for you. And it scares me to say even that much out loud because what if this isn't the same thing for you? What if you make it a habit to greet every new person to the island like this?"

Branson snorted, but I wasn't joking. If this was a one-and-done sort of thing, I needed to know that now. Even if it was weeks too early to be having this conversation.

He leaned forward to kiss me, and I pulled back. I wouldn't be distracted by my needs like I'd been with Blaine. I'd been so eager to believe everything Blaine had said to me; the fact that he was duping me had never crossed my mind. I'd rather go home right now and suffer the epic blue balls that would follow than fall into that trap again.

"It is completely natural for you to feel like this," Branson said. "I'm feeling some of it myself. When I think about my reactions toward you, I start to worry Nana's craziness is rubbing off on me—she's always talking about prophecies and soulmates. It sounded insane, until now."

I sighed heavily. Hearing his own doubt helped a little. He was riding this roller coaster right along with me. I kissed the very tip of his nose. "You'd tell me if there was something about you, about what you are, that I have to know, right?"

"Absolutely." His responding kiss held more intent. His tongue thrust through my open lips, reminding me how his dick felt when it entered me.

I wrapped my arms around his neck, wishing I'd already taken off my shorts. My erection was squished under a fold of loose fabric while my ass ached, clenching as if to remind me of how empty I was. But Branson was there. He saw what I needed, and he was willing to give just that to me. I didn't have to worry, not in his arms.

A second later, I was lighter. The shorts Branson had loaned me popped to the surface, torn along the side seam. "You ruined your trunks."

Branson tickled my ass, testing my tightness. "I don't care," he whispered hotly between kisses.

I felt like the water we soaked in, fluid, hot and form-less. I was whatever shape Branson wanted me to be, what-ever position. My knees clenched his hips like I was riding a horse as I lifted my body up and down on his fingers. He let me ride him gently, getting used to the intrusion.

He decided when we were finished. He pulled his hand free, grabbing my cock instead. He pulled my dick like a leash, guiding me until I was exactly where he wanted, poised with my ass hovering over his glistening rounded head. He tugged down, and I moaned, both because the stroke felt like it did when I touched myself, only a million times better, and because his dick lodged inside me, stretching me to my limits while igniting my nerve endings, sending pleasure racing through my synapses.

I felt him everywhere, and that wasn't only a euphemism. He fucked me so deep, the hair on my head tingled. The water splashed over the rim of the tub and against the bricks, but Branson didn't slow. He did exactly as he wanted, maneuvering me with a familiarity that made us seem more like old lovers, perfectly in tune and aware of every button to push, every angle to thrust.

I kissed him, licking the sweat and water from his face and neck. My lips were dry from all the panting, but Branson was my fountain. What more did I need when I had his rigid length so tight inside me I could feel his dick throbbing? He growled, his hazel eyes dark with his lust.

I cupped his face, swiping the moisture from his brow. His neck was tight, along with his jaw. His gaze was so primal, rugged. I couldn't take the intensity for very long and closed my eyes as my balls tightened, signaling my impending orgasm. "Branson, yes, please!" I lifted my arms to the cloudy sky.

We were outside, not quite where anyone could see us, but that didn't dampen how wild I felt. I wasn't Riley, downtrodden social worker who had run away with his tail between his legs; I was a wild animal with only a single care in the world. I howled along with my orgasm, wailing to the sky while I felt a different sort of heat pulsing from inside.

Branson latched onto my neck, sucking and biting as he thrust without really moving. His hips jerked, his thrusts stuttering while he filled me with his seed. I collapsed against him, exhausted, spent, but utterly satisfied. "That was... that was..." I lifted my face from his shoulder, panting but needing to see his eyes more. "That was way better than poker."

Branson smiled, but I could see he still hadn't quite come down from the frantic high of our lovemaking. His eyes flashed a golden amber color, looking more animal than man. He lowered his lips and sighed. He kissed lightly down my shoulder and then across my chest. When our gazes met again, his eyes were hazel once more. "I'm glad I measured up," he said, nuzzling the crook of my neck.

I sunk down to sit beside him, but he pulled me in his lap as we stared silently at the waves lapping the shore.

———

I PUSHED OPEN the window of my apartment, looking down at the street like Branson had asked me to do. He'd left me at my door, claiming he had one last surprise. It was late Sunday evening, and I had just enough time to throw on some pajamas and get a few hours, if I fell asleep right away. Though I'd spent the better part of the entire weekend, from Friday night to now, with Branson, I hadn't wanted to separate. I'd clung to him, peppering his face with kisses.

It made things easier that Branson hadn't wanted me to go either. "Look for me outside," he'd murmured, but he'd refused to give me a hint.

I stared at the empty street. Walkerton was the type of place that seemed to roll up their sidewalks by nine, and it was so much past nine. Across the street were shops, all closed; the only lights shining were the twinkling holiday displays that had been left to bring cheer overnight. But the sidewalk was empty. Had he already gone?

I frowned. He'd told me to wait here. It couldn't have taken me long to walk from my door to the window. Though I had paused to shuck off my coat. I squinted, but it wasn't like he'd shrunk. Then I saw it.

Him.

A wolf walked from the shadow of my apartment building into the middle of the vacant street. I'd never seen a wolf in the wild, but this one was bigger than I'd expected. He had mostly gray fur, speckled with bits of white, brown, and black. His tail swayed gently. No, not swayed. Wagged.

If I'd never met Branson and had randomly looked out my window at this moment, I would've thought he was a real wolf. He stared up at me without blinking, and I startled, realizing I'd seen those eyes. They weren't his normal hazel, but a warm amber, like he'd been in the hot tub.

I blinked. Because he was a real wolf. An actual wolf. I'd known for days, but seeing him was something else. My boyfriend could turn into a wolf.

Honestly, I'd heard stranger things.

I waved, tentative at first. The wolf bowed his head. He winked, making me giggle. I knew his claws and teeth could rip through me, but he looked so cute with one ear pointed up and the other flopped. He motioned with his head toward my apartment. I took it to mean *go to sleep.* "Goodnight," I whispered, retreating back into my apartment. A low whine wafted through, and I returned. Branson flicked his head to the side, another mimed message. *Close your window.*

I sent him a thumbs up, saying I *thought* I understood what he wanted me to do. I closed my window and went back into my bedroom to change, and when I came back out, he was gone. I must have gotten his message right.

I flopped down on the couch, knowing every moment spent here mindlessly scrolling my phone or watching television was one less moment for sleeping. I hadn't picked up my work phone since Friday, something that would've been impossible while I'd been positioned in Seattle. My cell service here was as bad as in the office, but I had decent Wi-Fi that let me stay connected to the things I needed.

Against my better judgment, I checked my work email. Before the transfer, I had no less than thirty unanswered emails waiting for me at any given time. This time, there were two. The first was an email from the state office confirming the report of my first case, and the second was from Hal.

Riley,

I tried calling your office, but your voicemail isn't set up yet. Someone came by looking for you. He'd asked half the department before I stepped in. Are you sure everything is okay there? This guy said he was your boyfriend, but he looked like trouble on two legs. I sent him away. No one could tell him where you'd gone, and I certainly wasn't going to. If this was the wrong choice, let me know. But if you are dating a guy like that, you and I need to talk.

In other news, I found more than seventy yards of copper tubing at a garage sale. Just what I needed for my mirror stand. Linda looks about ready to kill me every time I bring home more materials, but you never know, right?

Hope things are well up there in the great wild.

Hal

I dropped the phone. I didn't think not seeing the email would do anything about the events that had sparked its purpose, but not seeing it helped me concentrate on the wheezing coming from somewhere in my apartment.

Oh wait, that was me.

I'd begun to gasp for air, still feeling as if my lungs were screaming for it. Blaine had come to my work. It had only been a matter of time. I'd left, changing my last name in the process to hide from him. I hoped now his search would spread. He wouldn't think I would be stupid enough to remain employed in social services. He'd start looking elsewhere. If I was lucky, he'd find the false forwarding address I'd left with my old landlord and would head to the other side of the country.

I let my head fall against the couch cushion. Every

glowing, warm feeling I'd brought with me was gone. My insides were cold and clammy.

I launched from the couch with a ragged gasp, running to check the locks on my door. Unsatisfied, I circled to the window. The last time I'd stood here, I'd been over the moon that Branson had shown me his wolf side. Now, I eyed every shadowy corner on the street like Blaine was lurking, waiting for me to drop my guard.

I just had to get through the night. One night and then I'd be with people again. Branson would call. Maybe we'd meet for lunch.

Still, I found myself back on the couch clutching a large kitchen knife. I wouldn't sleep this night. But I only had to make it to tomorrow.

———

Monday came as quick as I'd suspected. I dragged myself to work, bags under my eyes, but at least my outfit was clean and pressed, my hair combed. I couldn't let my home life make me useless at work. Even if I was looking at a lighter workload, each case deserved my absolute attention.

I busied myself for most of the morning reading over the case files of those who'd had repeat visits from the previous social worker. Chances were, I'd be seeing them again, and it would best if I didn't have to start from scratch. So much of my job was establishing connections so people would trust me enough to tell me the truth when it mattered.

My reading kept me busy until lunch. I still hadn't heard from Branson and was beginning to feel like my skin had shrunk on my bones. I caught lunch with some of the other employees. We were a hodgepodge of departments. There was Gladys from animal control and Maxwell who worked in sanitation. They were both friendly enough and kept the lunchtime conversation going at a pace that didn't require my input.

By the end of the day, I was pretty antsy to hear from Branson, I figured we could grab an early dinner, or maybe we could go back to his house and make something for everyone. His house had been so much warmer and more joyful than my apartment.

I gave a little cheer when my phone rang at half till end of day.

I yanked the phone free. "Hello? I mean, Mr. Monroe's desk."

"I'd like to speak to the man, not the desk, please," Branson said.

I snorted. "Sorry, he just stepped out. But I can take a message."

Branson sighed, but it wasn't a happy sound; it was a sound that made my stomach twist. "I don't want to..."

"What?"

"Something's come up, Riley. If I could get out of it, I would, but... it involves the pack and..."

I looked around as if I thought there was both someone in my office listening in and that person could hear what Branson's side of the conversation. There wasn't, and they couldn't.

"I thought you guys were done with all that?"

"We are. For the most part. But we get dragged in on occasion. Can I get a raincheck?"

I could go a day without seeing the man I'd just met, couldn't I?

Of course I could. That I had to mentally check was stupid. "Definitely, a raincheck."

"Riley, I mean it. If I could get out of this, I would."

I smiled, even though Branson couldn't see my face. The smile was fake and forced anyway. "I know. I believe you. I do. I just—was excited to see you. I still will be, when our schedules work out." He didn't deserve to be punished for my baggage.

"Are you sure everything is okay?" His tone dipped, sending shivers up my spine and down to my cock. "You'd tell me if it wasn't, right?"

Things were fine. I was a mess, but that hadn't been what Branson had asked. "Yes. I'm just settling still. Call me when you can meet up."

I set the phone back in its cradle, but what I wanted to do was slam it. I wasn't angry at Branson, but at me. I'd know falling head over heels after a *weekend* had been a bad move. Now I would pay the price.

My life seemed like a series of me paying prices. I had to come out ahead at some point. Right?

9

BRANSON

I HUNG UP, growling only after the line disconnected so I could be sure Riley didn't think it was for him.

"None of us want to do this," Nash said from the driver's seat. He took the turns on the winding road like an old pro.

We'd learned to drive on these back roads. That had been after we'd left the packs, of course. At sixteen, when I'd mentioned wanting to get my license, my mother had chastised me saying we'd buy the documentation like we had every other thing but that I had no reason to really learn how to drive. She never did.

Learning to drive had been my first direct rebellion against her after we'd left. I didn't count refusing to murder my cousins as a rebellion, just proof I had a heart.

"Delia got herself into this mess," I replied, slipping the phone in my pocket. Leaving Riley on Sunday had been difficult enough. I'd only managed by planning what we would do Monday night. I was going to suggest dinner at his place. We were going to make easy conversation while I cooked for us. I didn't know nearly enough about the man except that every so often, he'd retreat in on himself and I could tell he was remembering a time that he'd rather forget. He didn't talk a lot about friends he'd left behind. I knew he didn't have much in the way of family.

I had too much of that last thing, and nothing could stop them despite the barriers we erected. Case in point, this night. Alpha Walker had called, and the four of us jumped.

Well, Alpha Walker had called, I'd told him we were busy and that I didn't care about the claims that had been brought against my mother. But then Nana had called, and here we were.

I might not have been all that sure why we were racing back to pack lands, but I knew where I wasn't. With Riley.

This was a fragile time for him and us. I'd promised him, and now...

"If the sounds from this weekend are anything to go by, you don't have to worry, bro," Wyatt said, turning from the front passenger seat and bouncing his fist on my knee. "You've got that guy locked and loaded."

I jerked my knee out from under his hand. He had to be blind not to see how much more Riley meant to me than that. I didn't understand my draw, but I wasn't going to fight it, either. Riley was special to me in a way no one else was. I'd say it was a wolf thing, except none of the others would have any idea what I was talking about. It was an *us* thing, him and I. I didn't need anyone else to understand.

"He's trying to be helpful," Aver murmured, sitting next to me in the back.

In Wyatt's own annoying way, maybe, but Aver's quiet words brought me out of my pity party. None of us wanted to be going where we were heading. I could count the number of times I'd returned to pack lands after leaving on one hand. Aver had returned more often, and Wyatt and Nash had been back less than me. But Nana knew that, so if she'd insisted we come tonight, there had to be a reason.

It wasn't just that we were being reminded of that night. Operating within the pack wasn't like living our day-to-day lives. The obvious reasons aside, everything *meant something* when it came to the pack. A cigar was never just a cigar, and it didn't take long to accidentally offend someone. The speed with which you entered a room, who could sit first at a table, who could eat with whom—all of that was governed by rules and regulations. And that was before a single word was spoken.

I often thought pack life had been created to ensure my failure. And as an alpha son to an elder Walker family, the son of the Alpha until my dad died, I'd had it better than most growing up. But the stability of living within pack boundaries, as well as the money the elder families channeled into pack business, was worth it for everyone who stayed.

I didn't judge them; I just didn't want to be one of them. Or lead them.

"Tuesday night is one dollar Jell-O shot night. Bring Riley down then. I've never met a pair of pants that could fight the power of my Jell-O shots." Wyatt mimed like he was melting, though he looked more like one of those inflatable men outside of car dealerships with his arms waving through the air.

I grit my teeth while Aver tried to hide his grin.

I couldn't be upset. Until now, the four of us hadn't been on a date that I wouldn't firmly place in the *casual* category, excluding Aver's blind dates, which were a whole different ball of wax. "What do you guys make of his ability? His curse."

Nash grunted. "I get that. Sometimes I think we've been cursed."

That was a surprisingly unsarcastic response from Nash.

"I don't," Wyatt replied, going against his brother in yet another upset from the norm. "We have the best of both worlds."

I agreed with him there. I'd never heard of anyone having abilities outside the norm other than wolf shifters. Which was what made Riley so unusual. I should ask him more about his parents. Maybe we could dig something up that would help us discover how aware they'd been of Riley's power. Were there others like him? If there were, Riley could talk to them, learn more about how to control what he could do. I decided to ask Nana about it later and looked through the windshield down the road. We were several minutes away from the bridge still.

We might have been able to see pack lands from our house, but getting there wasn't as easy. The river kept most traffic to one side or the other. There was one bridge, located almost on the other side of the island. We might have been able to see our old homes from where we lived, but we lived as far away as we could by car.

At the bridge, the road narrowed to one lane. There were no signs indicating the change, but the moment we crossed over the river and into pack lands, driving laws changed dramatically. Right of way was given to the Alpha —capital A—at all times, no matter what. From there, it was an intricate waterfall of privilege. At times, those in the lower rungs of the pack pecking order could wait for hours as a parade of cars rolled by, arranged in an order that really didn't matter any place else in the world.

I'd wondered about that immediately after the four of us

had first left. The rest of the world didn't play by their rules, didn't even know their rules existed, and yet around here, they governed every action.

No one was on the roads now. Or at least, we didn't run into anyone on our way to the main house. That was good since no one knew what to do when they saw us on the roads now anyway. Did they wait? Drive on? At this point, they were liable to get so confused they'd likely try to run us off the road before they passed.

There weren't shops or business, not like how they were in the rest of the world. Here, specific families were in charge of tasks. Some were tasked with taking and delivering grocery orders; others handled the landscaping and general maintenance. Mostly, the pack thrived on business thrummed up by the elder families. Wyatt and Nash's parents owned a large trucking company that brought goods from coast to coast. They had plans to expand internationally. My mother's money was in oil, not that she knew the first thing about the company. My father had expected me to take over the family business and had made that clear in his will.

When we left, I wanted nothing to do with my parent's money and had refused every call from my father's lawyers until they'd finally given up. I didn't know if my father had somehow know something like that would happen, but he'd made sure the company could go on without any input from Delia. She had enough people working under her that she didn't have to make a single decision other than how to spend the money. Aver's family was in politics, though how they made their vast amounts of wealth, I still wasn't sure. Apparently, there was a lot of money to be made in giving the right candidates money.

And each elder household was able to keep their overhead down thanks to the perks that came with being an elder family and the labor and services provided by the pack. In theory, it was a good system that kept the pack strong, but with the position of the future leader, the Alpha to take over when our grandfather passed, up in the air, everyone was concerned. I turned to face the window. The glass fogged under my breath. How the pack survived was no longer my concern.

"We're here," Nash said, though he didn't need to. We all knew where we were.

He'd stopped at the center of the driveway, ostentatiously lined with looming yew bushes, each formed and trimmed into the shape of a wolf. The way was lit by wrought iron lampposts, already decorated for the season with strings of holly twisted around each pole. The grand staircase leading to the main entrance was so gorgeously crafted, it nearly hurt to look at. But as beautiful as this mansion looked from the outside, I knew how cold it could get within.

I was the first to open my door. "Let's get this over with."

"There's Nana's junker," Wyatt said, indicating her old pickup with his forehead.

"Call it a junker to her face," Nash teased. "I dare you."

Wyatt winced. "I'd rather... I'd rather... face these dragons," he said solemnly as he got out.

We ascended the stairs as a team. That was how we would get through this night, as a combined force. It was how we'd left after all.

We were greeted by their butler—that was another service provided to the elder families by the pack—who took us directly to the grand dining room. The room wasn't empty. My grandfather and all of our parents sat around a table long enough to easily accommodate more. My grandfather was at the head.

He had a face that looked carved from stone. The severe lines around his eyes and mouth would've made any young child, even one groomed from a young age to become a leader, believe that they were hated. Later, I learned my grandfather didn't hate me in particular, as much as it was that he hated everything. As far as I'd been told, he'd been born surly, and the only change to that was living long enough to now be considered a curmudgeon.

My gaze passed over the other parents. I didn't care to look at them as much as they didn't me. My mother sat directly across from my grandfather but with the entire length of the table between them. The chair she sat in had been set back, far enough from the edge to make it very clear at first glance that she was a separate entity from those who sat around the table.

"Disgraced alpha sons, please take your seats," my grandfather said, resting his chin on the steeple made by resting his gnarled, wrinkled fingers together.

None of us moved.

"Oh, for goodness's sake," Nana said. She looked the same as she would if she'd stopped by our house randomly on a Sunday to drop off extra zucchini. Her brown corduroys were stained with mud and ripped, particularly at the bottoms. Her button-up had been made by sewing no less than four different shirts together. Her large, fur-lined jacket was homemade as well. I had no doubt she'd trapped whatever fur that was, skinned and treated it herself. She held her wooden walking stick in one hand.

It was never the same one. I figured when she got bored,

she went into the forest and found another that was the perfect size and length. Only her salt-and-pepper hair looked different, pulled up into a bun when normally she left it free around her face. She was the only one not sitting at the table. I wondered if she chose her spot in the corner or if that was where they wanted her. But then, Nana didn't do anything she didn't want to do. "Boys, please sit. We need to get this going. I've got dough rising at home."

"No one requested your presence, Great-grandmother Walker," Aver's mother said primly. She was a thin woman with shoulder-length blond hair that she curled under as if she were some fifties housewife. Aver's father matched her style and aesthetic with his neatly trimmed dark blond hair and cleanshaven face. They were picture perfect. Too bad that was the only time they were perfect.

"All the same," Nana said with a groan as she stretched her feet out in front of her. "I imagine I'll be more useful here than you will, Clarice."

Clarice, Aver's mother, took a shocked sip of her martini before grabbing her napkin and dabbing the red embarrassed splotches growing up her neck.

I grinned at Aver, but his face was an emotionless mask.

"What are we doing here?" I asked. I wouldn't sit before I knew. Not even for Nana. My tone and distinct lack of title was not lost on those around the table.

"I'm being framed!" my mother shouted. For as frazzled as she sounded, she looked ready to attend a holiday party. She had on a floor-length velvet red gown, white satin elbow-length gloves, and enough diamonds to fund a small country. Her hair had been swept back in a low bun pinned with something that glittered.

"How does that concern us?" I asked, knowing that I

spoke for the four of us. At times like this, I felt our solidarity as clearly as I'd felt my connection to Riley.

Wyatt and Nash's father snickered.

"You are here as witnesses. No more or less," Grandfather said. "The expulsion of an elder household is no light matter. The revenue loss is one thing, the dip in pack morale another. The pack operates under the belief that we have their best interests at heart. If something happens that leads them to stray from that thinking, we will have problems."

I shouldn't have been shocked by how cold my grandfather was. He didn't actually care about anyone from the pack, just what they thought of the elder families. I was pretty sure I knew what my mother was in trouble for. But I didn't know how anyone else had found out. I'd told my cousins, but none of them, even Aver, would repeat what happened to their parents. That was like pulling the pin of a grenade and tossing it into a crowd.

"What is the specific charge?" I asked, crossing my arms over my chest. The hairs at my nape prickled. I hated being here. This had been the room they'd brought the four of us on the eve of our eighteenth birthdays, informing us the next day the four of us would battle to the death. I felt Aver, Nash, and Wyatt around me, their body language likely mirroring mine.

"I received a call," John, Wyatt and Nash's father, said importantly. "I of course have trusted friends looking out for the welfare of our pack."

"You mean a spy," I snarled.

John straightened in his chair, attempting to look down his nose at me, but I was still standing. "There was a report made by someone in social services. It expressly stated

Delia Walker's name, Walkerton, and Walker County in connection with a possible sex trafficking ring. Our area is now under watch. There is a red flag in the system, which means in the future, we may come under the type of scrutiny we've been fortunate enough to avoid. Obviously, I had to inform Alpha Walker." He gave a sniveling little bow toward our grandfather.

I'd lost the ability to breathe. *Someone in social services* had to be Riley. If his name hadn't come up yet, I wasn't going to bring him up now. That these people were circling around him was worrisome enough. What if they wanted to question Riley and discovered what he knew? What he could do? If there were a group of people who wanted to keep their secrets, it was this group. I needed to do something before someone asked the question that would lead to Riley.

"I apologize, Nana, but I don't know what you thought the four of us could achieve here." I looked back at my three cousins. Each gave me slight nod as if to say they understood what we had to do and were on board. "I don't have anything to add here—"

"But the boy was sent to you! As a gift! It was all there in the report," John seethed. His dark black hair was the exact same shade as both Wyatt and Nash, but that was where their similarities ended.

"Then I must be lying," I said without remorse.

John looked mad enough to bite off his own tongue. "You speak like this, in Alpha Walker's home no less, during an official pack proceeding—"

"Weren't you listening, Dad?" Nash snarled. "We're the disgraced sons. I'd drop my pants and take a deuce on this table if the urge hit."

"Okay, okay." Nana got to her feet, unsuccessful in hiding her smile before the rest of us saw it. "I called for this reunion, so I'm gonna speed us along. Eustice, I know you've already made up your mind, so what is it?"

My grandfather's expression never changed. How could the son look so much older than his mother? Shifters lived longer than most people, but Nana had aged particularly gracefully.

"A punishment must be given," he said.

"What sort?" Clarice asked, unable to hide her zeal.

"I am the mate of our late Alpha—how dare you speak of suspending me!" Delia shrieked.

This sounded more like business as usual. I'd grown up listening to their sniping. The four of us had. What I couldn't figure out was why Nana had demanded our presence. This posturing and displaying of power could all be done just as well without us here.

"A suspension, for a week. And when you return, you must ask to speak with Paul and make sure this is something he's already forgotten."

The other elder families tittered, clearly displeased with the lightness of the punishment, while Delia squalled.

At that point, I was as ready to go as my cousins. This trip had clearly been a waste of time. Maybe I shouldn't have put so much stock in Nana's requests. She was getting up there in years.

"Where will I live?" Delia cried.

"Your son has a home, with an extra room," Nana said.

The four of us spun to face her. She was out of her mind. There was no other answer.

"Absolutely not," Aver started.

"No way in hell," Nash continued.

"Over my dead body," Wyatt added.

I'd been watching Nana. "Why?" I said only to her.

"Because it's the holidays?" Nana said, wiping her hands together. "Because whether you like it or not, you're family, and no amount of distance between you is going to change that. And because I said so, Branson Walker, how about that?" When I'd been younger, that tone meant I was dangerously close to being chased by a wooden spoon.

I didn't fear Nana's wrath, but I'd spent my life trusting her choices. Could I stop now because having Delia at our house during her suspension ensured a week of me not seeing Riley? How did I even begin to explain that to him? I couldn't risk Delia knowing without a doubt how important Riley had become to me. "Fine."

"What?"

"No way!"

My cousins weren't happy, but in that, we were the same. "If that's why we're here, fine. She can stay in the guest house." At the moment, that space was cluttered with pool equipment and spiders, but we could clear off the cot. "I'll bring her food. You guys won't even have to see her."

That mollified them, knowing only I would be subjected to her presence. "Is that all?" I asked the table, addressing my question to no one person.

My grandfather nodded. My mother was suspiciously quiet.

"Then we'll take our leave." I turned along with my cousins.

"I'll wait for Delia and bring her after she's grabbed some of her things," Nana said, reminding me we weren't leaving this house without the world's worst party favor.

I nodded, heading to the door the butler already held open.

"Aver, we haven't had a chance to talk. Karen was so excited after your date," Clarice chirped as we left.

Aver stopped immediately. I stood behind him so I only saw his shoulders bunch before he turned halfway. "I was less impressed. I don't require another date," Aver replied with a cold tone that sounded too much like his father.

"My boy! He won't be wooed by any woman but the best!" Glendon, Aver's father, boomed.

Aver turned too quickly for me to see his reaction. Ahead, Wyatt and Nash were already at the front door, rushing so quickly from the house someone might've thought it was haunted.

"I'll meet you at the guest house in an hour, Nana," I said before speeding up to walk by Aver's side.

"Fuck! I hate it there!" Nash shouted as he navigated the car with the four of us inside back down the driveway. He drove quickly, eager to put the opulent home behind us. "I need a shower, a beer, and someone bendy and eager to please," he said. "In that exact order."

As Wyatt and Nash made plans for how they would achieve those things the moment we returned, I turned my attention to Aver. "You okay?"

"Fine," he grunted.

He was silent for several moments before suddenly shouting, "Dammit!" and slamming his fist into the panel of his door. The plastic cracked under his bleeding knuckles. "I'm older than this, goddammit! How do I know exactly what to say at all times except for when I'm with them?" Aver's tortured gaze fell on each of us.

"There's a reason why we hate them," Wyatt replied, craning his neck to see into the back while Nash sped to get us off pack lands. "How are we supposed to know what to say in the face of true evil?"

"I'm not joking, Wyatt," Aver grumbled.

"Neither am I. It's amazing we aren't more fucked in the head than we are after what we went through. Each of us was raised with a silver spoon in our mouths, trained and shaped to be leaders. At least the two of you were on your own. For most of my life, I thought our parents were training us *both*, like we'd be co-Alphas or something stupid."

Early on, when the talk of which of us would claim the leader position had first begun, there had been whispers that the alpha most worthy among us would be appointed. After that, our days had been filled with lessons and extracurricular activities. We all spoke Spanish as well as English. Aver was fluent in Chinese as well. I knew a soup spoon from a salad spoon. We'd been taught all the skills to live that sort of lifestyle, but had none of the desire.

"You weren't stupid. I hoped the same thing," Nash said. "I see this all the time at work. People go through their worst days, and you can either choose to live and grow past that, or you can stay rooted in the past. I choose to grow. Preferably in the dick region with something hot and tight—"

The three of us groaned, Wyatt hitting Nash's shoulder. "We get it," he said with a smile. "You have sex."

"What are you going to say to Riley?" Aver asked.

Nash accelerated over the bridge. The four of us let out a combine sigh of relief.

"I don't know." I grimaced. The truth was the best policy, but it also made me look like a coward. I suspected that was why we hated going back so badly. In our lives, we could be the men we'd grown to be, but the moment we went back, it was like I fought the natural desire to revert back to the angry, obstinate personality I'd had as a teen.

The drive home took less time than there, thanks to

Nash's lead foot and his desire to get laid as soon as possible. I headed directly to the guest house, clearing some of the junk we'd thrown in there for quick storage. I hadn't asked for help, but Aver and Wyatt came with me. After a while, Nash popped in too.

We made quick work, uncovering the cot and clearing a path to the bathroom. She had working lights, running water, her own television with cable, and a small kitchen. Eventually, Nash left for the bar, taking Wyatt—who'd claimed he didn't need a shower since man and woman alike appreciated his natural odor—with him. Aver mumbled something about getting paperwork before bed, and then I was alone.

I couldn't be sure how long Nana would take, so I pulled out my phone. I only had Riley's work number, and there was no reason he should be at the office this late. I called it anyway; I could leave a message. Or several. However many it took to explain the situation sufficiently.

But someone answered after the first ring.

"Hello? Er... dang... Mr. Monroe speaking."

It felt good just to hear his voice. I sighed, expelling just a little of my stress. "Riley? What are you still doing at work?"

"I—um. Nothing. I mean, I'm reading up. For work." He paused, and I could picture the way his face would clench first from worry, then into a smile. "What are you doing calling me if you didn't think I was here?"

My mood had made me apprehensive. I didn't like the way he sounded, like he was hiding something. Was it a big something? Or was it my own mood coloring the moment? "I know your cell doesn't get great service," I said, wishing I could just skip what I had to say next.

"And?" Riley prompted when I didn't immediately continue. His voice had dipped, becoming suspicious.

I just needed to give it to him straight. We'd built what we had on honesty; there was no reason to stop now. Even if I did end up looking a little yellow. "Something has come up."

"Another something?" His voice had gotten quiet and higher in pitch.

"A big something. My mother has been... well to spare you all the boring details, she needs to live with us for the week. I'm putting her up in the guest house. You don't have a single thing to worry about—"

"Why would I worry about your mother staying with you?" Riley asked. I forgot he hadn't developed the same psychological response to hearing talk about my mom.

"Remember what I said about the pack finding out that you know? That still applies here. And if my mom found out you knew at a time like this, she wouldn't hesitate to tell my grandfather to try and get back into his good graces." It sounded ludicrous saying the situation out loud.

"Your family reminds me of one of those TV shows, where everyone is plotting against each other because they all have more money than sense."

I laughed. I would've given anything to see what Riley's face looked like while he'd said that. There was a fire in his words, almost like he was angry on my behalf. My chest warmed. "I swear I'll make it up to you. This weekend when she leaves. If you thought our first date was great, you'll love the second."

Riley didn't reply right away. I prayed during the silence that I hadn't ruined things already. I wished I could head to his office right then, but I had no idea when my mother would show up. "That's a pretty big promise, Branson. I won't hold you to it. Our second date can just be as good as the first."

Relief warred with paranoia. He sounded fine, but that didn't stop the twisting in my gut. Like I'd eaten something I shouldn't have and had no idea of the bathroom terror that awaited me. "Are you sure you're okay? Wyatt and Nash are going into town. I can have them stop by."

"No, no, I'm fine. You don't need to send the paw patrol."

I snorted at the name. That was definitely what I would call those two from now on.

"I'm still getting used to things. It will... all work out."

I wanted to ask what exactly would work out. Us? His position on the island? But I couldn't as Nana's old truck lumbered down the driveway, taking the side road to the guest house. "I'll call you the first chance I can," I said. "You'll wait for me, right? I don't have to worry about some other guy swooping in pretending he just wants to show you the island?"

"Not right now. The office is empty," Riley joked.

"Ha ha. I don't like the idea of you there alone," I said quickly. Nana had parked her car.

"Then it's a good thing you have to hang up." Riley must have heard my growing dread. "Goodnight."

I said goodnight and hung up just as my mother closed Nana's passenger door. She wiped her hand on a handkerchief she pulled from her clutch. In the main house, no one batted an eye at her extravagant appearance. Here, she looked as out of place as a polar bear in Hawaii.

"Where are your things?" I asked, barely managing to catch a large duffel bag that Nana had hefted my direction. One bag? That was surprisingly light. Maybe my mother had changed a little and—

Nana yanked back the tarp from the battered bed of her

old truck, revealing a mound of suitcases. Oh yes, that seemed more like it.

My mother tiptoed down the cobbled path to the modest guest house. Her face never stopped scowling.

"I'll just get your bags then," I muttered, joining Nana, who had already grabbed two of the larger suitcase pieces. I took them from her, piling a few more in my arms to take inside. By the time we were finished—my mother never stepping out to help us—it was officially late.

"My dough's ruined by now," Nana said as I walked her back to the truck. "Like they always say, poor planning makes poor buns."

"That isn't actually a saying, Nana."

"Oh you shush. What makes a thing a saying 'cept people saying it? I've been dragging my heels for you, boy. You going to be okay with this?"

I frowned. "It's a little late to be asking that." I sighed. "But we'll be fine. I'll bring her a bottle of vodka. That should keep her fed for a few days."

Nana didn't laugh—she did the opposite, making me feel like a kid who'd spoken out of line. "She's your mother."

"And that means nothing when it comes to whether I want her in my life. I thought we'd sent that message when we left. I choose my life, who is in it, how it is lived." I hated being at odds with the old woman. Most times, she looked as solid as an ox, but she had the sneaky ability to appear frail at the exact moment of a disagreement. "Why, Nana? I'm trusting you and doing as you asked, but you got to tell me why."

"She wasn't always the Delia Walker you know, son. When dear Patrick met her, it was true love, I was sure of it. He soothed her, rounded her sharp edges. Our Patrick would've never asked you four to do what the others did. He was a good egg. He would've come up with something. But life doesn't work out how we want it. The world lost a good man, but that pack lost a powerful alpha and a fair leader that day. Maybe I want to see some of his glory returned."

I didn't know a lot about pack life directly after my father had taken charge after my grandfather. He'd died when I'd been so young, most of my memories were from after my grandfather reassumed the position. "This changes nothing. The second she can return, we'll be as glad to see her go as she is to go."

"Maybe," she said cryptically. She looked back at the guest house. The doors and windows were shut tight. Add that to the irritated groan of her truck's old engine, and everything we said would be sufficiently muffled. "When am I going to meet this new boy of yours?"

I narrowed my eyes, my gut clenching with panic. This was Nana, though. Throughout the years, she'd been my one constant. "Who told you?"

"Just Wyatt, then Aver, and finally Nash," she replied, lifting a finger with each new name mentioned.

"Everyone then. Great. I don't know when you'll meet him, Nana. I don't know when I'm going to meet him again. He isn't coming round while she's here."

Nana watched my face as I spoke, her expression growing more worried. I wasn't always sure how Nana knew the things she did. She claimed she heard the spirits whispering. I wondered if she was just really good at eavesdropping. "He isn't just your new boy, is he? There's something special about him."

How did I answer a question like that? Did she mean how he knew that I was a shifter and about the pack? Or did she mean my reaction to him? Or, the most obvious answer, did she somehow know what he could do? Who knew how much the others had told her? "There is," I said with a smile. "He's very special to me."

"Then I'll meet him when the time comes. Goodnight, Branson."

"Don't you mean *disgraced alpha son?*"

The wind whipped by, lifting the frizzy strands that had escaped her bun. She clenched the collar of her jacket with a shiver before climbing in. "No. I don't."

10

RILEY

I SLAMMED THE PHONE DOWN, pinching the bridge of my nose in frustration.

"Hard day?" Sheriff Maslow leaned against the doorway, his legs crossed casually.

"I'm sorry. I should've closed my door." Better yet, I shouldn't have lost my temper. It was Thursday, and the rest of the week hadn't gone much better than this moment. "The Seattle Office of Housing has zero low-income listings within a fifty-mile radius of us. When I explained how that could be a problem when I tried to help my clients, they just asked how many active clients I have in need of housing."

Sheriff Maslow grunted.

"Who cares if we have five or five hundred? There isn't a single place I could direct someone who needed that sort of information from me. How do they expect me to do my job if social services aren't even offered out here?" I eyed the phone, contemplating another outburst. But if I broke this phone, who knew what they'd have to replace it? Probably two cups and a string.

I was annoyed after a week of phone calls that all ended

the same way. The irony wasn't lost on me. I'd chosen this spot because of the isolation. This week had been isolating.

I'd tried to focus my mind on more important things than not seeing a man, and that worked well during office hours. But after and into to the night had been hard. After Hal's email, I'd been sure that Blaine was in every corner, waiting, watching.

"I know what you did! You know what you did!" My throat burned. *"If you won't tell, I will!"*

"I don't need an answer right away..." Maslow said. Dammit. I'd clearly missed everything that had come first.

"What?" I blinked, my face burning. What had I looked like while my mind had been a million miles away?

"Lunch? Are you in?"

I wasn't very hungry. Nothing seemed to hit my stomach right. "Where?"

"A bunch of us were going to go over to The White Otter. Have you been?"

I knew the town was small and that there wasn't an endless number of places to eat like in Seattle, but did it have to be that one? I felt like a jerk, though. I'd spent a great weekend with a guy, a really great weekend. And we would see each other again. Moping just because we'd been pulled apart for a few days was asinine. "I have. The food is really good there. When are you going?"

He looked back around the other parts of the office. All of us who worked in any capacity for the city were located on the same floor. I couldn't see, but I guessed the motion was meant to indicate we were the only ones left. "Now. I'll give you a ride."

I turned off my computer, more because of habit than because I thought anyone would come snooping. I locked my office and followed him out. He drove to The White

Otter, rather than walking, which I appreciated because of the rain. As I stamped the water from my boots and shook out my hair in the restaurant entrance, a waitress approached.

"I wondered when you'd be here!" Alexis said cheerily. I immediately recognized her as the waitress who had served Branson and I last Friday, the same one who had made an inappropriate confession because of me.

I frowned, though. Did she say that because the rest of the office was here already? Maslow only shrugged when I looked to him; he wasn't sure what she meant, either.

"We're here for—"

"Oh, I know, right this way." The waitress headed toward the dining area, leaving us no choice but to follow.

I heard Maxwell from sanitation's loud laughter and relaxed. But the waitress stopped before she reached the long table of coworkers next to the window. They saw us, dimming their conversations to wave us over before they also frowned.

"Here we are," the waitress said, stepping to the side and revealing the table she'd brought us to.

Branson Walker sat with his mother. A basket of bread sat untouched between them. His eyes widened when he saw me, flitting over to Maslow and narrowing. Branson had dressed nicely for the occasion, wearing a navy blue suit that screamed both wealth and style. He didn't look at all like the sexy woodsman I'd left.

"Here we are..." The waitress, oblivious to the sudden tension, laid down two menus at the four-person table.

"What are you doing?" Delia asked, gazing at me first like I was nothing. Then she recognized who I was and looked at me like trash. "Is this you, Branson? Did you set this up to humiliate me?" She sniffed as her eyes filled with tears that I didn't believe for one second.

"What's... going... on?" the waitress asked, lifting the menus she'd placed. "I thought... since last time that you two were—"

"What last time?" Delia asked as she studied her son's face.

I felt like a deer in the headlights, except I wasn't nearly so graceful. I was more of a water buffalo in the headlights. I knew the risk, or as much of the risks Branson had revealed to me. But I didn't know what exactly I could claim to know. Delia had seen me leaving Branson's home in the morning. Surely, she'd put two and two together. She didn't know I hadn't left his house after that for almost two days. And she didn't know that I knew exactly what her secret was.

"When Branson met with me to explain the case," I said, hoping my hesitation wouldn't add to her suspicion.

"I see," Delia replied primly. "A courtesy you didn't extend to me, I see."

Poor Maslow looked from Delia to me. "Mrs. Walker, it's good to see you. We don't normally see your kind this side of the river."

My eyes bugged out of my head at the mention of *her kind*, but Maslow only meant the pack as it was known by the humans, a tight-knit group of people with similar hobbies who lived in isolation. Still, the look on Delia's face told me he'd said the wrong thing.

"I don't see why it should be odd that I visit my son, Sheriff."

Maslow sputtered and looked down at his shoes, ripping every protective instinct from me. He was a nice man who didn't deserve this woman's ire. I set my hand on his shoulder, knowing the layer of his uniform would be enough to keep any spontaneous confessions from flying free. Both Branson and Delia watched the motion.

"He didn't mean it that way, Mother," Branson said tiredly. He looked up at me, but not how he'd looked at me before. Now, I felt disposable, used and discarded. "It was good to see you again, Riley," he added as if the thought had just occurred to him. "It's been a while..."

Oh Lord. In most circles, *it's been a while* was code for *sorry I never called like I said I would*, but even though I understood the facade Branson was attempting, it stung. The message, his uninterested tone, the dismissive way his gaze glided over me—I hated it all. "It has," I smiled, hoping it looked real. I pulled myself together and found the waitress. "There's been a mistake here. Our party is over there." I pointed to the table of coworkers, all silently gawking at us.

"I'm sorry." Alexis turned to lead us to the correct table. "This was my fault. I'm sorry." The poor girl looked so upset. I wished there was a way I could let her know that she hadn't lost her mind. In any other case, I would've loved to happen upon Branson during lunch.

"Enjoy your meal," Maslow said, guiding us behind the waitress with his hand between my shoulder blades.

"What was that?" Gladys asked immediately once we'd sat. She lifted the menu to cover her lips. "Looked tense. But also sexy."

I tried to laugh, but the noise got caught somewhere in my nose and came out sounding like a choking snort. "What? No."

Maslow arranged the utensils at his place. "Definitely strange."

"Oh, look!" Gladys nearly shouted. I wanted to lunge over the table and cover her mouth, but that would've just brought more attention. As it was, our entire table stared as an old woman dressed in a long brown skirt and matching long-sleeved top took one of the seats the waitress had tried to give us at Branson's table. Aver filled the last spot.

"I've never seen so many of them in one spot." Gladys wasn't the only one who couldn't seem to look away.

"C'mon, you guys, let them eat." I turned firmly away from the other table and shoved my menu in my face. If they wanted to gawk like the Walkers were animals in a zoo, fine, but I wouldn't add my face to them. Unless, by not staring, I was separating myself from the crowd? "Why is it so strange to see them together? The four cousins live together not far from here."

Gladys's smile sharpened. "You know a lot about them for just moving here."

"They were his first case," Maslow said.

I sent him a grateful look.

"It isn't strange to see the Walker cousins," Maslow explained. "And Nana Walker goes where she pleases when she wants, but it is strange to see them all together with Delia Walker. And her attitude toward me—she's normally cold, not flat-out rude."

I shoved a slice of bread from one of the two in the center of the table in my mouth to save myself from thinking of a reply. I knew, or thought I did, why Delia was here. I wasn't sure why the four of them were sitting for lunch. My stomach turned. I also knew why Branson had acted so cold to me, but that didn't help bring my appetite back. That had left the second I spotted Delia.

The waitress returned for everyone's orders. She was fast to bring back our meals but didn't linger around the table. At this point, I was pretty sure she wouldn't be ecstatic to see me again. That was my life. Even people I had no reason to interact with on a daily basis eventually learned I was best avoided.

Picking at my meal, I tried to do anything but turn and look at the other table. Every once in a while, their conversation would become more heated, loud enough for me to almost hear, but they always quieted again. My coworkers kept our own conversation going, needing almost no input from me. I ended up asking for a doggy bag because while I felt like I had angry butterflies inside me now, I would be hungry later.

"I'll take you back," Maslow said, pushing his empty plate further from him. He rubbed his stomach, pushing it out as if he had a baby in there. "Oh no, I've done it."

"What?"

His smile turned sweet and silly. "We're expecting." He patted his food baby.

"Ha!" I laughed, hovering my hand over his gut. "What should we name him?"

Maslow got to his feet along with everyone else at our table. "Cordon Bleu, after his father."

I smirked, thankful for Maslow's goofing around. He was older than me, in his early forties, but he still liked to play, a fact I was thankful for right about now.

We walked side by side back through the dining room. There was no way to avoid Branson's table. I'd hoped they would finish before us—they were just four against our much larger party—but they'd just gotten their entrees when we'd been delivered our checks. Not that I was paying attention or anything.

Look straight. Don't deviate. All things considered, bumping into Branson hadn't been a total disaster. It hadn't been pleasant, but Delia still seemed unaware of the depth of my relationship with her son, as well as my knowledge regarding exactly what she was. *How deep is your relationship?* a dark voice asked from within. *So deep he can't recognize you in public?* I wished I could shut the voice up. It only voiced my deepest fears, but—

My foot caught on something, and I fell forward. My gut dropped as my body slammed toward the ground. I was going to fall. It was going to hurt. Everyone was going to see.

I opened my eyes as warm arms caught me. I peered up to see Maslow, looking bewildered himself. "I actually caught you," he huffed, pulling us both straight.

"I'm so sorry!" Nana Walker stood, waving her hands as if in a panic. "You snagged my purse strap. I'm so sorry."

"Really, Nana, he looks fine," Delia drawled with a dismissive wave.

Aver was closer and had already gotten to his feet, while Branson, on the other side of the table, hovered in an irritated half-standing state. Deep lines carved out the shape of his mouth as he scowled at me.

I couldn't help tripping! It wasn't like I'd set out to make a spectacle of myself.

"It's fine, it's okay." I declined her outstretched hands, but only because she looked so frail. Her hand fell—I assumed because she didn't have the energy to hold it up—but her palm hovered over my stomach for a moment. I stepped back, bumping into Maslow. I didn't like how pale the old woman had gotten. "I didn't fall. Maslow had my back," I reassured her, shooting Maslow another smile over my shoulder.

"I told you to call me Jake," he replied.

"Thank you, Jake." Centered and balanced, he released my elbows. I took a deep breath and faced the table of four, looking at every face but Branson's. "See, no harm. Just a clumsy guy walking by. Enjoy your meals."

I pulled Maslow away, letting go the moment we crossed the hostess station.

"I wonder what Delia's been saying about you?" Maslow asked, stepping over a clump of deteriorating leaves in the parking lot.

"Why?"

"Branson. I've never seen him look so angry. For a second, I thought he was mad at me." He laughed it off. "I'm sorry I ever brought up the idea of dating him to you. Maybe they've got business problems. I never know with that group. Their lives are so intertwined. Talking to one of 'em is like talking to a ball of strings."

That was a good point that I was only just realizing. Branson had claimed this week was special, that his mother had never stayed there before, and that it wasn't something that happened often. But before that, Delia had just shown up at his home. She'd sent Paul to try to coax Branson out before that. What had she done before Paul to try to get Branson's attention? I was sure there was something, which meant these interruptions would never stop.

"Hey, I'm sure they're okay, and even if they aren't, it has nothing to do with us."

Ignorance was bliss. But I couldn't be ignorant. That didn't mean I had to make a big deal about it, either. "You're right. Let's get back to work. Almost Friday!" Early in my career, I'd learn the surefire way to derail any conversation was to mention the impending weekend. Maslow was no different.

"I'm not even on call." Maslow pulled the cruiser out onto the road toward our offices. "Do you have plans this weekend?"

Wouldn't I like to know. "Probably just settle in some more."

"Would you want to go back to The White Otter? On a date?" He parked in front of the office.

What? I hadn't gotten the idea Jake was gay. In fact, our earlier conversation had convinced me of the opposite. He wasn't bad looking. He had a full head of brown hair, gentle eyes, and the type of mouth that always looked seconds from lifting into a smile. More importantly, he had no meddling family. But he also did nothing to my insides. The only stirrings I felt near him were due to digestion.

This was tricky, though. If I jumped out and ran in now without saying anything, it would look rude. Too rude, and he might get angry. Jake didn't strike me as that type of guy, but I'd been surprised before. He'd asked me out, and I needed to give him an answer. "Oh, Jake, I'm flattered, but—"

His eyebrows furrowed. "Wait, wait, you got the wrong idea here. My friend is visiting this weekend. He likes to fish here when in the winter months. He's gay, and I think he just broke up with his boyfriend..."

"Oh!" *Awesome job, Riley. You're so twisted by this Branson thing you thought your friend was asking you out.* It was an honest mistake on my part, but that meant nothing to how awkward I felt. The emotion grew exponentially by the second. "Oh."

"Hold on, you thought I was asking you just now?"

I nodded.

Maslow chewed on the corner of his mouth. "I'm straight. I thought you knew that." He paused a moment, thinking over his next words. "But you weren't sure. And you were going to say no?" He got out, waiting at the front of the car for me to join him and walk to the building. "To all of this?" He emphasized his body with two hands, waving over himself like he was the big prize in a gameshow. "You were about to reject me!"

He didn't seem angry, or if he was, it wasn't serious. "Of course not," I rushed to his side. "I was just doublechecking because I was pretty sure you were straight."

Jake puffed his chest out at that, and I hid my smirk, passing through the door he held open.

"As it is—since it's not you after all," I added, "I'm going to decline for now. I just came from a big relationship, and I'm not ready for more."

His mouth dipped, curving the opposite direction it normally curved. "Did he act up? I'll tell you what I tell my friend—you don't need to endure through that shit. There are plenty of men out there who, you know, like other men. Never settle, Riley."

This work lunch had taken a weird turn immediately out of the gate. My *sort of* superior was trying to hook me up and give me dating advice. "Thank you, I'll keep that in mind." I pushed the button for the elevator.

"I hope you do. And if you have any trouble, just call me. I'll sort it out." He hooked his thumbs into the loops of his belt.

I leaned against the elevator wall. Between my relationship woes and the skeletons in my closet coming out to say boo, this week had been mostly a disaster. It wasn't over yet, but at least now it looked like I'd be ending the workdays with a friend.

———

I TIPTOED to my bed from the bathroom. My mouth was minty fresh, having just brushed my teeth before filling a glass of water to take with me to bed. Thanks to the near catastrophe with Jake, I'd had something to mull and chew over all afternoon and into evening. Even now, the memory of all that had happened made me smile. Unlike everything that had happened before that which had just made me feel like I had to throw up.

I thought some about that too, but didn't dwell on it like I would've normally. I simply wasn't meant for espionage or secrets. Hilarious given who I was. I could pretend to not know something, but the effect on my insides felt like knives let loose in a blender. Maybe that was a little dramatic. Like butter knives sloshed around in a bucket. Either way, it was uncomfortable.

I slid into bed, propping the pillows under my head how I liked them. In Seattle, I would spend my evening scrolling my phone until I fell asleep with it in my hand, but I was too mentally exhausted even for that. Even still, the moment my head hit the pillow, I heard something creak.

The wind. The building settling. It isn't a monster. It isn't Blaine. Please go to sleep!

I managed to close my eyes again, sighing tiredly when —*click—that* hadn't been the wind. That had been a lock or a door.

I threw the blankets back. Someone was inside my apartment. My heart pounded in my head. My hands were suddenly freezing and my fingers slow to move. I was scared stiff, literally.

I reached for my phone, but it wasn't like I got any service. What did I do? I'd deleted all my social media accounts and hadn't bothered creating any dummy accounts. Would the murderer in my apartment be kind enough to let me set up a new Facebook profile, find a friend, and then ask them to call 911? *Oh yeah, sure, maybe he could be in the profile pic.*

Somewhere in my apartment, something crashed. It sounded like glass. Now, it sounded broken. I rushed to my bedroom door, trying to peer down the dark hallway to whoever was bumbling on their way to kill me. I wouldn't go down without a fight. I looked down at my hands. I clutched a pillow and my cell phone to my chest. *Awesome.* If he was very still, maybe I could scratch his eye with the corner of my phone—

"Riley?" a deep voice whispered from much closer than I'd expected. I jolted back, still staring down the hall while Branson appeared from the shadows. His hair looked messy, like he'd spent a lot of time pushing his hands through it. He wore the same suit from earlier but had lost the jacket and undone the top few buttons of his white undershirt. "I'm sorry to break in."

My tongue felt too thick to reply. So many emotions pinged inside me. Relief, shock, confusion, desire. I didn't know which to latch onto, so I chose a new emotion, outrage. "You snuck into my apartment? You broke in? How?"

"I picked the lock," he said sheepishly.

The blood drained from my face. He'd picked the lock? It had been that easy? All this time I'd been a sitting duck. If Blaine and his friends had come by, nothing would've been there to stop—

"Riley, what is going on? You're shaking. Let go of the pillow, babe." He wrapped his arms around me, and that felt amazing, but I was too stuck in a mental downward spiral of fear to recognize that fully. "Are you okay? Did someone hurt you?" His tone dipped down into a growl ferocious enough to knock my thoughts free.

"No. I'm fine." My face turned up to his. Now that I knew it had been Branson and I wasn't about to die, I felt a little silly. I'd freaked out so quickly. But, it wasn't weird for me to be scared at the idea of someone breaking in. I smacked Branson's shoulder with my cell phone. "Why not knock? I would've let you in!" My legs shook as the adrenaline left my system.

"I'm sorry I scared you. I know I'm not supposed to be here." Branson's eyes traveled over me before he hugged me close. His tight embrace hadn't gotten looser. It felt like we were hugging after years apart, not days. I let my head rest against his chest as he spoke. "I was outside."

I lifted my head to peer up at him. "Doing what?"

He looked away. "Being weird."

"Huh?"

"I couldn't stand it after today. Your face today—it broke my heart, babe. And then *Maslow*," he snarled.

"I thought you two were pals?"

"We were... are. But watching him do the things I wished I was doing. Guiding you to your table, giving you a ride, catching you when you fall—"

"Isn't it just good that I didn't fall?"

"Of course it is, and I would rather Maslow catch you than that, but, babe, I'm not used to this. It feels so much like how life was on pack lands, where I'm bound by the people who were supposed to be my family. I left that life over ten years ago and have spent those years living exactly as I want." He nuzzled his face against my neck.

I'd been so concerned with how things had been from my side; I hadn't thought about Branson's. That lunch had been horrible for him too, just for different reasons. "That's a relief to hear. I was beginning to worry this was how our life would be."

Branson froze, lifting his face. Slowly, his lips stretched up into a broad smile. "You said *our life*." He squeezed me tightly, kissing up and down my neck and jaw. It tickled but also dusted off the remnants of the fear in my body, making room for desire.

I basked in his attention for several minutes, letting his touch wash away the fear from the week. This was where I'd wanted to be every day since he'd dropped me off. My skin prickled, reminding me of how little I had on. A thin white V-neck and black boxers. Branson's lips found mine, but he only kissed the edges of my lips. The tent in my boxers rose on its own, needing little help from me. But, as Branson grabbed the waistband of my boxers, I remembered the part about how Branson had broken into my home without my permission.

I turned my face to the side so his next kisses fell on my cheek. "I'm still waiting for you to explain why it was okay for you to break in."

"I was in the area?" Branson spoke between kisses.

"Nope, not good enough. I know we are playing this fast and loose, but we still need boundaries." Lord, I felt like a hypocrite. Here I was talking to him about boundaries when I'd only been so afraid because I'd thought he was my psycho ex here to murder me, a fear I wouldn't be sharing with him because—well, I didn't want the reality of my life to break into the pleasantness of what was happening between us. We were getting used to each other, and it would only worry him. Plus, Branson didn't strike me as the type of guy who worried well. The lock on my front door could attest to that.

"I really was in the area. I'd been talking to Nana and was going home." He brought us to the edge of the bed and sat down. "Okay, I was coming here first when Nana called. I made a quick stop and then continued here."

I smiled at the way he ratted himself out. "But why?

Tomorrow is Friday. If I'd known you could risk late-night visits this whole time, I would've demanded it."

"I really shouldn't. But after the lunch, and watching Maslow's hands on you, and your face, I had to see you. But when I got here, your lights were out, so I waited on the street."

"You watched my windows?"

"Not for long," Branson said with no remorse. "A cruiser kept creeping by. I worried someone had called in my loitering."

"So you left like a normal person?" I said with a smile.

Branson twisted his lips into an expression I had no word for. It wasn't happy or sarcastic—a mix of both. "No, brat." He hooked his hands under my arms, leading us both up my mattress so that we lay with our legs extended. I sunk into the warmth of his embrace. "I went in your building so he wouldn't be suspicious. But then your neighbor's dog started yapping nonstop, and I couldn't very well go out into the street."

It was an explanation. Not a good explanation, but I would've taken any reason if it meant we got to kiss. I should've been angrier that Branson saw doors I'd locked not as a sign to stay out, but as a challenge to break in, but now that I knew he wasn't someone here to kill me, I was ecstatic that he'd come. His kisses were like the touch of spring, thawing out the cold frost of winter. All week, I'd been irritable and twitchy. I'd blamed it on Blaine, but it was Branson. Being apart from him was like wearing a jumpsuit ten sizes too small. Now he was with me, kissing me, I could breathe again.

Though it wasn't long until those breaths turned uneven and shallow. He had a way with my body, stimulating every sense at once. His tight muscles rippled under my palms. His kisses tasted minty and masculine, while his scent made it not a necessity to breathe, but a joy. When I opened my eyes, his chiseled face peered down at me, dominance glinting in his eyes. Even the sounds he made, growls interrupted by a low purring noise, felt like strokes on my dick. I'd fallen for Branson, hard and fast, and now he was reminding me why.

"Please," I gripped his biceps, unsure what exactly I was pleading for other than for *more*.

More kisses, more touches, *less* clothing. He cupped me over my boxers, and my hips jerked into his hand. His callused hand squeezed my balls, and I gasped, thrusting harder immediately after. I knew he was a little possessive—he wouldn't have been here if he wasn't—but I liked the way that changed his caresses. He controlled everything, from the way we kissed to where, and I wouldn't have traded a single thing.

"I missed you so much this week," I confessed, knowing that my words wouldn't be met with derision. Branson wasn't the type to play it cool or downgrade his emotions.

I looked at the top of his dark head moving down my body. "It was hell for me. And yet, I feel like I should've expected it. I've never wanted anything more than you—of course they would try to take you from me." His grip turned hard. Not bruising, but I could feel his fingertips press into my skin. "I won't let them," he growled.

I cupped his head, gripping his hair to turn his face back to me. The rawness in his gaze softened. "Neither will I."

His expression was hot enough to melt the clothes from my body. "Because you're mine, Riley," he whispered, returning to his earlier journey of kissing down my chest. He caught a nipple, bunched in the fabric of my shirt, and bit down.

It hurt, but only for the flash of a second before my back bowed off the bed as I yelped my pleasure.

"I don't have nearly enough time," he snarled against my stomach, smoothly pulling my boxers down at the same time. He didn't remove them completely but left the elastic band to cup under my balls. "I want you like this forever. Boneless and aroused, completely at ease in bed. I could work all day happily if I knew I had you waiting at home for me."

"You work happily anyway," I said with a smirk. Branson devoted so much to his business; that he was able to come from everything, leave with nothing, and still make something of himself was a point of pride.

"But if I knew you were in bed, like this, waiting for me." He paused to stare at my exposed cock. His mouth opened as if he were in awe. He didn't fool me. I was intimately aware of how much larger and thicker he was. "Do you only bottom?" he asked.

I propped my upper half up on my elbows. "I've never topped," I said, my mouth suddenly dry. I liked bottoming and hadn't dwelled a lot on the alternative. And I'd never had a partner who'd brought it up. But everything was different with Branson. "Why do you ask?"

Thinking about him bending over in front of me, all that masculine prowess waiting for *me* to bring him pleasure. I shuddered as a bead of precum glided down my shaft. There wasn't any way I could make him feel as good as he did me, but I would try.

"I want to be your first."

My tongue felt too thick to swallow around. I tried anyway. "Do you... I mean, have you..." We'd had a lot of sex so far, all of it mind-blowing. I reached forward for his pants.

Branson chuckled and caught me by my wrists. "Soon, yes. I want to do that with you. I've never—as an alpha, I thought that meant I should always be the strong one. And topping meant that to me. But with you, I just want to be. I want every experience, if it includes you. Jesus, I sound like a teenager. I've only got so much time, and I'm wasting it blabbing."

Branson let me cup his face. He had no idea that this was exactly what I needed from him. I'd been a mess all week. But, clearly, Branson had too. I liked that. We could be messes together.

He kissed me sweetly. "Will you call me alpha?" he asked, but by the way he ducked his head, I thought he was slightly embarrassed by the request.

"Like with a capital A?" I asked, recalling the difference Branson had told me between being an alpha and being the Alpha.

"No, lowercase. It means something different in shifter culture. More like a term of endearment."

"Does that make me an omega?" I asked with a smile. I knew just enough Latin and had watched just enough Animal Planet to know the term. My smile evaporated from the heat of his gaze.

He closed his eyes and pressed his forehead against my stomach.

"What is it? Is that not a term?"

"No, it is," he said quickly. "Omegas are an alpha's chosen mate. The designation can be given only once. Considering how long our kind lives, that isn't a decision to take lightly."

"Oh, of course. That makes sense." My cheeks burned as I racked my mind trying to figure out how to bring the mood back to what it had been.

"I don't think it does," Branson replied. "You've been my omega in my mind from the beginning. There is nothing in my heart holding me back. But, if I make you my omega, that's like ripping you out of the frying pan and into the fire. I can't do that to you."

"But you can still be my alpha?"

He nodded, his eyes fluttering closed as I spoke the title.

I frowned. "That doesn't sound fair."

"Welcome to shifter life," he chuckled. He pulled up my shirt, nibbling my soft tummy.

I exhaled loudly. "Whatever, alpha." I'd meant it as a tease, but Branson let out a deep, sultry growl that went straight to my cock.

"Again," he commanded, slipping back down my body. He looked up at me, his mouth inches from my glistening head.

He was waiting for me to say it again. Well, if that's all it took. "You want me to call you alpha?" I teased. "Okay, *alpha*. Suck me, *alpha*." I was still teasing just a little, until Branson opened his mouth.

He silenced me with ease, showing with his actions what he didn't need to say with his words. It didn't matter if I was teasing, not quite understanding the full meaning of my words. This was just one more thing that brought us closer together. Branson's tongue laved up and down my length as his lips kept me encased in a wet, hot trap. One I never wanted free of.

"Oh, fuck, Branson!" My hips jerked, but it was no use. Branson wouldn't be happy until he'd claimed every inch of me. At this rate, there wouldn't be a spot on my body that hadn't been touched by him.

My orgasm approached quickly, like snow rolling down a hill. The days without him had taken their toll, and when my cock tightened, sending jolts of pleasure down to my toes, I knew that I'd have a lot to give him. "Wait, alpha, I'm going to come!"

Branson only snarled, the sound reverberating around my dick, followed quickly by an explosive climax. But, unlike most orgasms that flashed bright and petered out as quickly, this one stayed with me, extending far past anything I'd ever experienced before.

I flopped into the pillow beneath me, unable to even lift my head. Branson was still down there, licking my shaft clean while fondling my balls. I moaned, reaching blindly for him. I'd been tired before he came, I was exhausted now. But I knew Branson didn't have long. Though I didn't understand his reasons completely, staying the night was out of the question. I didn't want to waste any of my time with him sleeping.

When he was satisfied with his job, he lifted his body even with mine, kissing me long and hard, before he groaned.

"Don't say it," I mumbled with one eye closed.

He spoke with his lips pressed against my cheek. "I don't want to."

This was hard on us both; I didn't need to make things worse. I opened my eyes, waiting for them to focus on his face before I spoke. "When can we see each other again?"

"Delia is leaving this weekend," he said firmly. "And... Nana would like to meet you."

"We did, at the restaurant." She'd tripped me. Well, her purse had.

"No, she wants to make us dinner. I told her we'd be too busy since we hadn't seen each other all week—"

"You did not tell your great-grandmother you were too occupied having sex." Shock warred with mortification.

Branson just laughed.

"That isn't funny!"

"You don't know my Nana. She wouldn't bat an eye. But no, I didn't. I said we had date plans. She's insisting."

I hadn't had the same gut reaction to Branson's nana as I had his mother, and from what I'd heard of her, she was a lovely woman. "Okay, fine. When?"

"Sunday, dinner. I'll pick you up here."

"It's a good thing I turned down that date." I stretched my arms over my head, feeling Branson's gaze narrow on me.

"What date?" he asked through clenched teeth.

Jealousy, like everything else, looked good on Branson. But karma was a bitch, so I let him off quickly. "Maslow has a friend, and he thought we might hit it off. I told him no."

"Not Maslow?"

I punched his shoulder. "You've been friends with him longer than me! Has he ever seemed anything but straight?" I wouldn't mention the initial misunderstanding.

And Branson didn't look all that mollified. "You've changed me completely. Why should I doubt that you have that power over other people too?" He held my face, and I turned to kiss his palm. "You don't see your own greatness."

"Hm," I replied, uncomfortable with the topic. I grabbed his hand, wishing he didn't have to go.

"I'm late," he uttered. But one look at his face, and I knew he hadn't meant to say as much. I'd accidentally forced it out of him.

"Late for what?" I asked.

He groaned. "Nothing, just a meeting with the cousins. They need to talk about... everything. I told them to give me an hour."

I cocked my head to the side. "How long ago was that?"

"A few hours."

"Get out." I pushed him from my side, though all I wanted to do was pull him close.

He let me shove him off the bed before grabbing my hands and giving me a quick kiss. "Sunday. I'll be here. I'll come early. That way we can—"

"Come early?" I suggested.

He bent back down, giving me a kiss that wasn't so quick. "Exactly." He tucked the blanket around me before his feet turned to my bedroom window instead of the door.

"What are you doing?"

"Your apartment has a slanted roof beside it. It'll be easier to jump down and shift. Which is the way I would try to get into your apartment were I actually trying to break in."

I sat up, undoing the job he'd done. "What?" I sputtered. "What if you trip?" We were only two floors up, but that distance could easily break his leg. Or neck. "What about your clothes?" That last question had been one I'd wondered on a few times.

He opened my window and paused. The winter wind blew the curtains out, billowing around him so that he looked like something from a supernatural romance. "I won't trip." He winked. "And my clothes shift with me. Sometimes, they even influence what our fur looks like—" He started laughing. "Like that time Wyatt shifted, but he'd been wearing a thong and—huh, that guy has a thing for nice underwear."

The mention of his cousins reminded me this guy had somewhere to be. "Okay, okay go think about your cousin's kinks somewhere else." That wasn't something I ever pictured myself saying.

Branson blew me a kiss and jumped out the window, pausing on the other side to close it.

I sat there for as long as I could make myself before rushing to look out onto the street, but he was already gone. Locking the window, I padded back to my bed. I felt better than I had before, and now I knew when I would see Branson again. But things were only charging full steam ahead when it came to us. Soon, I'd have to tell him all about me. And I hated not knowing what he would think of me after he knew everything.

11

BRANSON

THE TIRES SQUEALED as I turned down Riley's street. A few people walking the streets turned and glared, but that was just tough. It was Sunday afternoon already, and I'd told Riley I was going to come early. But that had been before Nana had woken the house up at the crack of dawn, saying the house wasn't ready for guests.

I explained that Riley had already been over and that he'd transcended being a guest. Then she'd started on about how we hadn't done any decorating for the season. At least I had the joy of watching Nana rip Wyatt from his bed, only about an hour after I'd heard him come home and crawl into it. Aver had already been up, doing whatever Aver did. And Nash got up early every morning for his run anyway. But every time I broke away to get Riley, Nana had refused to let me, instead coming up with a new task I had to do. Sometime during that, my mother's driver appeared to take her home. Her suspension from pack lands had been brief, all things considered. Though she still needed to apologize to Paul and get him to accept that apology before she was back to her regular status as an esteemed Elder household.

Meanwhile, I'd hung the lights, cleared a space for the tree, and twisted garland around every twistable object in the house. Nana tried sending me to the back yard to decorate the trees there when I finally put my foot down. I was already too late for us to *come early*.

I knocked hard on Riley's door. He'd been so scared the last time. More frightened than I would've guessed. He hid something from me, something about his life from before he came here, which was fine, unless it was something that put him in danger.

Now Riley answered so quickly my fist was still raised for the third knock. "You're late."

"I know, I'm sorry." I hated how many times I'd had cause to apologize to him. "Nana was..."

He cocked his head to the side, raising one eyebrow as he folded his arms over his chest. "You're blaming a frail old woman?"

Were we talking about the same Nana? "No. I'm wasting no more of our time." My arms wound around him, settling at the small of his back. He lifted his face to mine, and we kissed. "I need to get you a signal booster for your apartment. If you aren't at work, I can't get a hold of you."

Riley's lips twisted in a frown. "That sounds expensive."

"A necessary expense," I said, looking around him for a bag. "You didn't pack anything?"

"For a dinner?"

We hadn't talked about it. I guessed I just assumed that Riley would stay after.

"Won't your great-grandmother be there?" he asked.

"Nana. You can call her that. Everyone does. And yes. I left her there actually."

"You *left* her there?" Riley yanked on his jacket and

shoved past me. "We're late then?" He took the stairs down two at a time.

I jumped after him, catching his elbow just as his foot missed the bottom step. "Slow down, Riley. I'm not early, but we aren't late. It's fine. We'll probably get there, and she will have just started cooking."

Riley was flushed, and his breaths were rapid but shallow.

I searched his face, my eyes scanning out to the rest of him when I found no injuries there. Had something happened? Maybe at work? But it was Sunday. I'd be getting him that signal booster; there would be no argument about that. I couldn't stand not knowing. "Talk to me, Riley. What's going on?" I wished his power could be reversed. But I didn't want to make him tell me; I wanted him to trust me enough to confide in me.

He scratched the back of his neck. "Nothing. I think just meeting your family..."

"But you've met Nash, Aver, and Wyatt with no problems."

"That isn't the same, Branson. This is your great-grand-mother. Your nana. From what you've said of her, she's a very important person to you. This isn't like meeting your cousins. She's... special." He kept his face down, angled toward his shoes. "You know what I mean," he mumbled sadly.

I held his chin between my forefinger and thumb, raising his face to look at me. My worry dissipated a fraction. "You're special, Riley. It's okay to worry, but there is no reason. You'll see."

He nodded, but nothing would mollify him except interacting with Nana.

The drive from his apartment to my house was quiet. Riley held my hand on the walk to the front door.

Once the door opened, I was enveloped by a wave of delicious smells. Sizzling beef, cheese, and something spicy. I helped Riley out of his coat. "I was wrong. She's already started."

Riley looked up at me, blowing an exasperated breath over his forehead.

I cursed my own boorishness. In the car, Riley had calmed down a little, but thanks to me, here he was winding up again. Since I'd picked him up, his moods seemed all over the place.

"Branson, you bring that man of yours inside this kitchen before I have to come out there and look for you!"

I smirked. "Now I'm in trouble," I said, hooking my arm around Riley's waist. "Coming, Nana!" I shouted back, loud enough to be heard over the exuberant Latin music that blared from the kitchens.

"Wyatt already left," Nana yelled back, her volume dipping to a conversational tone when she saw us walk in. "That cousin of yours will do anything to chase tail. Liquor inventory, my butt." She shook a dish towel at us. "He's going to wind up with some real trouble soon, if he hasn't already."

I'd known what to expect when Nana was in the kitchen, but Riley didn't. Nana couldn't cook without the kitchen becoming a disaster zone. She seemed to operate under the belief that if a job could be done in one pot, why not use two pans and three mixing bowls? Most times, she ended up with more tools littering the counter than the job required and a kitchen that took almost as long to clean as it had to prepare the meal.

But since she usually got one of us to do that part for her, there wasn't much cause for her to mind. Her own home was in a state of constant upheaval as she transitioned from her daily tasks—baking bread, cleaning fish, knitting, woodwork. She didn't believe in asking anyone else to do something for her that she was perfectly capable of doing herself. All in all, Nana Walker was the antithesis to my mother, and she was the only thing that kept us alive after we'd cut ties with our families.

"Riley, it is so nice to see you again." Nana ignored me as she pulled Riley into a hug. It would've been awkward with my arm pinned at his waist, but Nana's hugs were never awkward.

"Thank you, Na—Mrs. Walker... Great-grandmother—" Riley hissed like a punctured tire.

I couldn't understand Riley's apprehension. He didn't need to worry about what to call her.

"It's Nana, dear. You've got to trust that mate of yours." She turned and grabbed a rag, whisking a large pot from the burner a moment before whatever was inside frothed over. "I'm almost done here. Go get settled in the dining room. Branson, figure out what everyone wants to drink."

"Why ask?" The music got louder as the musicians paused for an energetic drum solo. "They're gonna want beer." I opened the refrigerator and reached for two bottles first, for Riley and myself.

Nana shook her head. "Oh no, none of that right now. I made you boys some lemonade. The pitcher's there. And if they don't want that, there's milk I can warm up..."

Lemonade or *warm milk*? I couldn't wait to deliver Aver and Nash their two choices. Nana didn't normally care what we drank. I guessed this was maybe more of a show for Riley's sake. But then, Nana wasn't the type to put on shows either. "See, that wasn't so bad," I whispered as we went from the kitchen to the dining room.

"I don't know," Riley said, leaning heavily against me. At least he wasn't trembling anymore. "I feel slightly as though I've been chastised. What was that term, mate?"

"It is a shifter thing. Think slightly more than boyfriend." That wasn't entirely correct, but for the sake of our conversation, it would have to do. I couldn't begin to go into the nuances of what it meant to be a mate. Depending on where you sat in the pack hierarchy, being a mate could mean something very little, or it could change every part of your life.

"Hey, Riley." Aver nodded our way. To me, he added, "Can you believe how cool Nana is being with Wyatt missing this? No way I could pull the same thing."

It was the unofficial grumble between the three of us that Wyatt was Nana's favorite. "What do you guys want to drink?" I asked, already grinning.

"Beer," Nash grunted. Aver said the same.

"No can do. Nana has spoken. It's a lemonade or warm milk." As I suspected, the faces of my cousins were priceless.

"What is going on with her lately?" Nash wondered aloud. "She's been so strange the past, well... Since you got here, Riley."

Riley straightened at the direct mention of his name. I frowned at Nash, angry that he'd say anything to upset Riley just when he seemed to be settling in. But, now that he pointed it out, I had to agree.

"Maybe we'll find out tonight." I squeezed Riley's shoulder before heading back into the kitchen. I filled five glasses with ice and grabbed the lemonade pitcher. I hadn't actually asked everyone, but was warm milk really even an option?

When I returned, Nash was retelling one of his more exciting stories from his work as a fireman. Out here, the types of calls were often varied and quite dangerous, considering the isolation. The Walker County Fire Department was relied on more than most, simply because there wasn't anyone else around with the equipment to help. The calls they fielded in a week went from assisting large animal rescue missions to helping arrange search parties whenever anyone went missing.

Nana hollered for Aver and Nash to help her with bringing out the dishes. Riley and I followed, offering our help as well, but she shooed us back. "You especially, Riley, dear. You should stay off your feet."

Riley returned to his chair. "What could that mean?" He looked to me and narrowed his gaze. "What have you told her?"

I shrugged, lifting my hands in front of me as if I were a surrendering hostage. I understood his suspicion. That was a strange thing for her to say. Though I'd hinted to her belief in the mystical, I hadn't mentioned to Riley how, sometimes, Nana simply knew things before she'd been told. The same thing had happened when the four of us had refused to play our parents' games. Nana had been there, ready. She'd even cleared space for us to sleep in her house, a task that would've taken days, though our choice to leave had been a split-second decision.

Moments later, the table was weighed down with several dishes. "Taco bowls are a standard around here," Nana said to Riley. She lifted the lid from the large pot in the center of the table with a flourish.

"My own recipe," she declared. "Four kinds of beans, all

rich in folate, mixed with mild spices, tomatillos, and tomatoes."

"It sounds delicious," Riley said.

"You can make yours however you like." She handed Riley a bowl from the stack, the signal for the rest of us to dig in. "I've got all the fixings right here." She gestured to the other bowls of grilled steak, lettuce, and salsa. "Make sure you load yours up on cheese, Riley. You can't have enough dairy at a time like this."

Everyone but Nana frowned at that.

At a time like this?

Riley reached for the steak.

"Oh no, Riley, this one is yours." Nana took the serving fork away and revealed a plate of grilled salmon. She lifted a generously sized fillet and laid it on top of his bean mixture. "All those fatty acids."

Riley set his fork down. "Excuse me, Mrs—Nana, I appreciate your cooking so much, and it all looks delicious, but you really don't need to give me special treatment."

"Yeah, why does he get the fish?" Nash whined.

"Oh, shush you," Nana mumbled while simultaneously scooping Nash the second fillet. "I'm sorry, dear. I admit to being a little too eager. I've been so excited to meet you. Tell me a little about where you're from. What brought you to Walker County?"

Overall, it was a simple question that I would have thought Riley would have been relieved by, and yet his face went as white as snow.

"Babe? Didn't you say you were working in Seattle?" I prompted. Maybe he was just freezing up. I understood that my family was not always easy to be around.

"Seattle." Riley cleared his throat several times. "Yes, that's right. I came from Seattle... And now I'm here." He looked around the table. Aver had his face in his food, while Nash had started sneaking peeks of his phone under the table.

Nana busied herself stirring the creamy sour cream mixture in a bowl on the table. "That sounds nice," she said noncommittally.

The hairs on my neck stood up, and I got the idea that the conversation going on in front of me was just a front. But damned if I could understand the subtext. As far as I knew, Riley and Nana had never met, aside from that day at the restaurant, and yet now they spoke as if in code.

"Oh no, I forgot the guac," Nana said, jumping from the table.

The second she was out the door, Aver and Nash leaned forward. "What was that?" Nash asked. He'd eaten his salmon in a single bite and now eyed Riley's.

I couldn't even look at my food, not when Riley was acting so strange. "Really, babe, are you okay?"

"Yes, fine," Riley snapped, obviously irritated. He exhaled loudly and leaned in toward me. "It's just—I don't know. Maybe this wasn't a good idea." He pushed back from the table, the legs of his chair croaking over the wood floor. "Maybe we should've taken this week as a sign to cool things down. We're running full steam ahead without wondering if we're ready. Meeting your family is a big step, one we might not be prepared f—"

Nana returned at about the same moment panic clawed at my heart. Cool things down? Because my great-grandmother was acting odd? What the hell was going on here? More than what I was privy to, that was for damn sure. "Excuse me," I said to the table, fighting to keep my cool. "Riley, will you come with me into the other room?"

Riley mumbled a yes, jumping from his seat so quickly I

had to hurry to stay just behind him. I pulled him away from the living room, down the hallway to my bedroom where I shut the door.

"Babe, tell me what happened. Why are you acting so strange?"

"Me?" Riley gasped. "Your nana is making me feel crazy! What condition? She isn't making any sense." He stomped away from me toward the bed. "I'm sorry. I should've canceled. She's an old woman, and I'm freaking out about..." He looked around himself, eventually flouncing to the mattress.

"Freaking out about what?" I asked, staying where I was a few feet away. I wanted to hold him, but the energy he put out right now was like an electric wire covered in thorns. The message was clear: stay away.

"I—" He started, opening his mouth several more times before giving up. "I'm not telling you. I just need to go home, I think. My head is pounding, and my stomach can't decide if it is starved or wants to throw up what I've eaten already. Can you call me a taxi?"

No, I couldn't call him a fucking taxi. He had no reason to want to leave. He was safe here. If he was sick, he could lay down here. He didn't have a reason to want to go. All that told me was that he was hiding something, and as the seconds ticked on—with Nash, Aver, and Nana listening from the other room—I suspected it was something big. "Riley, none of my feelings for you have changed..."

"None of mine have either!" Riley shouted.

"Then why do you want to go home?" I asked, a little more loudly than I should have. The wolf in me demanded I stay near my mate, even if he didn't think he wanted to. I recognized the danger of that sort of thinking but was too mired in the mud of the moment to do anything about it.

There was a knock at my door. I stomped to it, ripping it open. Nash. I didn't need him here with his hero complex, trying to save someone who didn't need saving. "What?" I snarled.

"Nana suggested we skip dinner and go right to dessert," he said, his eyes darting from me to Riley, as if *I* would hurt the man I'd claimed as mine.

My chest rumbled. "Fine." I swung the door shut, and it bounced off Nash's shoe.

"Do we have a problem?" I asked, looking from his boot up to his face. His green eyes were cold.

"I think you should ask Riley that," Nash replied.

"I think you should shut the hell up and go eat more salmon. This has nothing to do with you."

Nash pushed me back. I stumbled, and in the mood I was in, that was enough to make me see red. I launched toward him, grappling around his middle as we slammed into the other wall. Riley shouted something behind me, but Nash shifted and snapped at my wrists. I grabbed his furry throat; his jaws clapped together with a menacing clacking sound. This wasn't our first fight, but it was the first time I felt a very real desire to rip Nash apart. He was trying to take what was mine. He didn't think Riley was safe in my care and was trying to take him.

More shouts joined ours. I heard Aver's low voice, trying to get us both to calm down. In the back of my mind, I sensed Riley was still there. My wolf wouldn't let him out of our mind.

"Stop this at once," Nana shouted.

Immediately, Nash shifted and shouted over my shoulder. "It isn't me! It's Branson! He's acting—"

Nana's responding glare shut him up. "He's following his instincts with his mate, something you have no business sticking your nose in." Her index finger jammed into Nash's chest after Aver used our distraction to pull us apart.

I didn't smile that Nana sided with me. I wasn't a pup. Though I wasn't sure what Riley could think of me now.

I turned to him, sheepish now that the anger of the moment had dissipated. "Riley, I—"

"I want to go home, Branson. I'm not above walking—"

"Not while you're pregnant, you won't," Nana replied.

I blinked once, then again, still waiting for what she'd said to make sense.

Aver laughed. "Nana, are you feeling okay?"

Nana's lined face soured.

"All right..." Aver used his deep voice, the same one he used to speak to our employees as well as his parents. It was his cool, calm, and collected voice. "This night is best ended, I think. I'll take Riley home and—"

"No," I snarled, looking only at Riley. I knew I was acting insane. Any more and I'd be tempted to save Riley from me. I couldn't explain this terror any more than I could my sudden attraction. I wasn't acting like myself; the normal me wouldn't have a single issue if Riley wanted to leave. I'd have been bummed, but what I felt right now was so much more than bummed. Like something bad would happen to Riley if he left.

"Is no one going to point out that your great-grand-mother thinks I am *pregnant?*" He stood farthest from the door with the four of us clustered on one side. His arms were folded tightly over his chest.

This wasn't a situation I'd thought I'd find myself in tonight. I was at an advantage in that I had often been confused by the things Nana said. When she got going about all that the spirits had whispered to her, she didn't always wind up making a lot of sense at the time. But things always had a way of clearing up in the end. I knew not to take what she said at face value. Riley wasn't pregnant. But maybe she'd meant he was full of potential or something.

"I'm sure she didn't mean it that way," I said.

"I definitely did, Branson Walker, and you better not be making excuses for me." She propped both hands up on her hips.

Riley pressed his mouth closed. His skin was a mottled red. "I need to go home now."

"I'll take you," Aver said over the sound of my growl.

"I'll go with him," Nash offered.

Riley paused in front of me. "Thank you for inviting me tonight. I'll... I'll call you later."

My fingers tightened. Adrenaline and testosterone pumped through me, making me feel shaky and light, but also large and cumbersome. Riley wanted to go. I needed to let him go. And yet, the only thing in my mind was fighting every person in this room and stealing Riley away somewhere where I could protect him.

But this was my *family*. Riley didn't need to be protected from them.

Nana stood beside me, her bony fingers cold on my forearm. "I'm sorry, dear one. This night was my fault."

The front door opened. The click of it shutting closed stirred me from my stupor. I lunged toward the hallway; Nana's hand tightened. "You will crush him without ever meaning to, my dear. You've always loved so much, and now you've found your blessed omega, you love even harder. But you can love *too hard*."

12

RILEY

"I've never seen Branson like that," Nash said as Aver drove the three of us back into downtown Walkerton.

I wasn't much in the mood to discuss how tonight was or wasn't outside of Branson's normal behavior. I just wanted to go back to my apartment.

Clearly, these people were insane. Pregnant? Sure, the three guys had been dubious at Nana's announcement, but not a one of them had the balls to stand up and say as much. Everyone had skeletons, baggage. I knew that more than most, but surely this was too much for anyone from the outside to handle.

Except I didn't want to break up with Branson. Even earlier, at his home, I hadn't wanted to leave. My gut had told me to stay with him, but my gut couldn't always be trusted. I just needed to get back to my apartment, where I could be alone to think for a second. My mind felt scattered: terrified that I'd never see Branson again in one second; angry that the night had turned out like it had in the next. I'd been agitated from the moment Branson had picked me up, but I'd accounted that to not seeing him as much as I wanted.

Maybe there was something wrong with me.

Aver pulled up in front of my apartment. I looked up to my window and gasped. The light was on. Had I left the light on?

"What is it?" Aver asked, leaning across Nash to look out the passenger side window.

My cheeks burned. What these guys must think of me? I was acting as fragile as a flower. But I was made of tougher stuff than this. "Nothing, I just remembered some work stuff..."

"Mhmm," Aver replied. "Let me walk you up."

I didn't ask how Aver knew where I lived.

"Why didn't you touch Nana? Branson? Then you would know the truth." Nash turned around, looking at me from over the headrest. Lines crossed his forehead.

The idea had never crossed my mind. My curse was like the monkey's paw. Any time I tried using it for my own benefit, I always wound up wishing I hadn't. "It isn't a superpower."

"No, I didn't think it was. But it is a tool unique to you. Take me. I am extraordinarily good-looking. I use that tool to calm people down when I'm rescuing them from dangerous situations." Nash smirked.

"Leave him alone, Nash. He's had a night," Aver murmured.

But what Nash said stuck with me. As a child, my curse made my guardians fear me. But I already knew what they would've said had I ever touched them. *We wish it was you.* They'd done a kind thing, bringing me in after my parents died, and had been punished for it by losing their own son.

Later, in college, I'd only wanted to be considered normal. But I had used my curse on Branson, during our first date, because I thought he'd say something to make it easier for me to walk away.

As much as I thought I didn't use my ability, I realized I did, but only when I thought I already knew the truth.

Right now, I didn't know which way was up, much less what was going on. "Thank you for taking me home," I said, pushing the door open. Aver hurried around, walking me to the front door of the building.

"You don't have to come in," I told him, but as I pushed the door open, my hand shook.

"I'm here because Branson lost his damn mind tonight. He loves you. That's probably scary to hear after about a week, but to anyone who knows him, that fact is clear. When I get back, he's going to ask me every single thing that happened. Every word you spoke, if you looked sad or scared. And he's going to torture himself for hours. If I don't walk you inside, he's gonna know and be mad at me. Please, Riley, save me the trouble."

These damn Walker men were too charming for their own good. "Come on," I said, going first up the stairs. I slid my key into the lock, but Aver stepped between me and the door.

"Do you know if you left the light on when Branson came to get you?" he asked.

Charming and observant. "I'm not sure. It's probably nothing." I felt foolish. Even if there was someone in my apartment, I'd fight them off. I wasn't helpless. "This probably isn't necessary."

"All the same," Aver said, cracking the door open. He paused in the doorway, his nostrils flaring. I realized he was trying to *sniff out* an intruder. How was it so easy to forget these men were wolves? I'd seen one of the transformations tonight.

Nash's metamorphosis from man to animal had been seamless, like jumping in a pool and coming out the other side. No wonder he talked of using his strengths.

"Seems clear. I just smell you and Branson," Aver said. "I'm not a bloodhound, though, so I'll feel better if I check each room."

I figured I could've argued and then let him convince me to let him check each room anyway or just let him check them. I gestured him forward with a sweep of my arm.

He stalked into the kitchen, though I doubted anyone was hiding in the dishwasher. As he continued on into the living room, his phone rang. *He had service?* "Hi," Aver said after the second ring. "Yeah, we're here."

Was that Branson? Was he asking about me? Did I care?

Yes. I cared. Because after everything that had happened tonight—the weirdness with his Nana, his heavy-handed possessive behavior—I still felt the same draw toward him. If anything, it felt stronger now.

"I'm just checking his apartment now," Aver said, glancing quickly at me. "No, you don't need to call the police. There isn't anyone here." Aver sighed. "I don't know, Branson. You'll have to ask him. Okay, fine." He hung up the phone and shoved it back in his pocket. "If you need me to get rid of him," he said to me, "I'm pretty willing."

I knew he was joking but appreciated the gesture. I still didn't know what I wanted. Part of me wanted to be back where I'd been, letting Nana shovel more pregnancy-healthy foods onto my plate. The idea was ludicrous. Didn't she realize I didn't have the parts to become pregnant? I knew that sex education was a little backwards in some parts, but this was silly. "No, thank you."

"All right, well, the coast is clear here," Aver said, after peeking back into the bedroom and bathroom. He even opened the hallway linen closet, making me feel like a five-year-old who'd spotted a monster. "Any chance you're going to tell me why you were so concerned?"

I shook my head. I'd thought Blaine was here, waiting. If not him, then one of his pals. But why would he wait for me with the lights on? "I'm going to go take a shower, and..." My stomach growled.

"You didn't get a chance to have dinner," Aver said.

"That's okay." He'd already been so kind, and my head was beginning to pound again. "I'll snack on something around here."

Though his expression remained dubious, Aver said goodnight. I watched them drive away out my window, pulling the blinds quickly after they were gone. In the silence of my apartment, doubt crept in. Had it been that strange? If I'd been so worried, why hadn't I used my ability like Nash asked?

Even if I threw all logic out the window and operated under the belief that I could carry a child, the timing didn't add up. We'd had a lot of sex, all of it unprotected, but not enough days had passed. At least, I didn't think so. I'd admit my reproductive knowledge was limited. I'd always known I was gay, and frankly, the idea of carrying another person inside of your body squicked me out.

Exhausted, I flopped down on my couch. I hadn't asked for Aver to search the apartment, but I was glad now that he could. I didn't think I'd be eating anything tonight. I didn't think I'd even make it to the bed. I set my phone alarm for work, just in case, and rolled so I could see the door.

Maybe it was nerves, or maybe I was hoping Branson would break through and hold me, but I watched the knob. Willing it both to turn and stay still. Eventually, my eyelids became too heavy, and I passed out.

13

BRANSON

"But why is he worried? What is there to fear?" I asked Aver over the phone.

"I don't know, Branson. You'll have to ask him," Aver said.

It had taken me about five minutes to calm down after Nash and Aver took Riley home and another five to begin worrying without end. Nana was with me, humming into her tea. I scowled at her. How did she seem so peaceful at a time like this? She wasn't without blame here, going on about pregnancy and singling Riley out.

"I want you to remember every detail," I said. "Be ready to tell me everything when you come back."

"Okay, fine," Aver said before hanging up.

"You'll worry yourself silly," Nana said contentedly.

I clenched my hands under the table. "Nana," I said through gritted teeth, "can you explain to me a little about today? Why did you have me invite him? What did your spirits tell you?"

"Do you still not understand, my boy?"

How could I when she wasn't saying anything?

She smiled and looked up, her eyes tilted down in the corners, surrounded by laugh lines. "It's finally happening. The dark days of the pack are coming to an end."

The pack? What the hell did Riley and I have to do with the pack?

"The wolves in this region have operated under darkness for so long. Things came to a head with you and your cousins, and the pack has wavered all these years on a precipice." She balanced her spoon on the rim of her mug, letting it sway from one side to the other. "Our people are waiting for a push. But in which direction?" She looked up sharply, like someone had called her name. The spoon fell from her hand, clattering to the table.

"Nana?"

"Be ready to go when Nash and Aver return," she said, getting to her feet.

"What?" I got up, following her to the coat rack where she put on her jacket. I had twenty-eight years of believing in my great-grandmother, but tonight, I began to doubt. There were just too many questions. Why say that about Riley if it wasn't true? More importantly, *how* could that be a possibility? But instead of giving me any answers, here she was, being cryptic again.

She fussed with her jacket, untangling the bunched fabric in the sleeves. "My keys. I need my keys." She patted the front of her coat.

"Nana, stop." I moved between her and the door, grabbing her forearms to stop her nervous movements. She peered up at me, as familiar as she'd ever been. Her wrinkled skin looked as soft as silk, her irises a single shade above black. She had thin eyebrows that were often arched, especially when she was waiting for one of us to fess up to whatever it was that we'd done. But right now, she wasn't knowing or peaceful or any of the things I'd grown up used to her being. She was scared.

I hugged her instead of yelling at her. "It's okay, Nana. Whatever this is, whatever's going on, we'll figure it out. Why are you putting on your jacket?"

My phone rang, and my stomach dropped. I wasn't even surprised to see my mom's name on the ID. "Hello?"

"Branson, you must come," she said, her voice trembling.

I knew without a doubt this was related to whatever Nana had sensed.

"What's happened?"

"The doctor is on his way. Alpha Walker has collapsed!"

Nana winced.

"We're on our way." I hung up, guiding Nana outside just in time for Aver and Nash to pull in. Aver looked at my face through the windshield and kept the engine running.

"What now?" Nash asked with irritation.

"My son," Nana gasped, clutching her collar together.

"It's Alpha Walker. He's collapsed," I said, helping Nana into the backseat.

"And we're going back? If he dies..."

"I know, Nash." We didn't need this right now, and couldn't he tell how much he was upsetting Nana?

"...they'll be without an Alpha."

"I know, Nash!"

Aver pulled us back down the driveway.

"Look, we're adults now. They can't make us do anything we don't want to. We already put a stop to that." Neither of my cousins replied. I was glad to see the bickering end, but when I looked up at their faces, reflected off the windshield, I could tell they weren't convinced. "Nash, can you let Wyatt know?"

"He ended up having to work after all, so I'll text him after the late rush. I don't want him losing out on business."

I nodded and kept my arm over Nana's frail shoulders. The way Nash spoke might have seemed tactless and crude, especially considering this was Nana's son we discussed, but I didn't fault Nash. I didn't think Nana did, either. We'd all been hurt, pushed passed our limits by the pack. It had been Alpha Walker's decree that had ultimately pit the four of us together. And yet, here we were, rushing back.

It was exactly as Nana had said. The pack was broken. But, unlike Nana, I didn't think there was a way of fixing it.

———

THE MAIN HOUSE was dark from the outside. All the twinkling fairy lights had been turned off, and, despite the late hour, members of the pack gathered in the front yard. Some stood in clusters, clutching candles as they prayed for their Alpha's health, while others stood without moving.

We parked well behind them, skirting around the crowds to the front door. The whispers started as soon as the pack members saw who was attempting to get through. But though we were disgraced, Nana was mother to their Alpha, and she was not disgraced. Just gossiped about.

Inside, the halls were just as packed, and news of our arrival had traveled ahead of us. Those inside were higher up in the pack hierarchy, which mostly meant they would have more to lose if the leadership of the pack came into question. I understood the fear. Transitioning Alphas was a difficult time on its own. Each Alpha brought absolute power with them, and often, they wanted to start from a blank slate. At this point, there wasn't a Walker eligible to assume leadership, which meant there would be an even greater upheaval. The new Alpha would be responsible for bringing their close family, who would become the new Elder families. The existing Elder families would be stripped of their benefits and relocated—either to another house within pack lands or, more often, to another pack entirely, where the change of roles wouldn't be as obvious. There would be a lot of anxiety, but my cousins and I weren't here to fix anything. We were here for Nana. Half the people we passed seemed to understand that, looking at Nash, Aver, and me like we'd caused this. I preferred that. I couldn't stand the hope I saw in the faces of the other half.

"What is he doing here?" Aver's father, Glendon, snarled as he saw me escort Nana to the stairs. He stood in a loose huddle with the other Elders.

Delia burst forward. She appeared completely recovered from her short time-out. "I called him, as the rightful Walker Alpha successor—"

"You vulture," Glendon replied. Of all the Elders, Glendon hated me the most. He was older than my father, Alpha Walker's firstborn son. But he hadn't been born an alpha and had been ineligible to lead. I'd heard the very moment Aver was born and confirmed an alpha he'd begun preparing for his son to achieve what he never could.

"Father, stop," Aver said quietly, rejoining us after he'd hung Nana's jacket in the coat closet.

Glendon's face brightened. "Aver, my son! It's a good thing you're here."

Nash muttered something, but I didn't need to hear it to know it wasn't pleasant. He never looked directly at his parents. "Where is he? Nana will want to be with him."

The pack doctor ambled down the stairs. As old as my grandfather, he'd been appointed during his rule. It was widely known that the pack doctor answered to the Alpha first, but no amount of influence could help my grandfather if this was his time. He was relatively young for a shifter. It wasn't uncommon for us to live well over one hundred. I could only guess that Grandfather was sick and had used his appointed physician to conceal that until they couldn't.

"What has happened?" Nana asked, ignoring the death glares and posturing on either side of her.

Behind us, the pack quieted, eager to hear.

"Follow me upstairs—Elders only."

It was possible he meant to stem the flood of people behind us, but it felt like a direct attack on Aver, Nash, and I. Still, Nana's death grip on my hand and Aver's arm ensured we would be walking with her. I looked back at Nash, wanting to keep him close while we were here.

On enemy territory.

Walking upstairs was like walking into a different house. Up here, it was deathly still and quiet. The air in the dark hallway was cold.

"Shouldn't you have the heat on?" Julie, Nash and Wyatt's mother, asked. She was a thin woman, petite to the extreme.

"This is a large home, Elder. It's difficult to keep every room warm. Right now, Alpha Walker's room is the perfect temperature. He's severely dehydrated and exhausted due to his duties as—"

"Cut the bullshit," Nana snapped. "What is wrong with my son?"

The doctor could not be used to being spoken to that way, but he gave no outward indication of anger. "I'm not sure, Nana Walker. The butler reports that he was acting normally until after dinner. He didn't eat much and retired to his study. It was thirty minutes before the butler returned and found him unconscious. He's had some heart problems in the past, but we've been working on those with medicine. His symptoms indicate he's contracted influenza, though his body should be able to do a better job of fighting it than it is."

To think, the mighty Alpha Walker, killed by the flu. The story would be passed from region to region.

Nana tightened her grip on my arm, reminding me that, while I'd given up on the man, she couldn't give up on being his mother. "Can I see him?"

"As long as you are healthy, you can all see him. Though we need to limit the number of visitors. He is very tired."

"But is he going to make it?" Delia asked, with all the tact of a creditor at a funeral.

"If he makes it through this night, I'll feel a lot better. This has happened fast. I need to get more information about the specific strain. This could be an isolated incident or the beginning of an epidemic."

"Has anyone else reported that they feel unwell?" Nash asked, using his fireman-on-duty voice.

The doctor's face remained blank.

"Did anyone think to ask?" Aver's eyes looked ready to bulge from his head.

The doctor was here talking about an epidemic, and all the Elder families could think of was making sure their choice of alpha was around if grandfather died. I'd been sickened by them before; this was just one more time. "They won't answer if I ask," I said. "But one of you should. Like, now."

There wasn't a chance in hell that John, Julia, Glendon, or Clarice would obey an order I've given. It would be too close to accepting me as leader. Finally, Delia rolled her eyes.

"Oh, all right." She huffed by, descending the stairs like a teenager ordered to clean her room.

"I'll be staying by my son's side tonight," Nana told us. "If you need to leave before you have a chance to visit, I will understand." She looked to Aver and Nash, and that was all it took for them to slide in front of us, blocking whatever Nana had to say next from those standing at the other end of the hallway. "You take care of Riley. I gave him a fright, but I wasn't being metaphorical. He's blessed—you both are. I'll explain more about what that means later." She reached around my nape and tugged me down so our faces were level. "Keep your omega close, Branson. Especially now," she whispered before kissing my cheek. She did the same with Aver and Nash before walking stoically by the Elders and in to see Alpha Walker.

I didn't try to peek in at the sick old man. I knew what a sick person looked like, but my attention was pulled away almost immediately after Nana walked in, shutting the door behind her.

"Get the fuck away from me!" Wyatt yelled from somewhere downstairs.

Aver grabbed Nash before he could break his neck jumping down.

"Brother!" Wyatt yelled, the word boomed up the stairs.

"We're here, Wyatt," I called back, finally spotting Wyatt fighting through a throng of people. He wore his work uniform: a dark shirt, dark pants, and black apron. He still had a towel tucked in his back pocket as he pushed off the men trying to hold him back. His eyes lit up with his fury as he searched for Nash. "What did you say in your text?" I asked, but Nash wasn't listening to me. He met Wyatt at the top of the stairs. The two didn't embrace as much as they looked the other over.

"Why would you bring him here? Again?" Wyatt growled at me after seemingly being satisfied that Nash was unharmed. "If you and Aver want to keep playing go-between, one foot in, one foot out, that's your fucking choice, but don't drag us back into this." He stood to the side, but slightly ahead of his brother. Like Nash, he didn't acknowledge his parents.

"It's Alpha Walker, Wyatt. He's ill."

"Of course it is," he sniped. "That's why they called us here. That's the only reason they ever call us back, Branson, to try to trick us into staying. They aren't stupid. A fake trial one day, an illness the next. It will just keep going until they've got us back under their thumbs. It ends. I'm putting my foot down on this slippery slope right—fucking—now."

I kept waiting for Julie and John to make a scene, but they remained motionless in my peripheral. They weren't quite as overt in their manipulations as the others, but I didn't mistake that as remorse. Every year, they sent Wyatt and Nash birthday cards, like they hadn't asked one to murder the other. In the beginning years after leaving, getting those cards in the mail used to send both brothers into a depression it took days to help them crawl out of. Now we had a tradition. Any birthday, Christmas, or what-ever cards got folded into ships, set afire, and sent into Walker Bay. Later, we added an element of betting to see whose would sink the fastest.

But while Nash and Wyatt had developed coping mechanisms, the pain was still raw, and they were extremely protective of the other. There wasn't a one of us who wouldn't take the pain from the other three if we could.

"Come on," Wyatt grunted. His shoulders lifted like hackles on a dog.

While I had no problems with leaving—and had

guessed Nana had excused us already because she'd somehow known Wyatt was coming, like she knew everything else—I experienced the strangest urge to defy him. Not just that, but to reject his order and give him one from me to follow instead.

I ignored the strange urge. They'd just tell me I was letting the Elders and this house get to me. Nana wouldn't come out of Alpha Walker's room until morning, and I wasn't going to subject us to being near our relatives for longer than we had to. I had more important things to do, like make up for my disastrous behavior with my mate.

"Let's go."

We didn't have anyone to say bye to. Instead, we were stared at as we left the main house. The Elders remained inside. I spotted Delia's butler weaving through people, murmuring to them as he went. I hoped he was getting record of the sick, notating similar symptoms. Those people would need to be quarantined for safety until the doctor had more answers. Maybe Alpha Walker's sickness was unrelated, but better to be cautious now than regretful later.

We were nearly at the end of the crowd back, where I'd parked. Wyatt's vehicle sat beside mine, the lights on, door open, engine still running. I finally stepped free of the throng, and it was like a small weight lifted from my shoulders.

"Excuse me." A soft, high-pitched voice brought my attention back to the last line of shifters huddled outside. A child stood a foot from the others, looking directly at us.

I looked to my cousins. Wyatt's scowl softened, but none of them rushed forward to answer. And maybe I wouldn't have, either, if it hadn't been a child who asked. "Yes?" I asked. My voice sounded strange in my ears.

"Is Alpha Walker dead?"

I couldn't believe someone hadn't been sent around relaying to the pack what was happening. Their lives would be twisted upside down as much as anyone else if Alpha Walker was gone. "I didn't see him, kid," I said. Those around the child glanced at us while making it seem like that wasn't what was happening. I spoke loud enough for them to hear as well. "The doctor told us he might have the flu. You should check yourselves for symptoms. Those of you who feel ill should report to the main house."

A few of them nodded; most acted like they hadn't heard me.

Wyatt and Nash piled into Wyatt's vehicle, while Aver slid into the passenger seat, letting me drive. I was thankful for it. I needed something to do while my head spun around all that had happened. What a night.

Not my best second date.

"He isn't being honest," Aver said, once I'd driven us over the bridge and off pack lands.

I didn't have to ask who Aver spoke about—I knew. And I'd thought the same thing. As late as it was, my night was long from over. Riley needed space; he would get it. But I couldn't stop protecting him, especially when he was so clearly keeping something from me.

14

RILEY

I PEELED myself off the couch the next morning and went through my morning routine like a zombie. All through my shower, my stomach rumbled. Maybe I could pick something up on the way to work. I wasn't running late.

My mind buzzed with the events of the night before. What did it mean that Branson hadn't broken in like I halfway expected him to? I should've been glad he'd obeyed my wishes, but instead, I was just worried. Had something happened? There was a wobbly feeling in my gut, like I wasn't quite balanced and it would take the slightest push for me to topple over. But today was Monday, a work day. I would not let my personal life influence my work—my job was too important for that. Even if I helped less people out here, what if I was stuck in my own head, worrying about my own problems, and ended up missing the signs that a client needed some serious help?

I rinsed the glass I'd used for water and left it in the sink, catching the time on the oven clock. If I left now, I'd be early. My stomach growled, making up my mind. At least this way I could grab something on my way in. I pulled on my jacket and opened the door.

Something fell over that had been leaned against the floor outside my door. There was no one else there, and the two bags—one plastic, the other paper—looked clearly huddled in front of my apartment, like whoever had left them had done so for me. Inside the plastic bag, there was something wrapped in a thick, plastic blister pack, the packaging saying it was a cell signal booster. The device itself looked most like a small router with a long cord. The selling points written with exclamation points on the outside claimed the device could ensure a strong signal throughout your home while reducing the number of dropped or missed calls.

I didn't have to pick up the small card to know who had sent it.

Riley,

I'm sorry for my behavior last night. I'm not trying to buy your affection, nor do I think this excuses me, but I would be so relieved if you used the signal booster. The doughnuts are from the bakery near your house. I'd planned on introducing you to them already and still wanted to take that chance, even if I don't get to see your face when you take that first bite.

Please don't give up on me. I'll figure out everything.

Branson

I opened the bag immediately, pulling out a fluffy glazed doughnut. My hunger drove my mouth open, and I chomped down, moaning at the sugary, fried cloud of dough. Before I knew it, I'd consumed the first and grabbed a second. I pocketed the other items before heading to the street toward work. It wasn't like I'd be installing the booster now, if I was going to at all.

This situation was unlike any I'd experienced, and I was still gathering my options.

I hadn't discounted the possibility that Branson and his entire family were insane and I was well rid of them. But not only did that not feel right, I'd witnessed them turning into wolves. The impossible had proved true once already. How far of a stretch was it to believe this? I mean, I clearly wasn't pregnant. I had nothing against babies, but I also didn't have a uterus or tubes, or whatever else it was that women kept tucked in their baby factories. I couldn't believe what they said was true, but I could believe they thought it was true.

But that only cropped up more questions. Why would they think that? What did that mean? In nine months, would they expect me to pretend to have a baby? I was openminded, but that was ridiculous.

I got to work with enough doughnuts left to offer Jake. He accepted the whole bag, scurrying into his room before the vultures came—his words. I unlocked my office and booted up my computer. Mondays weren't quite so bad in Walker County. I wasn't hit with that overwhelming wave of work I'd dared to miss during my few days off. There weren't a thousand fires that needed putting out. Instead, there were a few emails. Some of the programs I'd called the previous week were going to make the first steps in establishing resources closer to the island, which was better news than I'd hoped for.

I had an email from Hal telling me no one had come back to the office asking for me. Hal had also finished a recent project, a corkboard for his wife he'd constructed out of an old frame and wine corks. I made a note to call him later and tell him how good it looked. I hadn't done much making since I'd gotten to Walker County. Maybe Branson would like a—

You still haven't made your choice when it comes to Branson.

Who was I kidding? I'd made my choice that first day when I'd said yes to a date. He was caring and protective. The signal booster in my pocket was proof of that.

I checked my voicemails. A representative from the state office wanted to talk about clarifying some points on my report about Paul. I frowned at that. They sounded angry. The next message started playing automatically. I pulled the phone from my ear when it sounded like whoever had called had dropped the phone.

"Shit, damn!" That was clearly Branson's voice. "I wasn't sure if I should leave a note or a voicemail, but since I'm still on the phone, I guess I'm doing both. Sorry, this is excessive. I'm on a job site all day today, so you don't have to worry about me barging in. I'll give us space. It will be good for us both." There was a long pause, but I could still hear Branson's breath. I closed my eyes. He sounded so concerned. I wished I could help alleviate some of that. "My grandpa fell last night," he said, sounding as if the words were being wrenched from him. "I thought I wouldn't care if he died, that I wouldn't care about what that meant for everyone, but —I don't know. I want to hate them. Nash and Wyatt do a pretty good job of it. Anyway, I'm sorry for unloading this on you. If you don't already have plans, you don't have to worry about lunch today. Just stay in your office. And if you do, go about your business as you planned. I love you, Riley, still and forever. And it's okay if you don't feel the same way right now. I'll wait until you tell me not to."

The line clicked. Branson had hung up. I reminded myself he hadn't really been there; it was a recording. I grabbed my chest as an ache spread from my heart. I set the phone back in its cradle before yanking it up again, my fingers poised to dial Branson's number.

"Oh, hey," Gladys said, hanging off the doorway of my open door. "I heard you had doughnuts."

I swallowed all the emotions that Branson's call had drummed up and smirked. "You'll have to talk to Jake. He took the bag."

Gladys narrowed her eyes. She looked right to left and then poked her head inside. "Between you and me, he should avoid the stereotype."

There was no way I was responding to that. I liked everyone I worked with in our small office. That had never happened to me before and I wasn't doing anything to upset that. *You'll need friends to invite to your baby shower*, I thought with thick sarcasm. As Gladys got to work sniffing out the doughnuts, I started making calls.

Thankfully for my workload, my first call made me angry enough to power through the rest of the morning. After being transferred several times, I finally spoke to the assistant to some Seattle politician from the Department of Tourism. He had issue with me linking someone from this area with a possible sex trafficking ring, something I hadn't done in the slightest. I'd simply mentioned in Paul's report that I'd double-checked the database to make sure his name wasn't listed as a former victim, and, based on the manner he was dressed when I met him, that had been necessary.

I hadn't been able to get the assistant to see reason, and the assistant gave up on trying to bully me, ending the call with an ominous, "I'll let my boss know."

"Ready for lunch?" Jake asked hours later.

I jerked my face up from my desk toward him. "Already?" I checked the time. Hadn't Branson said something about lunch? He hadn't invited me, but he'd claimed I didn't need to worry...

"Mr. Monroe?" someone asked from outside my office.

"In here." Jake looked over, his eyes bugging. "What's all that?" he asked.

My curiosity wouldn't let me sit for any longer. I joined the other half circle of employees gathered around a man with a dolly carrying a stack of food platters. "What is this?"

"Lunch for the office. You're a kind man," the delivery worker said. He handed me the form, and I read it through. Someone had ordered a catered lunch of Mexican food. I scanned the itemized list. There were enough beans, rice, burritos, enchiladas, and fajitas to keep our office full for the day and tomorrow. "I didn't order this."

"Well, someone ordered it. Paid for it already too."

I investigated the form a second time. At the bottom, someone had made a note: paid in full, Walker Construction. Branson.

I could sense every eye boring into me. Their stares felt hopeful. "I mean, if it's paid for. Food's gotta go somewhere," I said.

The other employees gave a little cheer as the delivery worker began unloading the platters onto a long table. Branson had made sure of everything, and the delivery man didn't leave until he'd set out all the food, plates, drinks, and the assortment of mint candies for people to eat after.

I went back to grab my wallet for a tip, but the delivery man stopped me. "I can't accept that. I've been tipped." By the tone of voice, I assumed he'd been tipped well. He left, and I gestured for the others to dig in. They descended on the table like extremely pleased locusts, and I was just happy from all the joy. Who knew free food would spur such a celebration?

I made my own plate but didn't quite feel like joining everyone at the break table, so I took it back to my office. Should I call Branson? Say thank you? Tell him to stop meddling in my life? Ask him over? Suggest a quickie?

The last thing wasn't a possibility, even if it was a deep wish. It was like now that I had a taste of what Branson's body could do, I was addicted. But I couldn't rely on our sex to pull us through these moments.

"Everything good?" Jake asked, snacking on the chips and salsa he'd piled on his plate. "What are you getting me for dinner?"

"Ha ha." I flung a rubber band toward him, and it hit one of his chips, bringing it tumbling to the floor.

Jake bent down and picked it up, popping the chip in his mouth. "Five second rule."

"That rule doesn't exist." I didn't want to begin to think about how dirty this floor was. "It's a silly concept anyway. Do you have to wait five seconds after someone commits a crime before you can bust them?"

He snorted, likely at my use of the word *bust*. Sheriff Maslow wasn't taking down the heavy hitters in a place like this. Most of his calls were false alarms. "I do, in fact. Work on your sprints, and you too can live a life of crime." He sat down on the other side of my desk, and I found I wasn't annoyed in the slightest. Jake was as good a friend I could've hoped for at a time like this. "You never answered my first question. How are you?"

My boyfriend thinks I'm pregnant. He was over-controlling when I tried to leave his house. He can turn into a wolf, and if his family finds out I know, something bad will happen.

"Fine."

"Mhm." Jake didn't argue my answer; he just leaned back and took another bite.

"It's just... let's say you have a girlfriend. And she's awesome, right?" I tried to figure out how to translate everything I felt with Branson but in a way Jake would understand. "She's caring and understanding but has really big boobs too—"

"I'm more of an ass man," Jake deadpanned.

I'd let that slide. "Okay, forget the boobs—"

"Now let's not be hasty," Jake said.

"Jake! She's hot, okay? That's the takeaway here. She's an attractive, perfect young woman."

"But?"

"But she... has this belief. And it's really crazy."

Jake winced. "Super religious? You can't change a person, Riley. And I would never stand between someone and their faith, no matter their boob size."

Gladys poked her head in at that moment. She blinked as if convincing herself she'd heard what she thought she heard before shaking her head, clearly choosing to ignore it. "Wanted to check you didn't want more. They're going to town out here."

"Eat it up," I said.

At the same time, Jake hopped up. "I'm gonna grab a platter. We're splitting it," he said, when I opened my mouth to tell him just to take it.

It would be smarter if I listened to him. Then I would have food for later too. "Good idea."

He left and returned with two platters, a bag of churros, and a sheepish expression. "Getting back to your question. I'd say, like with anything when someone has faith that doesn't mirror yours, you have to decide how much it is all worth to you. Is the person worth more than the troubles they might cause? I can't say yes or no. You have to do that. How long have you been dating Branson?"

I cringed behind my monitor. "I'm that obvious?"

"Yes. I'm even more curious about what this could mean about that lunch and how rude he was..." He took a deep breath, obviously affected by thinking about that day. "...but you've got a good head on your shoulders, Riley. I trust you and what you choose."

I changed the subject to his friend's visit but kept what Jake had said fresh in my thoughts. How much was Branson worth to me?

———

AFTER WORK, I headed home, half expecting a full steak dinner waiting at my door. There wasn't one, but I was still full from lunch, and my arms ached from carrying all the food home. It was good Jake had grabbed the food when he did; the table had been completely clean the next time I'd gone out to the break room.

I was ready to call Branson. At least, I was ready to install my booster and wait to see if he would call. And if he did, I would answer. I didn't know what I felt about the whole pregnancy thing, but I'd give him a chance to explain what it all meant. He deserved at least that much.

When I got to my front door, there was no food, but there was a little old lady waiting for me.

"Hello, Riley," Nana said warmly.

She opened her arms, and I was surprised by how quickly I fell into her hug.

"Are you feeling well?" she asked.

Her eyes stretched down in the corners, weighed down

by worry. Branson had mentioned his grandfather's illness. "Please don't worry about me, Nana. How are you? How is your son?"

She smiled, looking pleased. "Branson told you."

"Sort of. He left a message. We haven't talked... since..." This should've felt more awkward than it did. But my mood had already been light. I'd had a really good day, made better by Branson. Nothing seemed so insurmountable now.

"It's good he told you anyhow. You need to be brought into his life."

I unlocked my front door and gestured for Nana to walk in first.

"I thought that was dangerous?" I asked, knowing this was okay to speak about around Nana. "The *others* can't know that I know their secret, or else they will have to bring me in and vote on whether I'm worthy to know. And I'm not real sure what happens if that vote comes back no."

Nana nodded and sat down on my couch. "That's the way they do it." She watched me move around the space, hanging my jacket and putting the food away.

"Can I get you anything to drink?"

"Do you have tea?" she asked.

I rummaged through my cupboards, but my unpacking had mostly been putting boxes in the places I wanted the stuff to go, not actually putting anything away. I found a mug and a dusty box of chamomile tea. I paused, deciding at the last minute to put everything on a tray, which I couldn't find at the moment, so I grabbed a cookie sheet from the drawer on the bottom of the oven. I put the microwaved cup, tea bag, and bottle of lemon juice on the cookie sheet and walked it into the living room.

If Nana thought there was anything odd about the presentation, she didn't mention it. She tore open the tea bag packet and dipped the bag into the water. "Thank you. Do you not drink tea?" she asked.

"Oh!" I'd only prepared one cup. I jumped up, but Nana settled me with her hand on my arm.

"Don't drink tea on my account, child. Have you eaten today?" she asked.

I nodded. "Branson dropped off breakfast and lunch."

Her look turned quizzical so I explained, making her frown. "Doughnuts are a part of breakfast, not the whole breakfast. Especially now."

There it was. *Especially now. In my condition.* So she still believed this delusion.

What's it worth to you? Jake had asked.

I decided not to fight the point. "I was thankful for the doughnuts. And my employees were thankful for the food." Really. They'd treated me like a king for the rest of the day. Though I'd figured some of them were sorrier for pigging out so much than they were thankful to me.

Nana nodded contentedly. She sipped her tea, setting it down again. "My son, Alpha Walker as you may know him, is improving. The doctor believes it was the flu, but thankfully, it isn't spreading. Not so much as a cold from anyone else."

She spoke with a familiarity that I didn't think I deserved. I hardly knew of Alpha Walker and had never met the other shifters that lived in their pack, though I had spent some time imagining them. They always ended up looking like versions of Branson in my imaginings, and by the time I conjured the mental image of being surrounded by a pack of Bransons, I'd been thoroughly distracted.

I looked up at Nana, noting her smirk.

She couldn't know what I was thinking... could she?

"That's good news." My throat was dry. I'd been shocked

at her presence, but now that some of that had worn off, I was just confused. Was she here to talk about that night? Shoot the shit?

"I wanted to check in on you," she said, answering the question I hadn't actually asked. "And apologize." She smiled, and it brightened her face, making her seem decades younger. "I was so excited. It's been so long since we've welcomed a Walker with joy into the pack."

I squirmed. I didn't have to confront the delusion, but I couldn't actively participate in it. "Nana, I don't want you to be disappointed."

"I won't be," she replied happily.

I grabbed one of my throw pillows. I'd made it by knotting old shirts and stuffing it with the stuffing from discarded toys. It cost me nothing but time to make. It wasn't fancy, but it did its job. Right now, that job was to give me something to fiddle with. "Why don't you tell me more about the Walkers? They seem... varied."

She smiled at my choice of word. "They are that."

"But you don't live with them? On pack lands?"

"No. I always had land on the other side. For a while, the entire island belonged to the Walkers." She paused, and I could almost see her travel back in time to one where her family wasn't quite as fractured as it was now. "But, that was many years ago. We've sold most of what we had, on this side of the river, anyway. When my Eustice died, I knew I'd be needed elsewhere."

"Do you always go where you're needed?" I'd never had a grandma—or grandpa, for that matter—but when I was young, I'd imagined them being a little like that. Going where they were needed.

"Not always." She frowned.

I knew immediately what she referred to. "You weren't

there? That night?" The night four young men had been thrown in a pit and instructed to fight until one of them remained.

"No. For all that I hear, I wasn't made aware that would happen until it was too late." Her face fell, and I wanted very much to change the subject. "Something broke that day. Not just in the boys, but in the pack."

For a fight that had ended with refusal, the injuries from that night still seemed to haunt everyone today. "Do they regret it?"

"In their way." She picked up her mug again. "If I was as intuitive as I'd like, I would've picked up on the decline when it started."

I'd assumed the pack problems had begun that night. "What do you mean?"

"Patrick, bless his soul, was a kind man and a good Alpha. But he didn't understand diplomacy. He'd been raised to rule the pack. His brothers hadn't been. They grew to resent him, which meant they resented everything Patrick chose when it came to the pack. He couldn't see the resentment. To Patrick, he was doing what was best. To the others, he was making reckless changes. The seeds sowed in those days grew into thorny vines that are suffocating the pack today."

It felt almost like she was making excuses for the parents. I crossed my arms over my chest.

Nana smiled at the gesture. "You're loyal. That's good. I suppose I should get to the point of my visit. You've been so kind when I clearly popped up out of nowhere."

I didn't answer, which might have seemed rude, but I hadn't intended it that way. I was just giving her time to say what she'd come here to say.

"Tell me you'll stay. You'll let my great-grandson take care of you."

I blinked, unsure what else I could say in response. Was she asking me to stay forever? To not leave because of her? "Shouldn't Branson get a say? Maybe he'll wake up and realize this was all a flash in the pan." Was this what they meant about well-meaning grandparents?

"Shifter ways may seem odd to you, and I understand that. They seem odd to us sometimes as well, and we were born into this life. But there are traditions that have been passed down through the generations, and some that have simply tapered off. When I was a young girl, a blessed omega was a rare thing, but one to be cherished. I have not seen another one in a very long time. But I knew what it meant the moment I did." She tipped her mug back, emptying its contents.

"What does it mean?"

She smiled again, that same face-brightening grin. "You're going to fix my family."

My forehead started to sweat, along with my hands as I grew hot all over. "Nana, I don't—"

"Shh. I know the doubt in you." She gave me a knowing gaze. "It nearly eclipses your fear. But don't fret. It took years to break. It will take a while to fix. But the mending has begun. Just stay. Make an old woman's heart happy."

The promise felt like an easy one to give, since it required no immediate effort from me. Who knew if I would go or leave? Maybe Blaine would pop up and take the choice away from all of us. I wondered how Nana hadn't seen him, since she seemed to see so much. Her powers could only extend to shifter business—or she could be a charlatan, and I was just beginning to believe her. Either way, I nodded. "I promise."

She left shortly after that, but not before demanding she wash the dishes she'd used and then set me some food in the oven to warm. While it cooked, I tore into the cell booster package. I skimmed over the installation instructions and found the best spot near the window. I needed a chair to reach the shelf.

The moment I set my foot on the floor, my phone trilled with an incoming call. I scrambled to my jacket, where I'd left it in the pocket. Was Branson watching in through my window?

I swiped to answer. "Hello?"

"If you call him all the time, you'll scare him," Branson said, but his voice wasn't clear like it would have been if he spoke into the phone. He sounded like he spoke from far away.

"Branson?"

"Or," Branson continued arguing with himself, "you'll show him how much you care. That you're always thinking of him." There was a rustling, maybe like he'd started walking. "He needs space," Branson muttered. "You told him you'll give him space."

I grinned, pretty sure Branson had butt-dialed me. "Branson! Pick up your phone." Weren't they supposed to have super hearing?

"You love him. And you'll love him while you wait as much as you would if you didn't. Be patient."

I couldn't stand him not knowing I was there. Throughout our relationship, I kept trying to trick him into saying the thing that would make it easier to walk away. And without fail, Branson came back only saying something that made me want to continue being by his side. "Branson! It's Riley! I'm in your pocket!" I yelled as loud as I dared without disturbing my neighbor.

There was much more rustling and then a quiet, "Hello?"

I smiled. "Hey, it's me."

"Did I call you? Where are you? This is your cell number. Did you install the booster?"

"Slow down with the questions," I said with a laugh. "You called me. Butt-dialed, I think. I'm at my apartment. This is my cell number, and I installed the booster. Your nana was just here. Where are you?"

"Nana was there? Why?" His voice deepened with suspicion.

"She wanted me to promise not to leave Walker County."

"Oh." There was a long pause. "I won't... I mean, what you two talk about is your own..."

"I'll tell you if you come over." I was done thinking it over. For all the weird moments, whatever this was with Branson was still a thousand times better than anything I'd ever had. Giving it up before I gave it a chance felt like a mistake, one that would stay with me for the rest of my life.

"What would you say if I said I'm just down the street?" Branson asked.

"I'd say run."

Branson hung up, but not before I heard his feet pounding down the sidewalk. I smirked. I'd meant a figurative run, but if Branson wanted to show up sweaty, possibly shirtless...

I ran into the bathroom, ripping my shirt off to splash water on the smelliest parts of me. Halfway through my sponge bath, I gave up, dressing down to hop into the shower for a thirty-second rinse down. I'd just got my clothes back on and run a comb through my hair when my cell rang again.

I jumped over the coffee table, answering it before the first ring finished. "What now?" I asked.

"Is that any way to greet your long-lost love?"

My body reacted to hearing Blaine's voice before my mind could catch up. My heart pounded as my stomach turned. My knees wobbled, and I sat down. "How did you find me?" The words came from my mouth as if they were being spoken by a dead man.

"Find you? Baby? I didn't know you were missing," Blaine chuckled. "I'm right outside your window."

I ran to the curtains and ripped them back. There was no one on the street, though my skin prickled anyway.

On the other side of the phone, Blaine laughed hysterically. "You just checked, didn't you?" His guffaws continued, so loud the speaker shook in the phone.

"Why won't you leave me alone?"

The laughing stopped. "You know why. You've definitely made this more difficult than I'd expected. There's no sign of you, Riley. I'd almost believed you changed your name. But do you know what you didn't do? Change cell carriers. You just switched numbers, didn't you?"

I squeezed my eyes shut. I wouldn't confirm what he'd said, though he was spot on. Was there a way to track that sort of thing?

"I had no idea you were so good at disappearing."

"Yeah, so I'm gone. The cops didn't believe me anyway, and now you can leave me the fuck alone!"

Unfortunately, Branson's heavy steps sounded up the stairs a moment before I spoke, leaving him directly next to the door to witness my outburst. He started knocking, quietly at first, but with each second I didn't answer, it grew more insistent. "Riley? Are you okay in there?"

"Who's that?" Blaine asked as if he didn't care.

He was too good at playing bored, disinterested. "No one. Just like me. I'm gone, Blaine. So don't call back!" I hung up the phone, but that didn't feel final enough, so I turned it off as well, tossing it on the bed as arms reached around me from behind.

15

BRANSON

Riley fought me like his life depended on it. I was afraid he'd hurt himself. "Riley, it's me!"

The moment he heard my voice, he turned to me. "Branson, I'm sorry. I thought you were..."

"Blaine?" I growled the name. I had no idea who the man was to Riley, but I knew Riley was afraid of him, so that was enough for me.

"You heard," he whispered.

"The apartment building heard, Riley. You sounded so afraid. Babe, my heart jumped into my throat. I thought someone was in here at first." I'd been frantic. Riley had gotten angry the last time I'd taken liberties with his locked door. But, finally, the tone of his fear had driven me inside. Now that he was settled in my arms, my heart soared while my instinct told me I needed to get the whole story, here and now.

A scent drifted to me, light, but distinct.

"Is something burning?"

Riley cursed and ducked out of my arms. He opened his oven, using the end of his shirt as a potholder.

"Babe!" I hissed, lunging for him as he hopped and dropped the pan on the counter.

"Nana put it in for me to eat."

While I loved the idea of my entire family caring for Riley, I couldn't let myself get distracted. I checked Riley's hand, running it under cold water until I was satisfied he hadn't burned himself more than he thought. He grabbed a plate, and I scooped the leftovers onto it, carrying it to the table where I sat him down with a knife and fork. "Can you eat and talk?" I asked.

Riley picked up the fork but set it down. "I probably shouldn't."

I didn't know if he meant he shouldn't eat or he shouldn't talk, so I waited.

"Talking about Blaine turns my stomach."

I stifled my growl. I'd known Riley was hiding something from me but hadn't ever thought he was hiding someone. That this person obviously meant Riley harm made me hate him more.

"He's an ex. My last ex," Riley said.

"Did he hurt you?" I snarled, losing the fight to keep the growl from my words.

Riley shook his head. "Not how you're thinking. As a boyfriend, he was unremarkable. But I didn't realize that at the time. I was too happy someone wanted to be with me even after..."

"He knew about your abilities?" Jealousy flared. As juvenile as the feeling felt, I couldn't squash it. Blaine had known Riley well then. Enough to know his secret.

"I think he did before I ever decided to tell him. Blaine was sneakier than I ever gave him credit for. It wasn't until the end, when I really started digging, that I was able to unravel all the lies he'd told me throughout our relationship. He hadn't been faithful—"

My hands clenched under the table. "And now he wants you back?"

Riley exhaled sharply, like an airy laugh that held no humor. "Not for the reason you think. I caught on to one of his tricks and went back to confront him. I saw... something." He paused, staring at the table. He abruptly stood and dashed for the bathroom.

I followed a few steps behind, and he ran in, barely making it to the toilet before he heaved. He'd said Blaine turned his stomach. I got a towel and moistened it before standing by Riley's side, rubbing his back all the while. When he was done, he sat back, grabbing the towel and wiping his face with it.

"Thanks," he muttered. After a moment, he stood. "On the last day, Blaine took me to meet one of his friends."

I'd started this, but watching him grip the sink, avoiding his own gaze in the mirror—it broke my heart. "Babe, you don't have to keep going."

He faced me, his expression determined. "I want to tell you," he croaked.

I closed my mouth.

"I'd met his friends before, tons of times. I didn't think anything of it. We got there. A few of his buddies I'd met were there. But this time, Blaine insisted I shake hands with one person in particular. He was so weird about it, even after knowing what would happen. We did, and his friend said two words, *San Jose*. It seemed odd to me, but Blaine just thanked me and told me to wait in the car. I was so stupid, I did. Then, when it started taking a while, I crept back in. The man was on the floor, not breathing. Blaine and his friends were breathing hard and—"

"You ran?" I asked, my heart in my throat.

Hysterical laughter bubbled out of Riley's mouth. "I should've, huh? No. I was so mad. I'd known then what he'd done and could only wonder how many times he'd already used me. I told him that I knew what he'd done, that I knew what they'd all done. I'd reminded them that my touch could make them tell the truth, that they would confess. And if they wouldn't, I would."

My lips turned down in a wince. That had been a brave but foolhardy thing to say. Riley didn't need me beating him up, though.

"Then, when Blaine pointed out that I couldn't do any of that if I was also dead, I ran."

I wanted desperately to know how he'd gotten away, but I didn't think I could handle listening to the story. I'd already started mentally listing all the identifying information. Later, I'd give that all to Aver, and he'd find out a last name for this Blaine, and the four of us would pay him a visit. "You were so brave, babe."

Riley scoffed but accepted my embrace. "Brave?" he said, his face stuffed against my chest. "More like stupid and cowardly."

"Don't say that about yourself. You were stuck in a situation and made the best choices possible."

Riley grunted. "You're biased."

That was definitely true, but it changed nothing. If this was the secret Riley hid from me, that was fine. I would handle it. I was just glad he'd told me. "Do you feel better now?"

He nodded. "Just let me brush my teeth. I think I'm actually hungry again." He frowned. "Is that weird? I shouldn't want to eat after that..." He waved to the toilet. "But I'm so hungry."

He'd removed everything in his stomach; it didn't seem weird to me that he was hungry. I led him back into the dining room when he was finished brushing and reheated the food while he waited. He let me re-plate it and scoop the first forkful before taking the fork from me, his brow raised.

I let him have it with a sheepish shrug. It turned out I was like a mouse with a cookie, too, except I just wanted to care for Riley. He ate while I was mostly quiet. "Do you want some?" he asked, and I shook my head.

"Is that from the lunch?"

Riley nodded. "Jake made sure I had some leftovers. The office really liked the food."

I knew that because the Mexican restaurant was a town favorite. I stifled any jealousy I might've felt toward Sheriff Maslow since the end result of his actions had been Riley getting food. "You two are turning into good friends," I said as casually as I could.

Riley still wasn't fooled. "He is, and I want to keep it that way."

I sighed. "I'm sorry, babe, that I made it seem like I don't like you having friends. I am overjoyed. And Maslow is a good guy. A good, straight guy."

Riley snorted. He leaned back, his plate empty, and patted his stomach. Either the angle or the food made Riley's stomach a little rounder, and I froze as a sense of *meaning* overwhelmed me. This was important, this moment. This man. He was the type of guy who found beauty in everything. Who was honest and good. "I'm going to tell my grandfather about you," I said.

Riley's eyes rounded, but he didn't speak.

"You aren't something for me to hide, and I'm so sorry I tried. You're it for me, Riley."

His face crumpled, and I lunged forward, afraid I'd blabbed all the wrong things.

"I'm sorry, babe. Does that make you upset?"

"No." He shook his head as his eyes spilled over with unshed tears. "I was so scared that my secret would scare you away. But you know and you still want me—us. I'm happy." He lifted his face and tried to smile, but the tears streaming over his cheeks somewhat dampened the effect.

"I can tell." I stood, new energy buzzing in my veins. I was with Riley again. He was still mine.

"You mean now?" Riley asked, his question rising in the end to express his panic. "Isn't he sick?" He stood with me.

"Nana said he is feeling better. He's back doing his regular tasks. There's no time like the present."

"What if he gets mad? Votes no on me knowing?"

I shook my head. "It won't matter. I'm going to tell him he can vote until their hands fall off. I don't have to recognize the decision. If I need to fight them after this—"

"Hold up." His hand flattened on my chest. "Fight? I don't want to cause more drama. Especially not after Nana won't drop this pregnancy thing and is convinced I'm the second coming for your pack."

I still hadn't had a chance to pin Nana and get the details of that. "She said you're blessed."

"She said the same thing to me. But Branson..."

His words trailed off, but I heard what he didn't say. How crazy that sounded. At this point, I had no idea why she kept pushing the issue. It made me start to believe the impossible. But that only spurred me to want to go to my grandfather even more. If something odd was happening to Riley because of me, I wouldn't be able to keep it a secret. I already wanted to move all his things into my house, and if I thought he would let me, I would've gotten my truck that moment.

The point was, Riley was going to be in my life, and I needed to start acting that way. I knew one thing for sure—I would never be forced to stand aside again while some other man had to care for what was mine. "I won't do this without your permission, Riley, but if you're ready... I am."

He nibbled on his lower lip as a frown wrinkled his forehead. "You aren't worried Blaine will find me and cause more trouble for you?"

Was that what he worried about? "I'm hoping for it."

Riley hit my shoulder. "Branson! He's dangerous."

I let the growl rumble through me with a little more primal force than I normally let slip. I wasn't afraid of Blaine, not past the danger he posed for Riley. If he was coming here, it was an even better idea for Riley to be by my side. "I can handle him. And if I need help, I've got it."

That pacified him, and when he looked back up at me, his face carried hope. "Okay. Let's do it."

———

RILEY SHIVERED, and I peeled off my jacket to give to him. He tried pushing it away, but his hands shook as I draped it over his shoulders. "Y-y-you'll be cold."

I stood for a moment, showing him how not cold I was.

"Sh-show off."

"You can wait in the—"

"I'm not waiting in the truck," he snapped before sighing. "I'm sorry. I'm nervous. And starting to doubt how smart eating that food was. Maybe I am getting sick."

I had my own thoughts on that, but I was keeping them to myself. Since our talk, I watched Riley with new eyes. At first, I'd assumed the stress from talking about Blaine had spurred his upset stomach. Since then, he'd mentioned the overwhelming smell of old fries that he detected in the cab of my truck. I had eaten fries, but so long ago the smell was faint even to my nose.

My phone rang, and I switched it to silent without looking.

"You don't want to tell them where you are?" Riley asked again.

We were at the bridge between pack land and the rest of the island. Riley and I waited on the island side, but when my grandpa arrived, we'd walk to the middle. It was an older way of handling negotiations between packs that weren't friendly. If I were to go to his side of the island, the pack side, I'd be subjected to obey the laws of the pack. I couldn't worry about that with Riley by my side. And he'd made his presence mandatory.

"If I told them, they'd get angry," I said.

"And you don't want them to talk you out of it?" Riley asked.

"No, I didn't want them to come. It hurts them. Just being on pack land hurts them."

"It hurts you too."

That was true, but not in the same way. I was spared having to explain that by headlights in the distance. "They're here." I grabbed Riley's hand, pulling him directly to my side, where I clamped my arm over his shoulders to keep him there.

I counted our steps over the dark bridge. It was a clear night, letting us see a sky of stars, but also making our breath come out in puffs of smoke. Alpha Walker stepped out of the black town car, followed by two shifters in their wolf form, as well as Glendon, Aver's father, and John, Nash and

Wyatt's father. I'd specifically told them to leave my mother behind. I didn't need her here trying to twist things for her benefit.

"Thank you for meeting me, Alpha Walker," I said loudly and clearly.

My grandfather stared at Riley. He had to know he was human, which meant he already knew that Riley was aware of our secret.

"What have you done, disgraced alpha son?" he asked.

"Don't call him that," Riley snarled. "He isn't disgraced."

Alpha Walker's eyes dropped to Riley's feet, checking which side of the pack boundary he stood on. He frowned, but we were on the human side; there was nothing he could do right now. That didn't mean he wasn't planning something for later.

"This is Riley. He's my mate. I claim him as my omega."

Glendon and John hissed.

"He isn't a member of our pack." Glendon surged forward and pointed at us. "You aren't a member of any pack. We aren't required to recognize any claim."

I didn't satisfy him by looking his direction. My gaze remained on my grandfather. "Are you finished speaking for me?" he asked his son.

Glendon bowed his head immediately and stepped back in line with the others.

"Why have you come, Branson Walker?" Grandfather asked. "You know our laws and that what Elder Walker says is true."

"Yes, but he's not going anywhere. We're not going anywhere." My voice turned hard as my emotions got the best of me. "Aver, Nash, and Wyatt, we've made this island our home, and won't be run out."

"You turned my son against me!" Glendon shouted.

Alpha Walker spun, backhanding Glendon across his face. "Silence!"

Riley squeaked, but I remained motionless. Glendon was letting his emotions control him as well. He rubbed his face as Alpha Walker turned back to us, panting from the slight effort. "I tire of this. What is your point?"

"My point is, you're the Alpha. You tell your pack how to think and feel. If you accept Riley as my omega, they all will."

He arched his brow. "Why would I do that?"

"There must be something you want."

Riley gasped. He hadn't known about this part. I had a list of things I was willing to trade for this. It wasn't a pleasant idea, and I dreaded having to fulfill my end of the bargain, whatever it ended up being. But something had to give. I couldn't worry about danger coming from all sides now that Riley was in my life. This was another reason why I hadn't asked my cousins to be here. They wouldn't want to be kept from negotiations, and they shouldn't have to offer anything they weren't already willing to give.

"The Winter Solstice Celebration," Alpha Walker said.

I wondered what he would want in combination with the celebration. Was I to serve people showing them how far we *disgraced* sons had fallen?

"I want you to attend," he continued.

I scowled, waiting for him to finish his request. "And?"

"That is all. Just attend. Be cordial."

I looked into each face standing across from us looking for signs of deception or that they'd already conjured this plan up and I'd given them the perfect opportunity. Glendon and John looked as angry as I was confused. They wouldn't speak up against what the Alpha had asked for, though, not while Glendon's cheek was still a red reminder.

"And if I attend, I will be treated in the same manner I treat others?"

He waved away my worries with a lazy twitch of his hand. "You have my word as Alpha that no harm will come to you or your new mate."

My snarl alone could've been viewed as a punishable offense against the Alpha if I were a few steps forward. "No. Riley stays out of this."

Alpha Walker turned away. "Then no deal. Take me back," he instructed his driver.

"Wait!" Riley called out, and I tugged him behind me.

"No. You don't get placed in danger," I whispered, pressing my forehead to his.

"He said there wouldn't be any. Why does it matter? I can go to a party. You'll stay with me. We'll leave. It will be fine."

I never stopped shaking my head.

He grabbed my biceps and shook me. "Listen, Branson. If this is what it takes, I want to do it. Let me do this. Your nana said I could help you guys fix things. What if this is what she meant?"

It wasn't. It couldn't be. Nana would never want Riley to be in a situation that could be dangerous for him.

"If I go, does your promise extend to me? I will also be safe?" Riley asked over my shoulder. My grandfather acted like he hadn't heard him until Riley added, "Alpha Walker."

Though mostly I was worried for Riley, part of me was also possessive. Not just of his attentions, but of those he obeyed. Even hearing him use my grandfather's correct name made my jaw tic. I was Riley's alpha, no other man. I wanted to be Riley's Alpha, too.

Alpha Walker narrowed his gaze as he looked from

Riley and then back to me. "Is there something I should know? A reason why you might not be safe?"

The fact that Riley could force someone to tell the truth by touching them? Or that Nana believed him to be on par with a savior poised to save all of our lives? Oh, and that he was pregnant?

"Can't think of anything," Riley said in a high-pitched tone that fooled no one.

But Alpha Walker must've decided that whatever Riley held back did not outweigh his desire to have us present. "You will both be my honored guests. You might not know what that means, Branson Walker's omega, but it means you have my word. You will not be harmed on this land during the Winter Solstice Celebration."

I wanted to take Riley back to the truck where we could talk this over, but he nodded his head. "We'll do it."

I knew they would wait for my acceptance as well. I nodded begrudgingly.

"It's settled. I'll be pleased to see you. Please send your RSVP to the party planner." He got back into the car without a goodbye.

I hadn't expected one.

"He's not pleasant," Riley whispered as we returned back to the truck.

He seemed fine, which was good because I felt like I'd been shoved through a woodchipper and then mashed.

I lifted him into the passenger seat, ignoring the glare I got. I knew he could get in on his own, just like he could buckle on his own. I still *wanted* to do it for him. He let me, and I left him with a peck on his forehead as I circled around.

Even though we hadn't quite entered pack lands, I felt the stain of it swirl in my head. My cousins were going to be pissed. But I would explain that it was for Riley. They would come around.

But had I just made the right choice? Or had I played into their hands?

The roads were empty as I drove us back to my house. "Will you let me sleep beside you tonight?" I asked him. I thought we'd made up, but it was best to be clear.

He hugged himself, still wearing my jacket. A fact that pleased me to no end. "I'm glad you asked."

I kept looking over at him and grinning. He was in my truck, going to my house, where he would sleep in my bed. I was over the moon. Only one dark cloud still lingered. I pulled the car over. We were minutes from home, but I needed to say this now. I put the car in park and turned toward Riley.

"What?"

"You were very brave tonight," I said. "Not just tonight. I've asked you to accept so much."

"Hey, I've had my own drama," he said, pushing the hair back from his face.

"That's true. But from now on, I want your drama to be my drama. Ours."

Riley looked nervously around the cab, and I knew what he searched for—something to lighten the moment. Not because he didn't feel the same way, but because he did, and that scared him. I felt like I understood Riley better now. I'd seen him interact enough and knew that his spine was strongest when he was defending others, but when the attention came back to him, he shrunk.

He couldn't see the prize I had in him, and I would do everything in my power to help him see.

I pulled him into a kiss, and my heart soared. He was in my arms. His warm mouth molded against mine, opening immediately. I was in no hurry and kissed him as thoroughly as my heart urged me. Riley was power and submission. In other words, he was my perfect match. With the strength to stand up for what was right and a vulnerability I would devote my life to protecting.

I caressed his face, rubbing my thumb along his jawline before cupping his neck to feel his pulse pound. I had to keep control of my desires. When it came to Riley, one touch was never enough. I wanted more—I wanted *all* of him.

My other hand found his hardness, and I rubbed him over his pants. His head fell back against the seat, and he closed his eyes while that purring sound I never remembered making before Riley started again deep in the back of my throat.

"I love that noise." Riley opened his eyes to stare down at where I touched him.

"I love you." I flicked open the button of his pants with my thumb. His cock was warm and throbbed even through the stiff material, and if I didn't get him in my mouth, I wasn't sure what would happen. I didn't want to wait and see.

I bent down at the waist. The angle was only awkward during the moments it took me to turn and accept his cock into my mouth, letting my head drop until I felt his short curly hairs tickle my nose. Riley groaned and brought his hand to the back of my head. His fingernails scraped against my scalp. "Someone is going to see," he urged. "We're right here."

I smiled but didn't stop. I flattened my tongue, running it along the underside of his dick. "I won't let anyone see what's mine," I murmured against the small rolls at his stomach. I loved those as much as I loved every other part of my

Riley. They made him more real, and for a man who constantly seemed ripped from my dreams, that was vital.

"Jesus, Mary, and Joseph," Riley muttered.

I smirked and peppered his erection with kisses as soft as a butterfly. "I didn't know you were so religious." But I couldn't wait to learn everything about him.

"How can I not be when that mouth makes me see God?"

I tsked jokingly. "Blasphemer." I winked.

But when he opened his mouth to respond, I took his dick back in the warm heat of my mouth, and whatever he'd been about to say turned into a wail. I could do this all night, and I might. For the moment, I needed to get my mate off the streets and into my bed.

I sucked hard, hollowing my cheeks. My hand found his balls and massaged tenderly. Riley's thrusts were uneven and without rhythm, leaking samples of the meal that was to come. I listened to the tone of his moans, the way his cock twitched a moment before he climaxed. It was like the ring of a dinner bell to me, and I readied myself to swallow every drop Riley was willing to give me.

When it came to my mate, I was the greediest man in the world.

He held my hair, kneading my scalp like a kitten. "Branson!"

I loved how my name was the last thing to leave his lips before he filled my mouth. I swallowed his essence, savoring the wild, masculine taste of him. He let go of my head, and I brought my face up to kiss him.

"Okay," I mumbled against his lips. "Now we can go home." Where I planned to do all this over again.

And again.

16

RILEY

"ARE you going to tell your cousins?" I asked. It was Tuesday morning, and though I needed to get up and get back to my house to dress for work, I wasn't eager to leave the cozy warmth of Branson's bed.

The night before, we'd made love until my eyes had refused to open. And even then, Branson wasn't ready to stop. He ended up falling asleep with his hand on my cock, and it was there when I woke up in the morning.

"If I don't, the pack will. They should hear it from me," Branson said. He had his shirt off and lay back on his pillow with his arms folded up under his head. My head fit in the ridges of his chest, and our twisted limbs tangled in the dark flannel sheets. It was the most comfortable that I remembered being since the last time we'd lain in his bed together.

"If you need my help with them—"

Branson dropped his arm over my side and clamped me down tight. Every firm, heated bulge on his body pressed into me. I was a kid in a candy store, and I didn't know where to dig in first.

"I can handle my cousins. You shouldn't be made into a

shield for me or anyone else." He turned toward me. His face was always gorgeous, but first thing in the morning with his soft full lips and eyes drowsy but filled with warmth, he was a thing of beauty. "That reminds me. Blaine."

I buried my face into his chest. Not that name. He had no place between us, or in this bed.

"When this business with the solstice is finished, I want you to tell me everything you know about him. If it's too hard for you to talk about, I can find him anyway, but it will be faster if you—"

I jerked upright. "Find him? I came here to get away from him, Branson."

"I know that, babe, but that was before you met me. I won't have my mate living in fear. I've never heard you so afraid as I did on that phone call. At the risk of ruining this perfect morning, can I ask a question about what happened?"

I shrugged, having crossed my arms tightly around my front. Branson's touch remained gentle on my shoulder.

"You said they didn't believe you. What did you mean?"

I snorted, though the noise hardly conveyed the fear and frustration that arose thinking of the moment. "I went to the police right after. I ran right to the station. And I told them everything that I had seen. I told them I could prove it beyond a shadow of a doubt, and the officer asked how. Which was when I explained my curse. They didn't believe me. Not a one of them. Suddenly, everything I told them turned into this big joke. Later, I tried to call it in anonymously, but obviously nothing happened since he's still around. I checked the police arrest database for weeks after. His name was never listed."

My anger boiled as I relived it in my mind. I wasn't sure

what made me angrier, that Blaine had used me or that he would get away with it *because of me*.

During this, Branson listened quietly. He dragged his palm from my shoulder down my arm, leaving goosebumps in his wake. "You aren't alone anymore, Riley. And if I have my way, you won't ever be again. Let me share this burden with you."

He didn't make any promises that he might not be able to keep, and I appreciated that. As always, his honesty won me over. "Okay," I relented, going immediately boneless as he pulled me back down to his side.

He kissed the side of my face, which turned into tiny nibbles down my neck.

"Oh no, don't start that. I have to go. I'm going to be late."

Branson continued his exploration.

I smirked. "I'm already pregnant. What more are you trying to do?" I laughed, waiting for Branson to join in. I'd meant what I said as a joke, and yet Branson stilled.

"What if you were?" he asked quietly.

I pulled back, pressing my chin to my chest to look at him. "Branson..."

"I know. Believe me. *I know*. But I turn into a wolf. I never questioned how. I just accepted that it was possible. What if Nana isn't being cryptic, and it isn't a metaphor? She claims to have seen it happen in her day."

Put that way, with the impossible already being true, it almost seemed not so farfetched. But, I couldn't start down this road. I was too afraid of where it would lead. "What would the pack do?" I asked.

Branson's eyebrows flared with surprise before narrowing. "I hate that you have to ask that. But you aren't wrong to worry. We must keep this between us. I don't even think

Nana will be so cavalier with what she suspects. The pack could—I actually don't have any idea what effect this would have on them. Until I do, it's our secret. You, me, and the three nosy dudes down the hall."

He kissed me, threading his fingers in my hair. He tugged lightly, but hard enough for my dick to twitch. I groaned, opening my mouth to him.

"Haven't you earned some time off? A sick day?" Branson murmured against my lips.

I slipped out of his arms and rolled off the bed in a tactical maneuver. Branson blinked, his arms still circled around where I'd been moments before. His eyes met mine, twinkling with a predatory edge. "Don't run from me," he warned playfully.

"Or?" I replied, adding as much sass as I dared. I wasn't sure how much I could trust Branson when he looked like a hunter sizing up his prey.

He leapt from the bed, reaching me in the time it took me to gasp and stumble back. Branson's hands covered my lower back. He was naked from head to toe, a fact I couldn't help but be aware of with so much contact. My heart pounded. Though he was playing around, my flight-or-fight reaction made me tremble. Branson winked, kissing my nose before letting me go. "Get dressed. I'll take you to your apartment and wait for you to get ready."

That didn't sound fair. Branson probably had work to do today too.

"I don't want to hear another word out of your mouth unless it's yes, Branson." He squinted as if deep in thought. "I would also accept yes, Master."

"Bite me," I replied, kissing his nose. "Master," I added with a wink, spinning to the bathroom in the next moment.

He smacked my ass playfully.

"I'll wait in the kitchen," he called after.

I did my business quickly, splashing water over my face. My toothbrush was at my apartment. I'd take a quick shower there too. It couldn't have been more than ten minutes later when I went to meet Branson in the kitchen. My footsteps slowed as angry voices sounded ahead.

"I didn't believe her," Aver yelled. "Not for a single second did I believe she was telling the truth. Branson, what the hell has gotten into you?"

I guessed they'd heard about last night's negotiations.

"I have to do what I must to protect Riley, Aver. You can't ask me to keep him hidden. He isn't a secret. He's my mate. I recognize him as my omega. Maybe that doesn't mean as much as it would've to the pack had I stayed, but it means the same to me. He's it for me, brother. He's my omega."

"Jesus, it's too early to be this dramatic," Wyatt grumbled next.

"And Riley is listening in the hallway anyway," Nash added.

I jumped forward and rounded the corner, my shoulders raised with my guilt. Branson grinned and dropped his arm over my shoulders. "I told you they'd know before I could tell them," he murmured in my ear.

I looked at each of them. Wyatt was barely upright at the kitchen table. Aver was fully dressed in a suit for the day, while Nash had on his crisp fireman's uniform. "I'm sorry I—"

Aver spoke up first. "You don't need to apologize. I'm sorry if anything you overheard made it seem we're upset with you. It's the bonehead next to you that we're concerned with."

"But, if I wasn't around..." I wasn't sure how to finish

that sentence. Not only did I dislike thinking about life without Branson, I didn't know what he would do in my absence.

"If you were around, he'd be harder to be around," Nash said. "None of us like this time of year that much. At the least, you're giving me a distraction. But I won't participate. Nothing against you. I just can't spend more time with those people. Every moment in their presence feels like a loss, like they've won."

"I understand completely," I replied before Branson could say anything. "Thank you, guys, for everything."

True to his word, Branson waited in the truck while I got ready for work. He drove me to the office, promising to be there at the end of the day.

I appreciated his attention but saw the underlying stress that fueled his actions. "I'll be okay, Branson."

He nodded. "I know you will," he promised, kissing me once more.

———

IN THE EVENING, I stumbled out, exhausted from a day of arguing over the phone. Branson was there, his clothes changed but dirty from the day's labor. He didn't question where we were going. He just kissed me before driving us to his home, casually mentioning along the way that I should pack some things at his house.

The rest of the week passed in the same way. Normally, Branson dropped me off and picked me back up after work. Sometimes he sent Aver or Nash if he had work to do for a client that kept him busy. None of them complained or even spoke about this new task that had been thrust in their laps. They simply accepted it as a part of their life now. Branson wanted it, so they did it. I figured the cousins would've done the same if any of them had asked. At least, I told myself they would so I wouldn't feel so bad.

Some people might have hated the extra attention, but I'd spent so much of life alone, I didn't mourn the loss of alone time now. I loved knowing someone was waiting for me.

One week grew into two. The five of us fell into a steady rhythm. Nights at Branson's, days at work. The weekends were spent hanging with the cousins or doing work around the house. Branson bought me a new phone, demanding I leave the other turned off. I shared my new number with Hal, who was glad to be able to talk to me more regularly. He said he worried about me *up there in the trees*, as he called it.

So, on the following Friday, when Nash stood on the sidewalk waiting for me instead of Branson, I didn't think twice. I'd had a harder day, a stomachache that would not stop as well as a headache. No matter how much I slept, I couldn't get through the workday without crashing.

Gladys had ridden the elevator down with me, and when she saw Nash, she whistled low under her breath. "I'd catch myself on fire if I knew he'd come to put me out. Preferably with a bottle of champagne." She fanned her face.

Nash winked, I guessed more for Gladys's benefit than my own. "You ready, champ?" he asked.

I smiled and said goodbye to Gladys as I took a seat in Nash's car.

"Where's Branson? Did that stone come in?" He'd been waiting on a delivery of supplies for a client. The material had been back-ordered and sent incorrectly twice already, and the client's well of patience was nearly dry.

"It did," Nash said. "And, he wanted to surprise you."

"With what?"

"If I told you it wouldn't be a—oh, who am I kidding. It's another dinner. He wants to make up for that last one."

I nodded, wishing I felt a little bit better. The mood I was in, I would've been happier if Branson had planned nothing but time for the two of us to cuddle on his couch. He couldn't know how I felt now. I'd been fine that morning. Whatever this was came on quick and lingered like a bad house guest.

"You feeling okay?" Nash asked halfway to home. "You aren't going to throw up, are you?"

"No." I waved off his worry and opened my window. "Thank you for asking."

"Don't thank me. I'm just worried about my interior. Just got this baby detailed," he said, rubbing his palm down the dash.

I smirked, deciding if I did have to throw up, I would definitely do so in the back seat.

But I made it back to the house without incident. Everyone was home. I'd learned during my stays that while the four didn't have a lot of chances to be all home together, when they did, they cherished it. At least this dinner would give them a chance to hang out with each other. I could endure it for that.

Except, the moment I walked in the door, assaulted by the spicy smells of whatever they were cooking, my stomach turned, and I sprinted for the bathroom. I barely made it in time, and when I was finished, Branson waited outside in the hallway with a glass of water. "Sorry," I said, my face red from both embarrassment and effort.

"Why are you apologizing for being sick?"

"Because I know you had dinner planned. Is Nana

coming?" I hadn't seen her old truck outside when we'd pulled up.

"She's on her way now. Says she has something for you. I'll tell her you're sick, though."

I grabbed my stomach. "Maybe it was something I ate? I feel better now."

Branson's gaze narrowed, but he didn't comment. He'd been doing that more often too, looking at me when he thought I wasn't paying attention. "Whatever you want to do."

I smiled through my exhaustion, which throwing up had done nothing to soothe. At least I could smell the delicious dinner cooking without—

I went back to the toilet.

"It's the food, I think. It just smells... so much. Not bad." I felt horrible, like I was complaining that someone had made me dinner, which was exactly what was happening.

Branson frowned but called for Aver to open all the windows. The frosty winter air breezed in the house, diffusing the scent but also freezing everyone out. "Don't worry, we're used to cold," Branson said.

Nana arrived shortly after, making no mention of the windows or the temperature inside. "Riley, dear, I'm glad you're here." She pulled out a large mason jar from a knit sack slung over her shoulder. "Here you go, dear."

I accepted the jar and peered at the murky yellow contents. "Thank you, Nana. This is great. What is it?"

Wyatt laughed, but Nana shushed him. "Good manners are never something to make fun of," she said. "It's a homemade recipe," she said to me.

"A recipe for what?"

Her gaze touched on Branson before she answered, and I knew what this was about. I didn't know what was in the jar, and if I'd been made to guess, I might've said aged urine from a severely dehydrated man. But if she didn't want to say right away, it could only mean this had something to do with the baby she was so convinced was inside me. At this point, I'd go get scanned if I thought it would convince her.

"It is supposed to help some of your symptoms. Though I had to dig deep in my grandmother's books for the recipe. There's nothing too unpalatable in there. Some herbs, berry juice, wolf fur—"

"Nana!" Branson grabbed the jar. "You can't feed my mate wolf fur."

"I definitely can if it will help him. Look at the poor man. He's green in the face, and your home is as cold as a tomb. Sensitivity to smells?" she asked me.

I nodded slowly.

"What about headaches? You getting them?"

I nodded again, but she didn't wait before she plowed on.

"Have you been tired? No matter how much sleep you get? How about your feet or hands? Are they swollen?"

I tucked my hands behind my back.

Nana just shook her head, giving us all the same level, take-no-prisoners stare. "My dear, you can say something isn't possible from now to Sunday, but if it looks like a duck and acts like a duck, grab your gun, or you'll miss dinner."

I didn't remember the saying going quite that way, but I understood her point. "Should I take a test? Would that make everyone happy?"

Branson hooked his arm around my waist. "Babe, no one is asking you to do that."

"I wouldn't mind if he did." Wyatt spoke up, and the rest of us stared at him.

"No one is joking about this, Wyatt," Branson snapped.

"He isn't either," Nash defended his brother. "I might have... well, we had some around the station, so I picked one up, and I was going to bet Wyatt, but if Riley is willing..."

I frowned, understanding only about seventy-five percent of what he said.

"You have a pregnancy test?" Branson translated the rest for me with his question. "More importantly, you were going to bet on it?"

I didn't know why he should have been surprised. These guys bet on everything.

"He was," Aver spoke up. "But none of us wanted to go against Nana."

"*Et tu*, Aver?" I gasped.

Aver shrugged.

Branson's hand was still hooked around my hip, but I already suspected what his thoughts were on the matter. "Let me get this straight," I said. "Even though I am a man, you think I am pregnant." It wasn't a question as I pointed to Nana, but she nodded anyway. "And you, you, and you?" I pointed to the other three. I wouldn't make Branson go against me in front of everyone, so I didn't ask him. "Fine," I sighed. "Get me the test. But, if I'm not... you all, except you Nana, have to unpack the rest of my apartment and... clean my bathroom for a week."

"Make it a month," Branson murmured. "They'll agree to a month."

"But you think I'm pregnant!" I reminded him.

Meanwhile, Nash jumped up and went outside to retrieve the test he'd kept in the truck. I grabbed it with the strange knowledge that this was the first time I'd ever held such an item. I'd never seen a pregnancy test outside of commercials, though I figured I understood the basics. "And if I do this, you'll all drop the subject, right?"

"What do we get if you are pregnant?" Wyatt asked.

Branson growled at him, but I figured it was only fair. "What do you want?"

"Name it after me," Wyatt said without missing a beat.

My lips turned up in a smile. "If I'm pregnant, I'll name it after all of you," I said, positive that this was one promise I would never have to fulfill.

Branson groaned, following me to the bathroom. All of them were in the hallway—even Nana, who looked excited but also mildly disapproving. I assumed she didn't take kindly to the betting. I decided to name my fictitious child after her too to make up for any annoyance.

"You aren't all coming with me. I can pee alone." I never thought I'd have to say those words, but here we were.

"No way. What if you fake it? There's a bet on the line," Wyatt said, backing up quickly when Branson growled and lunged for him.

"No one is watching my mate pee!"

"He could pee in a cup," Aver suggested.

"But how can we be sure it is his?" Wyatt countered.

I watched the cousins discuss where to put my pee and how to judge its authenticity with horror and amusement. I wasn't exactly shy about it, and if these guys wanted to play in a cup of my pee—another sentiment I never could've imagined having to think—then fine.

"Get me a cup. Let's get this over with." By now, I was excited to take the test. I'd felt mildly coerced at first, but really, where was the harm?

Wyatt returned with a plain white mug. "Handled for your pleasure."

I probably should've been relieved that they let me shut the door. When I reappeared with my mug, they were all there. Branson had the test, and he dipped it in as the others counted the seconds. He didn't look nearly as grossed out at holding a pee-covered stick as I would have thought, and as Aver started the timer, we moved as a unit into the dining room. "Are you coming?" Branson asked.

"Nah, go ahead. Let me know what it says," I called over my shoulder. I dumped the rest of the mug, dropping it in the trash after. I'd buy them a new one. It would be a great gift for when they were all sad that they'd lost. I washed my hands and changed out of my work clothes.

Figuring enough time had passed, I went back to the dining room, expecting a crowd of disappointed faces. "Has it been three minutes?" I asked as Aver's phone trilled, signaling the end of the timer.

No one moved. Wyatt glanced toward the test, sitting on five napkins in the center of the table. "I can't look first."

They made such a big deal out of it, and now none of them wanted to look? I stomped over, lifting the test. "It's two lines." I looked for the box—I'd forgotten what the symbols meant.

Nash handed it to me without a word.

"See, here it says two lines means... *pregnant?*" I read the box over, but the words stayed the same. Unfolding the instruction sheet took one second, even while my hands shook. I read every word, front and back, while the others in the room watched me silently. The information stayed the same, though. "It says something about a false positive," I said, looking up into four stunned faces and one smiling one. "Get me another test," I whispered, my brain buzzing too chaotically to speak any louder.

I didn't know who left but heard movements. Branson approached, but I ran at the last minute to the bathroom, where I locked the door. I sat on the side of the toilet in silence, listening to Branson pace outside in the hallway.

Time passed, long enough for whoever left to return from town.

"I bought one of each," Aver said quietly.

There was a knock on the door. Then Branson said, "Babe? I have the other tests. Open the door."

"No," I shouted, knowing I sounded like a kid throwing a tantrum. "Slide them under."

There was silence, and then, "Ba-abe." He managed to make the short word into two syllables.

"Branson Walker! You have infected me with your wolf sperm, and you're going to give me guff for how I handle this? You slide those tests under the door right. Now!"

One of them, I couldn't be sure who, muttered, "Sounds like a dude version of Nana."

Anger flared for a moment. I was freaking out, worried what this meant. Would it hurt? Would it kill me? Was there really a life growing inside me? I couldn't handle all those questions while the four Walker giants breathed down my neck.

The first of the tests slid under the door, followed by nine more.

"But are you going to pee for each one?" Branson asked. "That could take a while."

"Then get started with dinner without me." I couldn't eat like this anyway. "And hand me my phone."

I couldn't tell who, but someone slid my phone under the door too.

"I mean it. Go on without me," I called through the wood. No one answered.

Two hours later, I had ten positive pregnancy tests sitting on the counter in front of me. I'd stared at them from every direction, examined them close up and far away. One false positive I could understand, even two, if the brand was subpar, but eleven false positives seemed excessive, and though I had no idea what to do next, I knew what I had to say.

I opened the door, finding Branson sitting on the floor with his arms balancing on his knees up in front of him. His head jerked back. "Riley?" he asked, rising to his feet.

"Look for yourself," I said, waving at the counter behind me.

He passed by and returned moments later. "Are you okay?"

"No," I said.

"Are you mad?"

"No."

"Are you afraid?"

I probably should have been. But, "No."

"Then how do you feel?"

I inhaled and patted my stomach. "Hungry."

Branson led me into the kitchen. The others had eaten but still sat in the dining room around the empty table. Branson had me sit while he dished me a plate. I felt rather than saw the stares on me from the others in the room. No one wanted to say anything, but I felt their curiosity.

I ate my entire plate; it felt good in my stomach. When I was done, I patted the side of my mouth with a napkin and finally lifted my gaze. "So should it be, Branson Aver Wyatt Nash Walker? Or do you prefer a different order?"

Wyatt whooped, and Aver stood, his face almost as white as Branson's was.

Nana sat down next to me, handing me a cup of the drink she'd brought. "It's Evelyn, dear," she said.

"Huh?"

Nana smoothed her weathered hand over mine on the table. "Branson Evelyn Aver Nash Wyatt Walker."

"Hey! I got demoted!" Wyatt wailed, while the others laughed.

And, surprisingly, I found myself laughing along with them. This was *crazy*. More insane than anything I ever thought to worry about in my lifetime, but with Branson and his family, I thought maybe it wouldn't be so bad.

17

BRANSON

I closed the laptop lid, finally finished with the book-keeping for the week. Aver had been on me to hire an accountant, and I was moments from putting out an ad. I'd spent all day in my office while my pregnant mate puttered around the house. He'd spent the early Saturday morning selecting driftwood while we walked along the river and had spent every hour since then crafting it all together into a...

I wasn't sure what he was making, but I was ready to be impressed. Not just because Riley was my mate and I thought everything he did was amazing, but because Riley had a real skill for seeing something that others might look over and making it into something beautiful.

Now, though, I heard him muttering from the back patio. "Stupid stomach. I'm sorry, baby. You aren't stupid. This big, fat—"

"How's it going?" I asked, leaning up against the doorway to the outside.

It had been a week since our discovery. Nana came over every day to check on Riley. Sometimes she came in the

231

morning and sometimes after work. She'd already come today, so I didn't expect her back.

"Fine, I guess. I'm just." He flopped his arms out in a frustrated gesture at the mess around him. There were bits of wood, a hot glue gun, and a bucket of unopened spray paints.

"Should you be spray painting?" I asked, scooping the bucket from the cement.

"I haven't yet. Why? Am I not supposed to?" Riley was as clueless as the rest of us when it came to what he should and shouldn't do while pregnant. I'd gotten in the habit of turning to ask for Nana, since she spent so much more time here, but even though there was no Nana to ask, I was positive.

"No, I don't think you can. You can't clean a cat box, either."

Riley turned back to his log creation and cocked his head to the side as he stared at it. "You don't have a cat," he said absently.

"Well, if you come across a stray dirty cat box, don't clean it."

He nodded his understanding, and I joined him staring at the... *thing.* "What is it?"

"It was supposed to be a shelf, but the wood wasn't cooperating. So now it's a... coat rack!"

It was clear both from the way he spoke and the mass of unorganized wood in front of me that he'd just decided what it all was. I smiled anyway. "It's beautiful."

Riley rolled his eyes but stuck his cheek out for a kiss.

I gave him what he wanted, sliding up behind him to cup his stomach. He claimed it was already bigger, though I didn't see it. He just looked perfect to me. I was aware of my tendency to sound like a broken record of support when it came to Riley, and rather than irritate him with my cheer-leading, I tried offering a more silent support role.

"Can you even get your arms around me?" Riley asked, letting his head drift to the side so I could kiss his cheek.

Though his body was relaxed in my arms, I picked up on Riley's wistful tone. He was joking, but only slightly. "You are beautiful no matter your size, omega. That said, I can get my arms around you. And if I ever can't, I'll still try." I squeezed his middle gently. I would never say it out loud because I didn't think Riley would understand my mean-ing, but I loved his squishy middle, just as I would if he had a six-pack or a keg. And when I thought about why he might have been gaining weight, that only made him and his body more amazing to me. He carried my child, some-thing that should have been impossible. But it was possible, for us.

"Whatever you say, alpha," Riley murmured. I knew the grin that would bless his face when he sounded like that.

Just like he knew the effect hearing him call me alpha had on my body. It was like flipping a switch that Riley alone had access to. I was powerless against the testosterone that fueled me, reaffirming the knowledge that this man was mine, my omega. He was mine to protect, to pamper and to love.

Riley popped his ass back, and my dick pressed against the confines of my pants, searching for the glorious oasis that waited for me. "Is anyone home?" he whispered.

Were there three sexier words? I didn't think so. Spin-ning Riley to face me, I lifted him, and he groaned, hiding his face in my neck.

"We have an hour," I said, and Riley lifted his head.

"I should finish here," he said, tugging away.

I frowned but let him slip from my arms. "Are you

working on a deadline?" I'd heard him promising his friend from his old office to send pictures of his latest project.

"No." He shook his head but kept his gaze averted.

I slunk back, remaining near but giving him the space he seemed to want. He wiped at his forehead, and I zeroed in on the nervous gesture. "Riley," I said, sticking out my hand as he turned to me.

He looked down at it curiously.

"Shake my hand," I said.

"Why?" He frowned.

I smirked. "Chicken?"

"No. What? No. What's gotten into you?" He still stared at my hand like it was a snake.

"Then touch it. Let me tell you how I feel." I had a hunch, and every word Riley uttered only confirmed it. "Shake my hand."

Riley hmphed and rolled his eyes, but every action held a twinge of worry. I was surer now than I'd been that this was the right course. If Riley couldn't see how desirable he was, then I would tell him in a way that could not be refuted. He gripped my hand, tenderly at first.

I slid my hand deeper into his, prepared for the floaty calm that touching Riley hand to hand brought out of me. "I want you bouncing on my dick." My lips barely had to form the words; they flew out of my mouth.

Riley let go with a gasp. He tilted his head like a curious puppy and grabbed my hand again.

"I can't stop thinking about your lips on my dick."

Riley smirked as the second lewd and lusty truth popped out of me.

Once more, he grabbed my hand. "Thinking of you pregnant makes me hard."

He laughed, throwing his head back as his neck muscles

flexed. "You're a pervert." He wrapped his arms around my neck, and his lips fell against mine. "My pervert alpha."

I growled and lifted him. His legs loosely wrapped around my waist.

"Someone's ready to put their dick where their mouth is," Riley said, and I chuckled as he frowned, as if mentally working out what it was that he said. "Or something like that." He reached between our bodies, having to go around his tummy bulge to get to my pants, where he unbuttoned the top and pulled my dick free.

It poked insistently between Riley's legs, rubbing along the cloth at his crotch.

"I can feel you through the fabric," he moaned, wiggling his hips in an attempt to get more friction. His irises shrunk, leaving his gaze dark. He didn't seem to mind that we were outside or that he was humping me like a dog in heat. I certainly didn't mind. In fact, I very much did not mind. I loved every side to Riley. The creative, the smart, the horny.

But we both needed more friction. I carried him in the kitchen with doors to block us from anyone on the river. His pants, thin joggers, tore from his body easily. Now, when I rubbed my rigid shaft between his legs, I felt his balls. Hot and heavy, I continued the teasing thrusts while my omega mewled, planting kisses along my lips and eyes and down my nose.

"I need you to fuck me," Riley announced while I sucked on his neck.

This had been what I was waiting for. Riley, ready, begging and needy. His body was changing, but that was the only thing that had. "Tell me you're handsome," I whispered hotly into his ear.

"Just fuck me, Branson," Riley whined, sticking out his bottom lip.

That lip looked sexy as hell, and I had to take a moment to suck it into my mouth before continuing. "I will fuck you baby. I'll give you just what you need. My alpha cock right *here.*" With my hands clenching his ass cheeks, it wasn't difficult in this position to pet his pretty pucker. "As soon as you tell me you're handsome." Ideally, I'd have him say it while looking at his glorious body in the mirror, but I didn't want him out of my arms for the time it would take to do that.

I'd carried us through the house to my bedroom. The bed sat near, beckoning us.

"I'm handsome," he grunted, accentuating his displeasure with a sassy hip wiggle.

"And any man would be lucky to have me in their life." I added more for him to say.

He copied me, the same words tumbling from his lips much more quickly. "Now fuck me or put me down. Actually, no *or.* Just fuck me."

Little did he know, I'd already pushed my body to the edge. I could no sooner deny Riley my cock as I could decide to stop breathing. I dropped him gently to the mattress. "On your knees."

Riley scrambled to obey, stretching to his knees, facing me. He opened his mouth wide and waiting.

My brain short-circuited at the sight. His plump lips, parted and expectant. But I had other plans and grabbed his hips, spinning him around.

"Hands and knees," I amended, not bothering to wait for him to obey. I was too far gone, operating on pure animal instinct. It was a dangerous game, pushing my sexual control around Riley, but it was a game with no loser. I bent forward, covering his back with my chest. "Now, say *you're welcome*, so I know you realize what a gift you are," I growled, lining my cock up in the next moment.

Throbbing and flushed, my clock glistened before disappearing between the soft pillows of flesh. Riley's tight channel opened for my dick, sucking me deep. His muscles clenched, nearly bringing me to orgasm immediately.

"You're welcome," Riley gasped, and my dick twitched. He moaned deeper, driving his hips back as he balanced his forehead on his clenched hands.

"Thank you," I rumbled in reply. Though I was sure to tell Riley how much I adored him, I didn't thank him enough, which was a crime considering how much of my life Riley had been required to accept. His life would forever be altered, for me, and if that didn't deserve a thank you, I didn't know what did.

"You're welcome," Riley chanted with each forward pound.

Somewhere between lovemaking and a claiming, my thrusts lay in that middle road. I kept a brutal pace but tempered it with gentle kisses. My balls tightened, and I slowed, leaning back on my heels, listening to Riley's pants.

"I want you, Riley," I said, needing to say the words before I lost my nerve. "In *every* way. I want you to feel how good this feels. How good you make me feel."

"You do the same to me," he replied, turning back to peer at me over his shoulder. With his ass propped up and that impish stare, I couldn't stop my hand from gripping my base and stroking to the tip and back. We'd spoken about this once before. It wasn't something that he'd pushed or that I'd obsessed over, but the moment felt right, and honestly, I wanted this first.

We'd met each other so late in our lives. This would belong to us only.

I slid up the bed, kissing and licking his body on my way up. Riley leaned back and arched his brow. He was confused, and rightly so. I'd been moments from orgasm, the same as him. But I had no doubt that this would bring us closer, and, on top of that, it would allow me to truly express all that Riley meant to me. I trusted him with this when I'd been unable to trust anyone before.

I'd been afraid that it would make me less of an alpha, less of the man I was meant to be. It took having Riley in my life to truly wipe away the rest of the bullshit that clung to those types of thoughts. I was ready now *because* of Riley. "I want to feel you inside me."

Riley's gaze narrowed with desire, and his hand pumped on his dick, but as sweet as he was, he still worried. "Are you sure? I don't have to, Branson. It's something I've been curious about, sure, but it isn't anything I need to push."

I'd been expecting this response and was ready with a kiss and lube. "I want to experience this. Be my first, Riley, and I'll be yours."

I pushed away the dark sneer that wanted to mock me for begging for my omega's dick. Fuck preconceived notions of what I should enjoy. And maybe I wouldn't. Maybe I would hate it. But I wanted to try, and now was the time. If we waited much longer, his belly might be too big.

That mental image had me smiling as I lay back and lifted my legs, opening myself like a buffet on coupon Sunday.

Riley dropped, his mouth parting on the way down. It seemed someone had missed having my cock in their mouth. But, as he sucked, using his tongue all the while to massage my underside, his lubed fingers peeked between my cheeks. "If you're sure," he said slowly, but I sensed the excitement building in him. He liked the idea of this more than he wanted to admit.

"Show me how thankful you are."

His grin turned wicked as Riley dropped his hand, smoothing his fingers over my crack. When I felt his fingers first prod at my ass, I kept completely still.

Even motionless, Riley's finger felt too big. "How many is that?" I asked, lifting my upper half to peer down. I needed to install a mirror. Not only would it give me an unfettered view of his ass in this position, but I'd be able to see, and I was positive I didn't want to miss a second of what he was doing.

"One knuckle." He grimaced.

One? I frowned and took a deep breath.

But Riley had other ideas. He kissed my lips softly, neither taking charge nor waiting for me to take charge. His kisses were lazy. Each swipe of his tongue over mine helped me forget where his fingers were or what they were doing— stretching me open. "That's right, alpha. Concentrate on me. My touch. How does this feel?" he asked, letting me get used to the intrusion.

Except the pain that had flared at first had faded to a dull ache, and even that had been massaged away. My ass tingled, the sensation unfamiliar and yet wholly consuming. I licked my dry lips but couldn't respond.

"Fuck, Branson!" Riley mistook my silence for being in pain and jerked back, but I grabbed his wrist with a snarl and kept his finger in place.

My tongue twisted around the growls I couldn't stop from erupting, and I moved his wrist, directing his finger in and out. "I need it. Your cock."

"You aren't relaxed enough. Let me keep—"

I refused to come on his fingers my first time being

penetrated. "Now." If he didn't move soon, there was nothing I could do to stop my orgasm. It shocked me, rising so quickly without stimulating my dick. I didn't know that I could start calling myself a bottom, but I was pretty sure I could bottom, if the mood struck Riley. Of course, I was thinking all of this without having felt Riley's dick, which he pressed where his finger had been.

I wiped the sweat from Riley's forehead. Concentration had hardened on his face like a mask, but I watched his hands, clenching and unclenching in a pattern that spoke volumes. He said with his fingers what he could not get through his lips. This was affecting him as much as it was me.

He buried himself to his limit, connecting us in a way that was foreign and yet utterly familiar.

He cupped my face, and I turned to his palm to plant a kiss.

"Thank you," he whispered.

"You're welcome."

Riley's thrusts stuttered. As his orgasm approached, his control waned, and I took over, gripping his hips and lifting him in and out of my body. His body stiffened before he collapsed on my chest, shuddering as his climax took him over. "Mine, Riley. You're mine," I growled.

Feeling him fall apart in my arms, the hot liquid heat filling me, I lost it. I came with a roar. My body spasmed and shook. This moment was familiar, and yet everything felt different with Riley's cock in me. My muscles clenched as my desire shot hot and wet on my chest. It covered us both when Riley dropped down, boneless and satiated.

"Sorry, should I move?" He switched his momentum to try to roll over, but I held him in place.

"Just stay that way for a second," I whispered. I wasn't done feeling my omega. "I love you, Riley," I murmured.

Riley didn't respond with his words, but he didn't need to. I saw it in the way he trusted me, in his care for my well-being. Neither of us could be sure what the future held, what the pack would do, or if Blaine would find him before I found Blaine, but we'd get through it together.

18

RILEY

*THINKING OF YOU. **I want to try that position you mentioned. The Superman.***

I smirked and shielded my phone as if I was afraid someone would be walking by my open office and see the screen. Sexy midday texts weren't technically allowed, but when you'd recently had a sexual awakening, the lines tended to blur.

At least, I assumed they did.

I readjusted in my chair, trying to find a position that didn't make me constantly aware that I'd spent the weekend both fucking and being fucked by Branson. He'd always been a beast in the bedroom, but after our recent discovery, he was unquenchable.

"Should I ask how you're doing?" Jake asked.

"Of course? Why wouldn't you? I'm fine." I'd known while speaking that I needed to shut up, and yet...

Jake smirked. "Uh-huh." He yawned, stretching his arms over his head and sat down on the other side of my desk. Ever since that day Branson had catered lunch, we'd started spending the lunch break and most every other break chatting. Either he came into my office or I made my way over to his. Sometimes he was out on a call or at home if he'd been on call overnight, but normally, he was around.

I still thought it was funny that I'd moved from a city with over seven thousand people to one with a fraction of that, and yet I'd made more friends in Walkerton than I'd ever had before. I guessed that was what happened when you stopped living your life in fear.

"Big weekend?" Jake asked, glancing at my desk calendar. I had the day of the solstice party circled in red.

I wrung my fingers over the desk, realized what I was doing, and made myself stop.

"Nervous?" Jake asked, picking up on my not-so-subtle body language. "I'm shocked, to be honest. Not that you'd be nervous, but that you were invited—no offense."

Normally I hated when people said that; they always meant offense. But, this time, I didn't understand why I should be offended.

"It's just that they never ask anyone from this side of the island. They've invited other people in. Bigwigs from the big city, senators, politicians."

I frowned. "Ever heard of anyone from the Department of Tourism?"

"Oh yeah," Jake said. "I've heard he's close with Delia Walker."

That explained the odd call I'd gotten asking to amend my report on Paul to not include references to the specific location. I growled internally. I didn't know how to explain the situation to Jake without him knowing the key factors. But at least now I knew better about what type of a gathering this was. Something meant to impress people, I guessed. That made me hiding what was growing in me during the party even more important.

I stifled the urge to rub my tummy. I was trying not to be so obvious at work. I wasn't sure what would happen when I got any bigger. Already, I wore the largest size I had in my closet. Maybe I needed to start eating in front of people to explain the weight gain. Except I hated thinking of my child like he or she was something that needed hiding. It reminded me of how Branson had felt about me, how he'd been compelled to tell the pack. I wanted to scream it to the mountains. *I'm pregnant!*

It had taken me a few days to get over the shock. During that time I'd been like a horse with blinders, unable to look anywhere but forward. I felt better now. Branson's kind support and steady loyalty had helped me realize that he would stay with me, no matter what happened. Since then, I'd started reading. I couldn't know how much of the information was the same. The records from Nana's time were spotty at best. But I figured most of the stuff would remain the same. My symptoms had certainly followed a more typical pregnancy.

The only difference was the baby's size. He was larger—rather, I was larger—than most women would've been at the same point. After all, I was still within the period when most women were just finding out that they were pregnant. I also worried about labor. I had no vaginal canal for the baby to come out of, and thinking of it coming out the other option left me a little queasy.

"Riley? You there?" Jake snapped his fingers in front of my face.

"I'm sorry. I got lost in thought."

"I can see." He stood and yawned again. "I guess that's my cue then. Want me to grab you a coffee? I could use one anyway."

"No," I replied more emphatically than I'd needed to.

But I'd just read about caffeine and the effects on the baby. While my heart broke to have to miss my favorite morning routine, I wouldn't risk it. Not now that I knew. "Thank you, Jake. I mean, not just for the coffee. For everything."

Jake scratched the back of his head, and his cheeks blushed. "Uh. You're welcome." He was clearly uncomfortable, and no wonder. He'd asked if I wanted a coffee, and I'd thanked him for everything.

When he left, I looked back at the calendar, fixating on that red circle. Not going wasn't an option. I'd just have to hope Branson and I made it through the party without anyone realizing my skin could force them into spilling their deepest secrets and that I had their disgraced alpha's baby growing in my belly.

I sighed. Maybe they'd at least have cake.

19

BRANSON

"Just show me, Riley. It can't be that bad."

"No!" Riley's refusal sounded through the bathroom door.

We needed to leave within the hour, but Riley hadn't been able to find a suit that he both liked and hid enough of his baby bump. He tried the various jackets, shirts, pants, and accessories I'd ordered along with my own tuxedo, but he'd yet to find a combination he felt comfortable walking out of the bathroom with, much less to go to the solstice celebration.

"Babe, I don't want to rush you, but we have to go soon."

"I'm not ready! Just go wait in the other room."

I hated the stress in his tone, but I'd known this night wouldn't pass without at least a little stress, and if wardrobe woes were our biggest worry, I'd count this night as a success. He wasn't so large that he couldn't hide the bump, and, other than Nana, who had been mysterious regarding the topic of whether or not she would be there tonight, no one at the party would know.

It wasn't like Riley would leave my side for a single

second while we were on pack lands anyway. We'd make the appearance, Alpha Walker would get whatever it was that he thought he'd get from our attendance, and we'd go home, hopefully never to return.

I skidded to a stop in the kitchen, noticing first, I wasn't alone, and second, the guys were dressed up for a night in. Aver, Nash, and Wyatt lingered in the kitchen. I'd heard them moving around but hadn't spoken with them. Nash sat with his back to me, while the others lingered on either side of the kitchen island. Each was dressed in a tuxedo similar to the one I wore.

"You all have a party to go to too?" I asked, accepting a cup of coffee from Aver. I wouldn't be drinking this night. Not until we were back here, home and safe.

"Brave but not very bright," Nash said.

"What's that?" I asked, sure I already knew the answer.

Nash emptied his mug. "What I'm putting on your tombstone."

I drank down my cup in one gulp. Riley would be out soon, and I tried to not flaunt my caffeine-guzzling ways around him. I knew it was hard to go without.

"Where the hell do you think we're going, Branson?" Wyatt asked. Of the three of them, his face was the sullen-est. His bow tie was crooked, and he had no shoes yet, but a holey sock that allowed room for his big toe to poke through. "It isn't like we can let you go on your own, and we know this is for Riley, so..."

"You guys are coming with us?" I blinked under the weight of my relief, but quick on its heels came guilt. "You can't. It's going to be horrendous. I don't know what he has planned, but if he wanted me and Riley there, it's got to be bad."

"He really knows how to sell it, doesn't he?" Aver said to

the others. "Brother, we're going because you must go. But mostly, I'm going for Riley. He makes you happy. He's pregnant, however that works, and he's a good guy. The way I see it, his worst mistake was attracting you."

Aver couldn't have said he loved me any better. And though it was cowardly, I could handle the guys going if it was for Riley.

"Ditto," Wyatt said. "I'm here for Riley."

Nash turned back to face me. "Me too—oh my..."

His gaze rose over my shoulder to the hallway, and I turned, my heart pattering. I was excited to see Riley in his...

"Huh," I said, cocking my head to the side.

"What?" Riley stuck his hands out on either side of him as he searched his body. "It's big, I know."

Big was an understatement. The suit jacket swam on him. The pant legs were baggy, but only from the knees down. From thigh up, the pants were tight. I didn't mind that, since I'd see his ass more clearly like this, but he definitely painted a different picture than the men in the advertisements.

The sleeves of his jackets came to about mid-hand, while the bottom hem hit well below his waist, covering his baby pooch. It didn't stop until about the mid-thigh point.

"I look awful," he wailed.

That wasn't exactly true. While the cut and size were off, the man underneath was still gorgeous. Riley could wear a used trash bag and still be attractive. "Your bow tie is straight!" I effused, making my cousins laugh.

Riley spun, I presumed to lock himself back in the closet, and I leapt up, cutting him off in the hallway.

"Babe, we have to go. You look fine."

"I don't want to look fine!" Riley spat back.

He wasn't normally this obsessed with how he looked, but the event, combined with where it was and the secrecy required, had whipped him into a state of frenzy.

"Could it be possible that you don't look as bad as you think and that maybe your pregnancy is filling you with hormo—"

Riley's snarl drowned out the rest of the word.

I heard Aver whisper, "Pay up," from the kitchen. What had those jerks been betting on now?

"If you tell me to relax next, we won't make it because you'll be dead!" Riley said, much to the pleasure of everyone listening in.

I took a deep breath and let it out slowly. "Babe, I meant you look great. In fact, you should help Wyatt with his bow tie because *his looks like shit*," I yelled over my shoulder. "We need to go, though. The guys are coming now. Isn't that great?"

"They are?" Riley asked, accepting the arm I draped over his shoulders.

"We are," Nash said, appearing in the hallway. "What does it look like with the jacket off?"

I led Riley closer to the door, where he shrugged off his jacket for the others to see. The white button-up fit around his shoulders nicely. It followed his form all the way down to his waist, where the buttons began to strain. The worst of that section was covered by a pleated white cummerbund that looked one large exhale away from bursting out from underneath his stomach.

Riley stood there, expectant, while my cousins silently stared.

"Put the jacket back on," Nash finally said, making Riley wail and dash back for the hallway. This time, Aver and Wyatt joined me in catching him before he got too far.

Wyatt took the lead, giving the rest of us a wink that said, *Let me show you how it is done.*

"Riley." I was not wholly comfortable by the way Wyatt spoke Riley's name. Somehow he made it sound more familiar, intimate.

In response, Riley peeked up at him.

"The suit isn't great," Wyatt said, inching closer, which made Riley step back, closer to the door. "But you shine no matter what you wear, man. I mean, it's tight and loose, but you are bringing a life into this world. That's hard work. Your insides are working around the clock to nurture and grow that little guy or girl. Who cares about the outsides, when it's what's inside that is truly gorgeous?"

"I guess you're right," Riley said quietly.

"It's a stupid party anyway," Wyatt continued, having looped his arm in Riley's on his way out to the car. Riley followed by his side, and while I was irritated by his familiarity and didn't approve of his tactics, we really did have to go. "I tore my tie crooked on purpose," he shot back over his shoulder.

"It isn't that crooked," Riley agreed.

I growled and thrust myself between them. Immediately, Riley's expression changed. *What did I do?*

I decided not to take it personally and kissed his cheek. "I do think you look great," I murmured while helping him into the vehicle.

"You have to say that, though," Riley murmured back. "You knocked me up. It's a contractual obligation."

That seemed fair to me. I kissed his forehead before sliding into the driver's seat.

The ride to pack lands was quiet. We all knew the plan. Stay close, stay quiet. We would speak when spoken to and leave the moment we were able.

Just before we crossed the bridge, Riley cleared his throat. "You all look really nice. I wanted to say that, before we..." His words trailed, but we all filled in the blanks.

Before we entered the lion's den.

Or wolf's, as the case was.

The moment we drove over the bridge, I spotted the first home, glittering and glowing with all the dressings of the holidays. To most, they would look like Christmas decorations. To shifters, the solstice was close to the same concept. No baby Jesus, but we exchanged gifts similarly. Our decorations ran closely along the same lines, so much so that most visitors would just assume what they wanted.

The lighted houses continued, like lights down a runway. The driveway to the main house was barricaded and manned by a team of valets.

"Is that a horse-drawn carriage?" Riley asked, leaning forward.

It looked like the carriages were transporting the guests from the end of the driveway to the main house. It was an effective way to trap guests, and I'd expected this act of control, but still didn't enjoy handing my keys to a pack member who wouldn't even look me in the eye.

The five of us piled into a carriage. There was room left over, but Nash and Wyatt spread out, telling the others to wait for the next. We weren't making friends, but getting out of the night in one piece was our goal, not popularity. I watched Riley's face as he tried not to gawk at the lavish decorations. Before, the twinkling lights had been tasteful. Now they were a message. It was as if each glittering bulb represented the Alpha's power, his might. The front driveway shone like a small sun, and the opulent decorations didn't stop once we ascended the steps inside.

We were met by a butler who took our names, crossing

them off a list. I wondered how Alpha Walker had known Wyatt, Nash, and Aver would be coming as well but decided not to dwell on it. I probably wouldn't like the answer.

Inside, there were at least a hundred guests, all dressed for the occasion. They mingled and chatted while men and women from the pack dressed in all black circled the room, offering drinks and food. The entire first floor was open, allowing the party to flow seamlessly from the sitting room, the meeting room, and the dining room. Only the kitchen was corded off to keep guests from wandering too far. A thick red rope blocked the guests from ascending the stairs.

"Do you see them?" Aver murmured.

"Two o'clock," I replied. I didn't nod at the Elder families grouped together in the sitting room. They stared at us anyway.

Delia smiled, her lips glittering almost as brightly as the jewels that draped from her. Her smile grew pinched when she saw Riley, but the motion was so slight, I doubted anyone but myself noticed.

John and Julie were huddled together, probably trying to think of a scheme to separate Nash and Wyatt from our group, while Glendon and Clarice smiled wildly at their son.

There were enough strangers in attendance that the mood didn't immediately change by our arrival. But all those that were a part of the pack noticed. The servers mingling in and out of the crowds wouldn't step anywhere near us, unless expressly ordered to.

"I don't have eyes on Alpha Walker," I said, but before any of the others could ask, I heard his gravelly voice coming from the other side.

"Here they are," Alpha Walker was saying to the small

group of five people following them. I recognized a few from the news, senators and politicians who likely helped the pack out in exchange for funding. The others were shifters, likely representatives from other packs, sent to establish and maintain pack-to-pack relations.

Alpha Walker approached us, opening his arms wide in a welcoming gesture. He shook our hands, skipping over Riley with a polite nod. That wasn't as disrespectful as it might have looked. Since claiming Riley as my omega, pack law required another shifter, particularly another alpha, to ask permission before touching him. "Come, please, your families are waiting," he said to us, like this was a regular Sunday and we were just stopping by for a visit.

We shuffled in the direction Alpha Walker indicated, none of us saying a word until he had us relatively in the same space, though we remained clumped tightly together.

While the human guests barely looked at us, the shifter representatives gazes lingered. They looked each of us up and down. It wasn't unusual to think that the story of what had happened to us had traveled. They would know there was no Walker ready to take charge, and it was then that I understood my grandfather's game.

He wanted to quash the rumors. He wanted it to look like the Walker family was as in control as we'd always been.

"He's shrewd. I don't believe he was sick for a second," Wyatt muttered.

The five of us circled together, Riley wedged between me and Aver.

"Careful," Nash warned. "He's got ears everywhere."

"I don't care what they hear me say," Wyatt said, loud enough for the Elders to look over.

Delia split from the group and floated over. "My son,

you made it," she announced loudly. They clearly understood their part in all of this.

I nodded, and to my surprise, she didn't push for any more. I realized as her gaze flitted to Riley that his position clamped at my side was the reason why. My gut twisted as a cold wave washed over me. Delia had experienced the effect of Riley's ability. We hadn't spoken any more about that moment, and I didn't know what she suspected, but clearly, it was enough to keep her back.

Had she told the others?

Was this all a trap?

"Mr. Monroe, you're here as well," she said. "How... progressive."

Riley stiffened at my side.

"Of course he came, Elder Walker," Clarice oozed, coming to Delia's side. "Mr. Monroe is Branson's chosen omega, didn't he tell you?" Alpha Walker had moved on with his posse, and Clarice spoke only loud enough for those nearest to us to hear.

Delia's face paled. "He did not." She recovered quickly, affixing that awful smile across her face. "Welcome, Mr. Monroe," she said. "Have you seen Paul? He's around here somewhere, serving drinks. I imagine you'll be eager to check up on him."

Riley reached around my waist, holding me as surely as I clamped him to my side. "Thank you. I'll look forward to seeing him."

Delia turned, and Riley inhaled quickly, his shoulders jerking.

"I received an interesting call, Mrs. Walker, regarding Paul's case. You wouldn't have any idea what it was about, would you?"

I frowned but quickly erased the expression. It wouldn't

do letting these people know I had no idea what my mate was talking about. He hadn't mentioned Paul or his report to me.

"I'm not sure what you're asking, Mr. Monroe," Delia said, and even though I didn't know the whole situation, I *knew* she was lying. Seemed like I'd be asking Riley some questions when we got home.

Delia retreated after that, and other than a wave that Aver ignored, the other Elder families let us be.

We ended up closest to the piano. The woman worked the keys beautifully, playing pleasant winter melodies at a level that still allowed conversation. I mostly liked how the sound muffled our huddled conversation.

"Okay, we came. We've been seen here. Let's leave," Wyatt said.

"I'm with Wyatt," Aver agreed.

But Nash looked to me. "Branson?"

I'd seen no sign of Nana, though I wasn't sure if she'd come. This sort of celebration wasn't her thing, and she refused to dress up for any occasion, much less to impress strangers. "It looks like some people are leaving."

Delia had crossed the room to say goodbye to one of the human men in Alpha Walker's posse. She looked back at me and Riley with a smile. What had she planned?

When they left, I took stock of who remained. The shifter representatives and everyone from this pack. But other than Riley, there wasn't another human in attendance. Alpha Walker clapped his hands, and the entire level went immediately silent. "Shall we, as they say, switch gears?" he asked, garnering pleasant laughter.

The servants flooded the floors, though their trays held more shifter-friendly foods. Steak tartare and crackers with raw salmon. The party guests accepted the new fare with enthusiasm, while me and my cousins shuffled Riley closer to the door.

"Mr. Monroe!" a young man said, breaking from the throng with a tray of champagne in his hand. "Elder Walker said you were here."

"Paul," Riley said warmly. "I've been wondering about you. I kept leaving messages at the number you gave me. I heard back about those classes—"

"You don't have to worry about that, Mr. Monroe. They're teaching me here," he said proudly.

Riley looked him over. I'm sure he didn't mean to be rude, but to him, it likely looked like Paul was being taught how to be a servant. "When we spoke, you mentioned an interest in welding," Riley said.

"Oh, I know, but I have time later to learn that. I promise I am happy here, Mr. Monroe," Paul said, letting some of the hurt show.

Riley stepped forward, likely in a rush to make up for his slip. "I'm sorry, Paul. I am glad if you are. But do you like it here? Really?" He sounded so doubtful, anyone listening in might take offense. Unfortunately, everyone had stopped to hear the lone human speak.

"I'm sure we don't know what you mean," Delia replied loudly. "Why shouldn't Paul be happy here, *Mr. Monroe?*" That was the second time she refused to call Riley by the title he should've been addressed by while on pack lands. I hadn't thought to push it at first. I always hated how an omega lost their identity, becoming only so-and-so's omega, but now it was clear she meant it as a slight.

"I have claimed Riley as my omega, Mother. You will address him as such."

She lifted her chin, peering down her nose. "Of course,

dear. I'm just not used to it at all. I'll have my butler make a note."

As she lifted her hand to beckon her butler, the man rushed over and, in his hurry, knocked into Paul, who fell forward. The flutes on his tray splashed forward, covering Riley in champagne. He jumped back, likely out of instinct, but the floor was wet and his feet slipped out from under him.

I lunged for him, managing to catch him just before his butt landed on the ground. I'd succeeded in cushioning his fall, but not much else.

"What is going on here?" Alpha Walker asked, breaking to the front of the crowd. He spotted Riley on the ground, and before anyone could speak, he reached down to help him.

In any other case, this would've been seen as a show of respect. Though permission was needed to touch Riley under casual circumstances, he was within his right to help Riley from the ground. Except, the moment Alpha Walker gripped Riley's hand, his face relaxed before he said, "I regret it all." Alpha Walker gasped and released Riley. The calm that had taken him over cleared, replaced by something dark and vulnerable. He blinked, growling low in the next moment as his eyes narrowed, glowing yellow in his anger.

I saw it happening as if in slow motion. Alpha Walker stretched his arm, striking Riley at his chest hard enough to send him sliding a few feet back.

I dropped to his side while Nash, Wyatt, and Aver lowered into crouches, surrounding us from all sides. The wall protected our back from the packed room. Snarls echoed off the walls. A swarm of shifters surrounded Alpha Walker. They'd give their lives for him if it came to that.

Only the shifter representatives stood to the side, motionless. This wasn't their fight. Grandfather wasn't their Alpha to protect, but this was all information they'd be bringing back to their regions, and I believed it was that which spurred Grandfather to brush off his suit and raise his hands, demanding silence.

Except silence had come a split second before Alpha Walker had demanded it. Everyone still stared at us, so I hadn't noticed the subtle change as the shifters stopped growling and gawked instead. I looked around for what had gotten their attention.

"Branson," Aver hissed. "His stomach."

In the commotion, Riley's already too-big jacket had popped open, showing his front. The cummerbund had given up the fight, and the white dress shirt, soaked by a tray of champagne and transparent, clung to his stomach that was both too firm and too round to mistake.

"What is this?" Delia hissed, but she was the only one.

The others whispered with each other. I helped Riley to his feet, my cousins rejoined our sides, and we stood as a united front against the rest of the pack.

"I'll break the window, you throw Riley through, and I'll catch him," Wyatt said, but Nash grabbed his arm before he could put that plan into motion.

No one seemed to know what to do. They still stared, stuck in that half-alert state where they were sort of sure there wasn't danger, but now they didn't know what they were looking at.

I wished Nana was there, if only so I could ask her for advice, but as the pack continued to stare, I felt the answer come to me as clearly as if she'd spoken the words in my ear.

"My omega is pregnant. He is male. He is blessed. Please, let us leave." I didn't speak to one person—not Alpha

Walker, not the Elders—but to the pack. We'd need them all to stand aside to get out of here anyway.

Slowly, they began to move, splitting open and then dropping to their knees in respect.

The word *blessed* became like a chant, mumbled throughout the crowd that had grown since I last looked at them all. More poured in from outside. Every servant lingered, including Paul, whose mouth hung open. Like a wave, they parted and dropped, bowing their heads as the four of us guided Riley. The Elders stood in the back, upright and watching everything happen with calculating gazes.

I could see the door when I heard Alpha Walker speak. "Part for the blessed omega. Our pack has been given a gift this winter solstice." He spoke like he'd planned this all along, though it was clear to anyone watching he hadn't. I didn't care how much face he needed to save. I just wanted to get my mate out.

I couldn't say this was a mistake, not when so many looked up at Riley with almost as much devotion as I had for him.

Someone must have alerted the valet because our car was ready for us at the end of the driveway. We'd walked the path, forgoing the carriage, and though I didn't quite understand how this had happened and I couldn't begin to ponder the ramifications of this night, I sent up a silent thank you when we were all in the car, driving away.

"What the fuck was that?" Nash asked.

I felt like the question summed up what we were all wondering.

No one answered him. None of us knew what this meant. But I was beginning to realize that after tonight, everything was going to change.

20

RILEY

My heart pounded, and my hands shook. I stuffed them under my legs to both get them to stop and so Branson wouldn't notice.

I didn't think any of the guys realized that they hadn't stopped growling the entire way back to their house. We were almost there now.

"I'll build us a schedule. Until then, I'll take first watch. Wyatt, can you take mornings when you get back from work? Aver, you'll be from Wyatt's shift to midday, Nash, you're afternoons, and I'll fill in every moment in between." Branson spoke like the four of them had been communicating the whole ride.

Who knew? Maybe they had, and their growls held more meaning than I understood.

"Whoa, whoa, what are we talking about?" I asked, shrugging off the jacket. It hung open anyway and had done a horrible job of concealing my bump. I rubbed my stomach, picturing those men and women kneeling as we passed.

"Guarding you," Branson replied. His nostrils flared as his eyes darted back and forth across the dark road.

I frowned. I was used to being surrounded by these four, but guarding me sounded entirely more invasive. "What about work?"

"You'll have to quit," Branson replied, and I didn't know if he'd never understood my work or if he was so stressed he didn't realize how insensitive he was being.

"I can't quit, Branson."

"You would've quit anyway once the baby came," he said.

I would have? We hadn't discussed this. "Branson, I love my work. I knew there would be some changes, but I thought I'd work remotely a few days a week, not quit. I just took this position. I've finally got organizations working with me."

"And the person they hire to replace you will pick up where you left off, Riley. Were you or were you not just at that party where we nearly didn't walk out?"

It had been an anxiety-inducing time, but I hadn't once thought they wouldn't allow us to leave. Was I being naive, or was Branson overreacting? I wasn't sure. The kneeling and bowing, while odd, hadn't felt aggressive.

"And what was that question to my mom? About Paul's report?" Branson snapped.

I sucked in a deep breath and rubbed my tummy like a worry stone. The motion soothed me, but I still didn't appreciate the way Branson asked, like I'd hidden something from him. "I didn't tell you because it had nothing to do with you, Branson. Paul's case is between me and Paul. Apparently, your mother doesn't understand that either, since she obviously pulled some strings and tried to get them to put the heat on me and alter the report. I won't." My tone sounded like a petulant child, but I didn't care. "I won't be bullied any more than I will be used."

"Riley." Branson looked at me through the rear view. "I'm on your side. Always. But you don't understand our world. My mother pulled strings. You had that part right. She got someone from the government to look into you. We know that since you were contacted. She must have called your old office first. She wouldn't have wasted a favor unless she was pushed. Which must also mean..."

That she knew everything about me. The old me.

Instantly, I thought of Blaine. She couldn't have dug that deep, could she? If she'd found Blaine, though, and had spoken to him, then she knew more about me than even Branson. My alpha was right. I hadn't thought it through the way he would have if I'd told him.

"You're scaring him," Aver whispered.

"No, it's okay, Aver." My forehead wrinkled, pushing my brow down. "I..."

Branson pulled into the driveway, dark and solemn compared to the one that had circled the main house. No, I wouldn't start comparing my life to that horrendous display behind us.

We'd survived the party, mostly, and now I was exhausted. Branson helped me to bed, tucking me in before saying he would stay up with the guys to arrange everything. I wouldn't have to work the next day anyway, so nothing needed to be decided there. Branson was going to be disappointed, though. I wouldn't stop doing my job. I was finally starting to make a difference.

I slept in short bursts, waking up in a cold sweat when my nightmares became too intense. I couldn't remember what I dreamt. It had been all loud noises and flashes of color, like I was looking at the world through fuzzy eyes and from a different angle.

Morning came quickly, and yet it felt like it took forever.

My eyelids were heavy when I finally pulled myself from the empty bed. I wondered if my dreams would've been so bad if Branson had ever made it under the covers.

He'd woken me once in the wee hours to say that Aver was on watch. Nash was ready to pick up after Aver had to leave, and he asked me to stay in the house.

I looked at the letter's sign-off, a rushed *Love, Branson* scribbled along the bottom. That was the only part of his note that implied he cared for me. The rest was written matter-of-factly.

When I stumbled into the kitchen, searching for a glass of water, Nash nodded his hello.

"Where's Aver?" I asked.

"He had to leave early. I'm here all day."

"Maybe we could go into Walkerton. I wanted to get some baby things."

"Nope," Nash replied plainly. "Branson said you're supposed to stay here."

Anger flared in me, and I had to remind myself Nash was only following orders from my bossy, overbearing, controlling, insensitive—

"I can make you waffles, though," Nash added.

I sat down with a hmph. "Is there whipped cream?"

Nash smiled. "There is." He got to work, mixing the batter and heating the skillet.

Around fifteen minutes later, I had a plate of waffles with enough whipped cream piled on top that I didn't need to lean over to take a lick.

Nash smirked and handed me a napkin as something at his waist began to beep insistently.

"What's that?"

"Shit, my beeper. There's a call at the firehouse." He pressed a button and read the small screen. "It's big. They're calling in everyone who is available. Fuck!" He paced from the table to the back doors.

"Go, Nash. It will be fine," I said. His pacing was making me dizzy, and really, I would be fine a few hours alone. Especially in a home as well monitored as this one.

"Branson would kill me."

"So tell him. Or I will, once you've left. What do they say about asking permission?"

His lips stretched wide. "You're trouble, Riley, and you're trying to get me in trouble."

"I'm not. I'm just a grown man who can handle a few hours alone. Go, save lives. Be a hero." I stuffed a large bite of waffle and cream in my mouth and chewed slowly.

Nash wavered seconds longer, but I knew the urge to go rescue someone would be too strong. He grabbed his keys. "I'll text him. He'll probably rush right back anyway."

"What's he doing?"

"Finishing up the Forstein addition. I want you to lock the doors. Don't let anyone who isn't ruggedly handsome inside."

I laughed and covered my mouth before bits of waffle flung out. "Will do. Go. I mean it."

Nash left in the next moment, and though I knew he'd texted Branson, I enjoyed the silence.

For a whole ten minutes.

I'd just finished my waffles and was running water over the plate, as well as picking up Nash's mess, when there was a loud knock at the door. Nash must've secured it closed from the inside.

"Sorry, babe. Nash said I can only open the door for the ruggedly handsome," I said as I walked toward the front door.

The frosted glass obscured the image of the man on the

other side, but I knew at once that it wasn't Branson. My steps slowed, and my nostrils flared. I smelled cigarette smoke as clearly as if there were someone smoking right next to me. I stopped, still five feet from the door. There was a camera on the porch, one of many around the house, but I didn't know how to access it.

"Who's there?"

The person didn't answer, but they did move. I watched the shadowy figure walk from the front door, following the wall of the house to the dining room, where Blaine peered in through the dining room windows like he'd stepped out of my worst fears.

So much had happened, I'd been so caught up with the pack, I'd forgotten Blaine, and that pesky habit he had of wanting to kill me.

My heart beat in my throat as I tried to remember where I'd left my phone. Branson was on his way, right? Nash had said he would be. Even if help was coming that didn't help me now. "I don't know how you found me here but you need to go!" I shouted, trying to sound fierce.

Blaine just smiled. He looked so normal from the outside. Like a guy on his way to brunch. Too late, I'd learned of the darkness he hid within. "She said you'd be alone. Snooty bitch. I didn't know if I could trust her." Though he spoke from outside the house, I heard his words clearly.

"Who? Delia?" I cursed myself. I needed to keep Blaine talking. And preferably on the outside of the house. This situation was the exact thing Branson had worried about the night before. I hated to admit that time, and the Walker cousins, had lulled me into a sense of security.

Blaine didn't answer my question. He just moved his

jacket aside to flash the gun tucked into his waistband. "Let me in, Riley."

That sounded like a horrible idea. I cleared my throat. As long as there was a barrier between us, I was safe. He had a gun, but I could hide deeper in the house. If he tried to break in, the alarms would sound and the Walker cousins as well as Maslow and whoever else on duty would rush to my rescue. If he was working for Delia, then Blaine had to know that. All I had to do was wait. Blaine would still be looking for a way in by the time Branson—

Blaine lifted something small that he held between his fingers. It glinted in the cold sunlight. A key.

I turned, running to the first spot I thought of, the place that I felt safest. I slammed Branson's door shut, looking for something to drag in front of the door when I remembered it locked. I flipped the switch, turning and panting as I strained to hear signs that Blaine had gotten in.

I needed a weapon. No. I needed to hide. But what if I hid and he found me without a weapon? I looked around the room, but other than Branson's nail clippers, there wasn't a single thing with a sharp edge. There certainly weren't any guns. My phone trilled, and I jumped.

Think, Riley, shit! You're acting too stupid to live right now!

I lunged for the phone and answered the incoming call.

"Nash just called. I'm almost there, babe—"

"Blaine is here! He has a key and a gun!"

Branson growled. "Where are you?"

"In your bedroom, but—"

Loud footsteps sounded from down the hall. I didn't know why I could hear it so clearly, but that wasn't really the thing I was focusing on at the moment. "He's inside," I squeaked.

"Where are you hiding?" Blaine called out in a singsong tone.

"Get in the closet. There's a small door that leads to the ducts. Crawl in."

I ran to the closet, flinging open the door and pushing aside the clothes that blocked the opening. The small door might've been a tight squeeze before I'd been pregnant. Now, it might as well have been the eye of a needle. "I won't fit!"

"You have to, babe. You have to hide. I'm five minutes away."

I heard the engine roaring as he pushed the truck to its limits.

Meanwhile, Blaine had gotten to Branson's door. He knocked politely. "It didn't ever have to be like this, Riley. If only you knew how to keep your mouth closed." It sounded like he tapped the gun against the door instead of his fist. "I never had to look for you, did I? Just wait until you blabbed loud enough that you annoyed the right people to contact me to take care of you. I don't know what you did to that uppity chick, but she sure does hate you."

Awesome, Apparently, Delia and Blaine had bonded over their extreme abhorrence of me.

"My mate is on his way. He will kill you if you are still here when he gets home," I yelled back.

Blaine responded by shooting the lock on the door.

I screamed and stumbled back. Fear enveloped me like thick fog. I couldn't think. I couldn't move. I fell on my butt and stayed there as my limbs seemed to tangle under me, unfamiliar and awkward.

Blaine kicked the door open, but instead of raising his gun at where I was on the ground, he stared at me.

Why was he staring at me? There was nothing

between us but a few feet of carpet. I wasn't in a hurry to see what life held on the other side, and my heart broke for the pain this would cause Branson, but I didn't understand the way he lingered, confused like he didn't recognize me.

"Where'd he go, pooch?" Blaine asked me.

What? I opened my mouth to say the word on my mind, but a weird grunting noise was all I heard. When I tried again, the grunt became a bark, and I looked down at my body.

"Settle down, buddy, or you'll have to take the eternal sleep," Blaine continued, his voice high-pitched, like he was talking to a baby. "Where is he, huh? Where are you, Riley?" he called over my head.

Where my hands should have been, I had paws. In fact, I had four paws. I also had long legs covered in fur. I turned my head to the mirror Branson had installed and nearly fainted.

I was a—

"Riley!" Branson screamed, and I darted to him, not knowing what the hell was going on but sure that if I could get to Branson, he would know.

Blaine jumped back, and I darted in the space that he created, skidding over the hardwood floor on four legs. I fell when I tried to turn and couldn't get traction again, making me slip over the floor like a deer on a frozen lake. But I could smell Branson now, more than I'd ever been able to in my life. He looked at me, and the fury cleared for half a second, replaced by utter confusion.

"Riley?" he said, putting two and two together way faster than Blaine or me.

I yelped to confirm just as Blaine came up behind me. He had his gun raised and pointed to Branson. I spun around, letting loose a growling noise that felt great rumbling through my chest.

"Nice dog. I'm here for my boyfriend. Seen him?" Blaine asked, believing his weapon made him tough.

He didn't have any idea whose house he'd broken into.

In the distance, I heard more tires squealing and assumed that was the others, called back after my frantic talk with Branson. I didn't know why Blaine didn't take that moment to run. Couldn't he hear the guys coming?

"I know you," Branson said, stepping first to my side and then in front of me.

I tried to scurry past, but he gave me a look that clearly said that I was to stay.

"Riley's told me all about your line of work. You should turn yourself in. They'll be nicer to you in prison."

"Nicer than what?"

"Than me," Branson said before shifting. He dropped to all fours, hair raised, ears flat.

Blaine stumbled back, but Branson was on top of him before he could fire a shot. He dug into Blaine's body, blood soaking his clothes as Branson kicked away the gun with his powerful back legs. Blaine tried to fight back, but he was no match for Branson's teeth and claws.

Aver, Nash, and Wyatt burst in at that moment, rushing forward to separate Branson from Blaine, who had stopped screaming and lay on his side in a fetal position, whimpering with his head in his hands.

"The cops are on their way," Aver explained. "Better dress down."

Branson stalked to me, and I cowered back, though I wasn't sure why. It was as if something inside me immediately recognized the alpha inside of Branson. I ducked down, keeping my eyes averted as I followed my instincts.

Branson licked my face, and I looked up at him. *You're okay, mate. You're safe.* I heard his voice in my head, not spoken in English, but in a language I understood just the same.

He closed his eyes and shifted, straightening into the form of a man again.

That had looked easy, but when I tried, I squeezed my eyes shut, only to open them and still be a wolf.

I whimpered.

"That's Riley?" Aver asked. "How? He was a human, right?"

"Shit, the cops are here. Get the trash up," Wyatt snarled. His fists were clenched, and I suspected he was disappointed at having missed the action. "How is Riley a wolf right now?"

No one answered him. I figured no one knew. I didn't even know, but I couldn't very well shift while Aver went to the door. Sheriff Maslow waited with one of his deputies and Aver explained that they'd been broken into by an armed man.

My ears perked at the sight of Jake, who looked at me and then over to Blaine. "Where's Riley?" he asked with concern.

"Out," Branson replied. "He took a walk, thankfully."

Jake scowled. "He's on a walk? Right now? He didn't hear all this happening?"

"We own a lot of land here, Sheriff," Branson replied, and though I felt bad for Jake's confusion, I was glad when he continued to Blaine.

He had him cuffed, dragging him out of the house. Once outside, Blaine began to babble about men turning into wolves, and I winced, but neither Jake, nor the deputies who had come to assist him, seemed to be paying attention.

He sounded completely crazy. I just happened to know that he wasn't.

Jake returned, getting statements from everyone. While he'd been escorting Blaine to the car, Branson and the others had plotted. Wyatt gave his statement first. He'd shown up right when Branson had overpowered the intruder along with the help of his new dog, which was probably what Blaine was babbling about—according to Wyatt. Then he excused himself and turned to me.

"C'mon, Riley—"

Jake stopped writing and looked up, his eyes dropping on me again. "You named the dog Riley?"

"Came already named," Wyatt said. "Weird, huh? Only a little confusing." He kept walking and snapped his fingers, a sign I guessed that meant follow.

I rolled my eyes and stepped forward but froze when I realized Jake had watched that all happen. "Strange dog," he commented. "You know, if he's part wolf, you have to disclose that to Animal Control."

"Jake, we were robbed today. I'm very shaken up," Wyatt replied.

I hurried after him before Wyatt could say anything else.

The plan had been for him to take me down the hallway to Branson's room. We waited there while Jake continued getting statements before promising to keep us informed. Until today, I truly believed Blaine thought he was the biggest, baddest thing around. Being forcefully shown how wrong he was hadn't sat well with him and he tried repeatedly to explain how quickly he'd been overtaken. Except, he sounded deranged in the process. Add that to the gun Maslow had bagged as evidence and Jake didn't see there being any problems.

Maslow sent the deputy back to the station with Blaine, made sure Branson knew what to expect next and left.

Five minutes later, the four cousins stood in Branson's room, all huddled around me with varying thinking faces.

I sat on the floor on my haunches. It was comfortable, but I wanted to be a human again. I wanted to kiss Branson and hug all the guys and thank them with my words. I wanted to know how I was a freaking wolf right now, but mostly, I wanted to know how the hell I was going to change back.

21

BRANSON

"He's a cute wolf," Aver said, scratching Riley affectionately behind the ears.

Riley looked both annoyed and overjoyed by the gesture. He'd been a wolf for two hours now. No matter what we tried, he couldn't seem to relax enough to shift back. Not surprising since this shouldn't have been possible in the first place. I'd never heard of a shifter learning they were a shifter this late in life. And I'd been positive he was human, one hundred percent. He had other abilities that most humans didn't have too, and I was sure this had something to do with that.

"Had any of you suspected this?" I asked the others. I'd asked something similar several times before, and the answer was always the same. None of them had thought Riley was anything but a human.

This had to be related to the pregnancy. We'd wondered how that could've been possible. Maybe this change, this ability to shift, had always been there, waiting for Riley to experience an emotion extreme enough to spur the change. Younger shifters often had trouble regulating their transformations, and while Riley should've been well past the age where that was still a problem, it was the best guess we could come up with.

In the back of my mind, I worried about what this meant for the baby, but shifter mothers could shift without harm to their child. I thought back to my younger years, trying to recall any tricks I'd used to help me master my shifts. As an alpha, so much shifter stuff came naturally and easily. "Maybe if you pictured your happy place," I suggested.

"He's pictured a thousand happy places," Nash added.

Aver pulled out his phone. "That's it. I'm calling the big guns."

──────

Nana showed up an hour later. We'd coaxed Riley into the living room, and he sat on the couch waiting for her when she arrived.

"My dear boy," Nana said, sitting next to him without a word from or to any of us. "It's okay. You're okay." She slid her palm down his head, and Riley's form blurred, solidifying as a man in the next moment. "Shh, there you are," she said, hugging him as fiercely as he hugged her.

Riley stood and reached for me. I was there as he sobbed into my chest, letting loose all his fear, worry, and anger. "Your mother!" he snarled.

"Now he sounds like a Walker," Wyatt quipped.

Nana shot him a dirty look.

I was thankful for it but only because I would deal with my mother in the only way she would understand. With money. Or, rather, taking hers. My father had always set aside a lump of her fortune, intending for me to take over the pack and the business. I'd left both control of the company and the money when I left the pack. I could see now the mistake that was. She wouldn't be destitute, and she wouldn't be in jail, which was where she belonged after basically hiring a man to kill my mate, but I would make her life miserable until my mate was satisfied.

"I love you, Branson," Riley said finally. "All of you, I love you. Thank you."

The boys blushed, but Nana nodded.

"Blessed," she whispered with a smile.

"Did you know this would happen?" I asked.

"I hoped," Nana replied.

"And you didn't think to mention it?" Riley cried out. "A heads-up would be great next time. I thought I'd gone insane. Actually, I thought I was dead first, then insane."

I tightened my arm over Riley's side. I didn't want him to ever feel like that again.

"Do you think the baby is okay?" he asked.

Nana rushed to reassure him. "The blessed child is fine, my dear. Shifting actually helps strengthen him. You should try many more times before he is born. Though you are running out of time."

He was? It hadn't seemed that long since he'd been testing himself on every pregnancy test available on the island.

I looked to Riley and recognized the same fear I'd felt. But there was also excitement.

Nana left, claiming we'd pulled her from an important task.

"More important than helping me change back, I guess," Riley muttered as we closed the door.

He'd cursed my mother a while ago. Now he was

confused by Nana's antics. It seemed Wyatt's joke was truer than I'd thought.

My mate really was becoming a Walker.

————

"THE SHAREHOLDERS HAVE BEEN NOTIFIED, but they expressed concern regarding the dual leadership," my secretary said. I'd reached out to my lawyers the next business day and got the pieces moving to claim my half of the company.

Wyatt still thought it was a bad idea, but Aver agreed it was the only punishment we could hope to give her, and it would hurt worse than anything else.

"There is no dual leadership," I explained. "My mother has always been a silent owner. That cannot and will not change. She has no authority."

He confirmed the date and time of the next meeting where I would introduce how things were going to be changing. Since the idea struck me, I'd looked into the workings of my father's corporations. They operated under antiquated standards, doing only what law required them when it came to greenhouse emissions or protecting the environment. Walker Construction had made steps to go green whenever a project allowed for it.

It might mean a loss in profits, at first, but I could afford it and got a vindictive joy at how this would all affect Delia.

Hanging up, I tiptoed past the dining room where Riley sat with Paul. He'd asked to meet him to explain what he'd said, and I'd been successful in not lingering outside the door to eavesdrop the whole time. I'd appointed Wyatt, who Paul had been more than happy to see again.

"Thank you, Paul, for meeting me and listening to my

apology. I'm getting used to how things are around here, and I let my bias blind me in regard to how it might help you."

"That's okay, Branson Walker's omega," Paul replied. The title was proper, but his tone was still casual. "Can I... is it okay if I ask you a question now?"

I tensed.

"Sure," Riley said.

"You're really pregnant with Branson Walker's child? But you were male?"

"Seems so."

I peeked in as Riley leaned back to show off his belly. He'd grown rapidly in the weeks since the solstice, but without unexpected pain. Nana hadn't been at all surprised with how round he'd gotten or how quickly. She seemed to think he would pop any day.

Thankfully, he still wasn't so large that a jacket couldn't cover most of his belly. He'd gone down to part-time days at the office and spent the rest of his work hours beside me in the home office. Around the house, he made no attempt to hide his bulge.

We hadn't told anyone about his shift. I wanted to find someone who had experienced the same thing before I gave the pack any more reason to focus on Riley.

"When are you due?" Paul asked. "My sister had her baby before I left. I used to help her care for him. I could help you too."

Paul was too close to Delia for me to be comfortable with that, but Riley only said, "Thank you, Paul. I'll remember that."

I knocked softly on the door.

Paul jumped to his feet, his head bowed. I didn't address it. Ever since the solstice, things had gotten weird with the pack. The Elders treated us all the same, but the pack members had thawed. The day before, I'd found a basket of baked goods on the porch that smelled of the pack. And it hadn't even been poisoned.

"It's lunch time, babe."

Riley smiled, and while I hoped his happiness had to do with my presence, I knew it was partly at the mention of food. "Music to my ears. And it is good to see you out of the office. Everything sorted?"

I nodded, hating I had to wonder about Paul's allegiance. He had been happy to come over, and the invitation was Riley's idea, but I would be stupid not to suspect she'd at least coached him or told him to report everything that was said.

Riley stood, gripping the back of the chair in the next moment. His face went white as beads of sweat suddenly appeared on his forehead. "I don't feel so good..." he moaned, tossing his head to the side before throwing up all over the carpet. He grabbed his stomach. "Branson?"

He was in my arms in the next moment. "Paul, use my phone to call Nana Walker," I directed as I carried Riley to my bedroom. I'd been mentally preparing for this moment for weeks, and the words tumbled from me as if by rote. "Tell her it is Riley. Then call my cousins. Paul!"

He'd been staring at Riley, but hearing his name shouted made him jump. He looked around, "Where's your phone?"

"In my office, thank you."

I brought Riley into the bedroom, working to keep my hands from shaking. My mate needed me calm. This felt early. But everything with this pregnancy had defied expectations. I needed to keep a level head. Nana would come; she'd figure out what to do.

But the moment I set Riley on the bed, he cried out,

shifting into a wolf in the very next second. He'd yelped, somewhere between a shout and howl before going stiff. His head dropped to the pillow, his eyes closed.

I reached for him, unsure what I was going to do while my heart raced. Minutes ago he'd been talking, and now he wasn't moving. I bent over him my mind buzzing like angry wasps. Adrenaline made me shake. I examined his body, stretching him out of the fetal position when I spotted a small ball of fur, curled against Riley's stiff, furry body.

"Babe? Babe!"

Riley didn't move as I pulled the tiny puppy, so small his eyes were closed, from the mattress. It squeaked and wiggled, crying out for its father.

"Is that the baby?" Paul asked from the doorway. "Riley is a shifter?"

I didn't have time to answer these questions. Riley still hadn't moved. I dropped, holding the puppy in my hands as I petted Riley's head. "Riley, babe, please, wake up. I need you. Please." I kissed him, feeling odd until I scolded myself. This was Riley. This was my mate. He needed me to heal him.

The puppy squirmed and whined, and I brought him up to Riley's face. I was too stunned to put words to what had happened. Riley had shifted, and the baby appeared outside of his body. Was that supposed to happen? It wasn't the normal birthing process, but Riley was the most unique pregnancy I'd experienced.

I blocked out any noise that wasn't Riley or the puppy. I heard the puppy's heartbeat, rapid but alive. Riley's was slow and growing slower by the moment.

"Riley? Riley!"

Someone grabbed me, and I growled, baring my teeth. But Nana just blinked back, calm pouring from her. She looked at the puppy before looking over to Riley and frowning. "Be with him, Branson. Be his alpha," she urged, but I didn't know what she was talking about. Be an alpha? My mate was dying, and I was helpless to stop it. "Go!" she yelled, shocking me into motion.

I dropped back down to Riley's head, whispering whatever came to mind. Should I shift? Would that help? It hadn't before. "Riley, our baby is here, and it's a boy." *And also a puppy.* "Riley, please. I was so angry without you. I didn't realize my anger until you. But you've changed me. You've changed us all. Please, Riley."

I thought I heard someone sob, and I told myself it was Paul. If Nana was crying, I didn't know what I would do.

Riley's heart rate hadn't changed.

Tears filled my eyes, and I blinked them away, not caring who saw me as I kissed Riley's muzzle. "Please, my omega, come back." I kept kissing him, my eyes closed. When I felt him kiss me back with real human lips, my eyes flew open, and I looked into Riley's drowsy gaze.

"What happened?" he slurred.

I set our child on his chest, and Riley peered at him curiously. "We got a dog?"

"He's our child. Our son."

Riley smiled as the confusion cleared. If our spots were reversed I would've still had questions, but Riley just gazed at the tiny figure. "My son." He cuddled the puppy close, and I watched as the newborn dog transformed into a newborn baby.

A screaming newborn baby.

I hugged them both, pulling them into an embrace I wouldn't soon let them free of. When I did, Nana came in, checking over father and son. She wrote down the baby's measurements on his chart.

"That was so weird," Riley mumbled, cuddling his son the moment Nana handed him back. "How did I have the baby? *Where?*" Riley asked while Nana turned her attention to him.

A few minutes later and she stood, confident that other than nearly dying, Riley had experienced no other complications. His skin color had deepened but I wouldn't soon forget the powerlessness of listening to his heart beat slow.

When Aver, Nash, and Wyatt got home a while later, each sat in the room, content not to say much, but to stare at son and father.

"Congratulations," Aver said at some point a while later.

Nana got trays of food with Paul's help and brought them into the bedroom. I didn't think anyone was in a big hurry to leave.

"He definitely looks like a Wyatt," Wyatt said around the bite of sandwich he'd taken.

Paul chirped up. "I think that's a great name."

That stupid bet.

"I agree," Riley said before I could speak. "Branson Evelyn Aver Nash Wyatt Walker Junior." He looked up at me with such expectant joy that I couldn't bear to contradict him.

"It's a mouthful," Aver said.

"It's perfect," I said, kissing baby and Dad on the head.

Eventually, Paul sat down on the floor with Nana, and we all lingered, letting time pass without us. I kept Riley's hand in mine. He'd almost died today. He'd been in danger far more times than I was comfortable with.

"How are you doing?" Riley whispered as Nash and Aver argued the best way to change a diaper. They'd already planned to time each other to see who's method was fastest.

"Better now. You scared me, omega."

"I'm sorry, alpha. I'll try not to again." His gaze drifted to the others in the room and he looked at them each, his smile growing by the second. "This is perfect."

"This moment?" I asked, my own lips curling in response to his joy.

"Everything," Riley whispered. "I love you," he said, his eyes drifting closed.

We'd have to explain the baby at some point and my mother would surely retaliate after what I'd done. The pack was still a mess and I had no idea what news of Riley's spontaneous shift would do once the information spread.

Riley would have to take some time off work, though he already had a plan worked out with his office. There was nothing I could do about Paul and what he would say when he returned to pack lands, but in that moment, as my mate and son slumbered, I didn't worry about the pack either.

When the baby started to cry, Nana made him a bottle and showed Riley how to hold it at the right angle to make sure he didn't suck down too much gas. After, he lifted the baby to his shoulder, burping him like he'd done it a thousand times before.

"I've seen movies," he said to my impressed stare before settling against my side again.

Still, we lingered. No one was in a hurry to move on, to face the new problems that would definitely come now that the pack oscillated between hating and worshiping us.

As the sun set outside and people began to yawn, I half expected them to break apart. But Nana ducked out to grab more food, returning with steaming bowls and several blankets. The guys all accepted one, with a pillow.

Paul fell asleep first. Then Riley and Nash, followed by Wyatt and Aver. Soon, it was just me and Nana awake.

"What do the spirits whisper to you now, Nana?" I asked, staring at my child and mate, both sleeping soundly.

She sighed peacefully. "They're quiet. This is what they were telling me about."

"So they have no more to say?" I asked. That sounded good. A little peace and quiet.

"For now," she said.

When I looked back over at her, her eyes were closed. I let her rest, leaning my head back as I kept watch. I'd known these people were my family, my cousins and Nana, but it had taken Riley to teach me we were a pack. We didn't have Elder houses. We didn't have an Alpha leader. But we had each other. And while they slept, I would protect them.

The End

KEEP THE ROMANCE AND INTRIGUE GOING WITH HOPE!

Nash Walker is a simple wolf. His days are spent at the firehouse and he never has trouble finding someone to fill his nights. He isn't ashamed to admit he has an amazing body and though his cousins tease him for his hero complex, he does save lives. He's a popular guy on the isolated island he calls home and certainly doesn't need to be around anyone who isn't thrilled to be in his presence.

Until he meets Phineas.

Phineas is a nerd through and through. Not just a nerd, but as far as Nash is concerned, an angry one. All of the traits that normally make men fall at Nash's feet have no effect on Phineas, and though his head tells him there are plenty of fish in the sea, Nash's wolf only wants him. There's a sadness in Phineas that calls to Nash.

Phineas is used to being invisible. No one cares when he walks into a room and he prefers it that way. People in his life have a habit of getting hurt so he lives alone. All his friends are online where they can be safe from his curse. His touch heals, but not without making sure a price is paid. But when Phineas has a problem he asks Nash—the insanely gorgeous fireman who is everywhere Phineas turns —for help. He might as well learn what he can before Nash comes to his senses.

Meanwhile, a serial arsonist is targeting buildings in Walker County, particularly on pack lands. As much as Nash hates the idea of helping the wolf pack that he once called his, he must do his job. When the danger spills to the other side of the island, particularly at his human's door, Nash knows he must find the culprit or he might not ever have a chance to truly claim his mate.

Hope is the second book in the Wolves of Walker County with steam, humor, magic, and intrigue as well as a second surprise pregnancy that will continue to change everything. For maximum enjoyment, this quartet should be read in order.

Get it today!

Chapter One
NASH

I needed to get laid.

That was the thought that carried with me as I jumped over a long log, covered in moss, that must have fallen between my run the day before and now. Every day, my runs got longer. My regular five turned into my regular ten, and now I was up before the baby—if it happened to sleep at all that night—putting in fifteen miles before most people were even awake.

My tennis shoe landed in mud, and I cursed but kept moving forward. These shoes were circling the drain anyhow. Maybe I'd take the ferry off Walker and go to Seattle for the weekend. I'd find a larger selection out there.

Of shoes and of willing men to bury myself in. It was clear I needed a break, something to help work the edge off.

I broke through the line of trees to the yard of my house, experiencing that familiar wave of pride when I looked at the sturdy walls and windows that gleamed in the morning sun. The sprawling, modern log cabin sat directly where the Lynx River emptied into Walker Bay. We'd made that, the four Walker cousins. It had been our first home away from the only home we'd ever known. Branson and Aver had done most of the planning and preparing, leaving Wyatt and myself to do the grunt work, but that didn't change anything.

We'd built that home when we'd had nothing but each other—and Nana.

It looked big, but not when you considered everyone

who lived inside: four grown alpha shifters, a newly changed omega mate, and a baby.

A baby who had caused a lot of whispers on the other side of the bay.

I didn't need some asshole with a memo pad and a pencil, asking me how I felt to figure out that was the root of my recent excess energy. The nearer I got to the end of my run, the closer I was to the wraparound porch. Already, I could see a small pile forming on the mat in front of the door.

I snarled at the collection of baked goods, homemade baby toys, and clothing.

The influx of visitors and gifts was mostly Nana's doing, with all that talk of Riley, my cousin Branson's chosen omega, being *blessed*. According to her, Riley was blessed, his pregnancy was blessed, his spontaneous transformation from normal human to wolf shifter was blessed, and the wiggling bundle of poopy diapers and around-the-clock screams was blessed as well.

I supposed baby Branson wasn't so bad. He was the only child I knew to be birthed by a man via some kind of spontaneous shifter osmosis—though I was the only one who called it that. We'd all wondered *where* Riley's baby would exit his body when it became clear that the impossible was true and he was with child. As alpha wolf shifters who had been born at the same time and been tasked with battling each other to the death to discover who the pack's new leader was, the four of us cousins were used to strange. But picturing which of Riley's orifices the baby would make his debut out of had been a cause for squeamish, yet heated, debate. Whenever Riley had been out of earshot, of course.

I was glad we'd all been wrong. Even if we still didn't understand completely how it had all happened.

But now, the pack that we'd done a fan-fucking-tastic job of avoiding for over ten years was in our faces again. Not so much the elders or our grandfather, Alpha Walker, but the other shifters that belonged to the pack. They believed in that blessed business more than anyone and hadn't stopped dropping off gifts for the *blessed Walker baby* since his birth.

Ha. I was forsaken because I'd made the choice not to murder my cousins and brother, but the baby was blessed.

Jealous of a baby before seven, a new record.

I stepped over the pile of gifts instead of stomping on them. I'd have to remember I did that for the next time Aver accused me of being a selfish narcissist. I preferred the term "unarguably gorgeous" to narcissist anyway. I couldn't be selfish and be a fireman. Aver knew that. He just forgot every time I was forced to use the rest of his shitty almond milk when we were out of regular.

"Hey, Rye," I said, passing him in the living room on my way to the kitchen. I grabbed a bottle of water from the fridge and meandered back to where Riley was giving Bran Jr. his bottle. The baby suckled happily, his eyes closed.

"You're sweaty," Riley replied, eye-fucking me from top to bottom.

Maybe he wasn't eye-fucking me, since he seemed to see something in my cousin, but let's be honest, he was enjoying the show. I stuck up my foot and struck a pose.

Riley snorted. "How many miles today, Nash?" he asked as if the number would worry him.

I shrugged. I knew the number but didn't like the way the wrinkles formed between his eyebrows. He didn't need to be worrying about me when he had so much more to concern himself with. "I better shower." I spun around.

"Nash?"

My feet froze against the wood. The smarter thing would've been to go and leave Riley to care about the things that were important at the moment. But he was clearly upset, and that wouldn't change if I avoided the conversation. If anything, it would just get me yelled at later when Branson attempted to bust my balls for upsetting his mate. And I'd hate to have to kick his ass when he was just defending his mate. "Yeah?" I asked without turning.

"Are you sure you're okay with this party we're planning?"

He and Branson had decided the best way to celebrate their union and the baby was with a huge get-together. So far, the guest list was a hodgepodge of people Riley used to know, people around town, and certain shifters. "Of course."

Riley's pause told me he wasn't convinced. "Would it be easier for you if I divided our time more, some nights here, some at my apartment?"

He still had a few months left on his lease. He'd barely unpacked the first box when he'd met Branson, and the rest was history. Shame filled me. I'd made him feel unwelcome. I deserved to be yelled at. "No, Riley, you're one of us now. Not just a shifter, but a part of the family."

"So you have to endure me and the baby? That doesn't sound fair. I know you're not as on board with having an infant around."

That wasn't fair. I pitched in as often as any of the other guys—maybe not as much as Nana. But I'd changed as many diapers, fed as many bottles, and experienced as many wet burps as the other guys. I didn't have any problem with Bran Jr. Only with the attention he brought.

"I'm not saying you don't help. Branson and I couldn't do this without you guys."

"I thought you could only hear my thoughts when you

touched me." I made a lame attempt at joking to change the subject.

"I don't hear your thoughts. You speak your truth, and you're right, it is only when I touch you. You're safe from my curse, Nash."

That was a relief. I attempted to not allow that to show on my face, though. "I don't want you or the baby moving. Ever. You're staying here. Okay?"

Riley's frown didn't budge. "But..."

"No buts, and don't ask again. You'll send Branson into a tizzy. Poor fragile guy. We're out of smelling salts."

Riley snorted again while Branson walked up behind me. "What will send me into a tizzy?" he asked, passing me without a glance and making a beeline to his mate and son. He kissed both, his boxers hanging indecently low on his hips as he whispered something I was glad I couldn't hear.

I didn't need nor want someone to whisper endless declarations of love. Now, if they wanted to whisper all the dirty things they wanted me to do to them, that was a different story. "I'm going to Seattle this weekend. Try not to freak out."

Branson just stared at me. "So? Go to Seattle. Have fun. Don't get arrested."

"There's another pile of gifts from the pack outside," I said, watching a meaningful look pass between Riley and Branson. "That's all I'm saying." I lifted my hands in surren- der. "There is no judgment assigned to the message. Just they are there. Okay?"

I left for my room before those two could put their heads together and decide more things that might be wrong with me. I had no problem with the baby. I never brought my dates home anyway. But I hated how much more the pack across the bay was in our lives now because they believed Bran Jr. was blessed. We'd left those people, as well as our way of life, behind when the four of us had left the pack.

Now, I couldn't turn without the pack inserting itself back into my life in some way—without my consent.

My happy place was wherever the pack wasn't.

I reached for my towel when my department-issued cell beeped, alerting me to a recent call. I scanned the information on the screen. This was way easier than those beepers we'd been using until a few weeks ago. I hadn't realized how behind our department was in that regard. But we had new phones, with a built-in app that dispersed call information, and we were even getting a new fireman to come help with how busy things were becoming.

He wasn't set to come until tomorrow. I knew the guys had been on shift for over forty-eight hours, and they were nearing the end of that time period. It wasn't odd for me to take on extra calls that came through the Walkerton station. In exchange, they allowed me to avoid the majority of the calls that came through the station closer to pack lands. None of my crew knew why I avoided that part of the island. They understood that I'd grown up there, though, and likely had figured it was some sort of familial parting of ways.

The location of the call was familiar, and ironic. The same apartment building Riley was waiting out his lease for. Thanks to Branson and Aver and their construction company, I knew the apartment building contained twenty units, so I wasn't in a rush to let Riley know. He couldn't do anything at this stage anyway but worry and get in the way.

I changed direction, heading back out to the foyer, where I grabbed my coat and keys. "Got a call, need to run,"

I said over my shoulder, shutting the door gently on my way out.

I hopped in my car and sped down the winding roads toward town. By the time I got to the building, the truck was there, and Paster and Krat were already applying first aid to those of the occupants that needed it.

From the size of the crowd shivering in their robes on the sidewalk, I'd say they had everyone evacuated. Including a tiny dog that wouldn't stop yapping.

"What's the situation?" I asked Paster as he cleaned a nasty-looking cut on an elderly woman's face.

Paster looked up, frowning. "Small appliance fire inside Mrs. Boxer's bathroom."

"Hairdryer?" I asked, looking up at the apartments. There was no smoke or damage visible from the outside.

Paster's lips twitched. "Charcoal barbecue."

"Inside?"

"I just wanted my sausages," the old woman mumbled.

I looked to Paster.

"Mrs. Boxer had sausages gifted to her that she wanted to grill," he explained slowly, somehow managing to not let it be heard in his tone how idiotic of an idea that was.

"It is cold outside," I agreed, sending Mrs. Boxer a wink. Paster could reprimand her after.

She smiled, but it quickly faded. "I didn't mean to get anyone hurt. Where's Phin? I must apologize."

I followed her gaze up to the crowd, but she didn't seem to spot the person she was looking for. "You don't see Phin?" I asked, the hairs on my nape standing up. "Paster?"

"Krat did the sweep," Paster said. "Krat, you cleared it, right?" he called out.

This sort of thing wouldn't happen with a larger crew. But with only five of us to cover all the calls for Walkerton including the surrounding Walker County, there were times when things slid through.

Not normally people.

"I'll check it. What's the number?" I asked Mrs. Boxer.

"309, right next door. I don't see him." Her voice had risen with alarm.

I was already on my way to the entrance, strapping my ventilator over my face. The fire had been contained and extinguished, but if she was grilling indoors, that meant there could be carbon monoxide issues as well. By the time I climbed to the third floor, taking three steps at a time, I'd prepared myself to find the worst possible scenario.

The apartment door was already open, likely from when Krat had swept the rooms. The room looked clear, but I supposed it had when Krat came through as well. I went inside, opening the door to the bedroom. All these units were constructed mostly the same, and I knew from being in Riley's apartment roughly where the rooms were. The bed was unmade, the flannel sheets twisted at the foot like whoever had slept there hadn't done so comfortably.

There were a few posters on the wall for movies and games I wasn't familiar with and a desk with two monitors. I might have thought the room empty as well if it weren't for my shifter senses. I could hear someone breathing—softly, slowly, but they were here. Hurrying around to the other side of the bed, I lunged forward toward the mostly naked man who lay crumpled on the carpet.

I grabbed him, and he lifted his head, opening his lids to reveal soft gray eyes. "Monster?" he mumbled.

For the span of half of a second, I froze, paranoid that this young man had seen through my human facade to the wolf lurking below. But then I remembered my mask and ripped it off, pressing the mouthpiece against his face. That would've been a dangerous maneuver for anyone who wasn't also a shifter. "I'm a fireman. I'm here to rescue you. Don't be alarmed."

The man, Phin I assumed, mumbled something that sounded like, "Mkay," and passed out.

I tucked his unconscious body against my chest and rushed for the door, flying down the steps to the outside. I didn't like how slow his breathing had become, decreasing rapidly even as I sprinted.

Outside, the crowd pressed in when they saw me.

"Fuck," Krat spat. "Stay back, please, give him some room."

"I need the oxygen," I told him, laying Phin out on the grass. Poor guy would wake up freezing. I'd just be happy if he woke up. He was thin and pale. His arm fell open, revealing a tattoo on his inner wrist. The silhouette of a crow mid-flight.

His chest rose with each shallow breath.

"Fuck!" My gut clenched. This was hitting me harder than normal, and I had to take a moment to keep my head clear. He looked so helpless, fragile. They always looked that way, but this guy was so pale. His cartoon rocket ship boxers only made him look more precious. And there was so much of him on display. I found myself wanting to curl over him both for warmth and to keep his body out of view.

I spotted a matching tattoo on the inside of the man's other wrist. A second crow, its wings spread as if it were seconds from lifting from his skin. I needed to know why he chose that tattoo, what it meant to him.

Krat rushed over with the gurney and the oxygen. I fit the mouthpiece over Phin's mouth and told him to breathe deeply. He inhaled, his eyes fluttering. Krat got into position to help me lift him up on the gurney, but I disobeyed protocol and lifted the young man myself. There wasn't any reason more people had to touch him at a time like this.

He stirred when his back hit the gurney, almost like he was trying to climb off.

"Just wait a second," I told him quietly. "Take in a few more big breaths. You passed out for a while there." I pushed his dark brown hair back off his forehead.

He mumbled something that I couldn't understand. I wouldn't let him take off the mask yet, so whatever it was would have to wait.

"Phin!" Mrs. Boxer rushed over. Paster hadn't bandaged her forehead yet, but the wound had stopped bleeding. "I'm so sorry, son." Her wrinkled hands fluttered in front of her. "I know you told me it was dangerous to keep grilling, but I didn't think anyone would notice if I cooked up a few. They were a gift." She seemed to add the last part as a reason that would explain everything else.

Meanwhile, I was biting back my growls. Mrs. Boxer was sorry; that much was clear. Her eyes were watery, and her hands still shook. "We generally frown against people using charcoal grills inside, Mrs. Boxers. Is there something wrong with your stove?"

"No, but the smoky flavor is what brings out the seasonings."

I didn't think that was true but wasn't going to argue with the old woman. "If you do it again, you may receive a ticket. Even if it doesn't end with having to evacuate your entire building." We should've given her a ticket immediately. I'd made up my mind to do just that when Phin's hand collided with my arm.

I looked down at where we'd touched. He'd shoved me. Because I wouldn't tell Mrs. Boxer everything was fine? Fuck that. He could've been killed. I wouldn't think about what might've happened if I'd gone to the firehouse at the beginning of my shift instead of rushing in early to help.

Mrs. Boxer went back to where she'd been waiting. Except now her frail shoulders shook. I'd probably feel horrible about that later.

"You didn't have to be so rough with her," Phin croaked.

My joy that he looked like he was responding well to the oxygen faded with his tone. "Did you want me to tell her it's okay? Let her burn down the whole place next time?" I put the mask back over his mouth.

He lifted it immediately. "She's a lonely old woman. She didn't mean anything by it."

"And yet you're still sitting there sucking down pure oxygen in nothing but your rocket boxers because a lonely old woman *didn't mean anything by it.*" Anger flashed a second time.

Phin pushed up off the gurney, and I moved, landing between his legs in my effort to stop him. His bare thighs cradled my hips. A few seconds longer and I'd spring the most inappropriate boner in the history of boners. I didn't get it. Phin wasn't my type at all. For one, he wasn't falling at my feet for saving his life. I didn't require the gratitude, but it felt nice when most people were appropriately thankful. Judging from his physique and coloring, he wasn't a big outdoors type either. I remembered the setup he had upstairs, and while I didn't know heads or tails about computers, it had certainly seemed impressive. That made him more Aver's type than anything. Aver liked those quiet nerdy ones. When he wasn't pretending he wasn't gay anyway.

But Aver was too diplomatic to tell it like it was to Phin. And apparently, he needed a big dose of reality. "You realize you were almost dead there, right?"

"We all die." He shrugged.

That just made me angrier. "Is that what you want on your tombstone? Suffocated to death in pursuit of smoky wieners?" I shoved the mask in his face, knowing I needed to relax. More than that, I needed to step back from where our bodies pressed together, but I could do neither.

"What do I care? I won't be around to read it."

"Well, *someone* will care. Worry about them." I should've just dropped it. Why did it matter to me that this guy seemed to care so little about himself? Perhaps because he seemed so very blasé about the whole topic. Like he lived in constant danger and had come to terms with the idea that he might not live the day every morning he woke up. He wasn't a cop. I knew all the police in Walker County. "Where did you come from?"

"I moved here a few weeks ago from Spokane."

That explained why I'd never seen the man before.

He frowned. "I should probably let my friends know I am okay."

Thank the lord, the guy had friends. So maybe a lot of what he was saying was just the shock talking. I lifted my face to the crowd of other tenants. They'd stopped focusing on us. Some had left, while those with no place to go lingered on the sidewalk. "I'll bring them over. Point them out."

"Online," he clarified.

I groaned. He was one of *those*.

"What?" Phin snapped.

One thing was for sure, he didn't take shit. But what had I expected? Him to open his eyes and immediately begin worshiping me?

Kind of.

"Nothing," I said, and I really, really, *really* should've left it at that, but I couldn't. "Just—I meant real friends."

Phin's face twisted into a glorious mask of anger. I felt his ferocity like a challenge that I was more than eager to meet. My heart pounded as my senses sharpened as if danger were nearby. "You know, thank you so much. I'm so glad that I know now. It is possible to save people while also being a complete and utter asshole."

Continue Reading...

THANK YOU!

My most sincere thanks go to you for picking up Truth!
This book was an insane experience, from plotting to writing, I'd never had a book so sure of what it wanted to be, and
at times I wondered if we were working together or against
each other. Now that this book is finished, I cannot wait to
see where the other three books take us. I'd also like to thank
my cover designer, Adrien Rose for being so amazing, my
beta reader, Jena Wade and my editor, MA Hinkle of Les
Court Author Services!

———

About Me

Kiki Burrelli lives in the Pacific Northwest with the
bears and raccoons. She dreams of owning a pack of goats
that she can cuddle and dress in form-fitting sweaters. Kiki
loves writing and reading and is always chasing that next
character that will make her insides shiver. Consider getting
to know Kiki at her website, kikiburrelli.net, on Facebook, in

her Facebook fan group or send her an email to kiki@kikiburrelli.net

Omega Assassins Club

(Wolf Shifter Omegaverse)

Wolves of Walker County

(Wolf Shifter Mpreg)

Wolves of Royal Paynes

(Wolf Shifter Mpreg)

Printed in Great Britain
by Amazon

47117345R00184